Born in Brooklyn, NY, Stephen Lewis holds a doctorate from New York University in the literature of 17th century New England Puritanism, and he is a professor of English Emeritus at Suffolk County Community College on Long Island, NY. His memoir, *Dementia, a Love Story*, was a finalist in 2021's BookLife non-fiction competition. He has published eight print novels, both genre and literary, for large (Berkley), medium (Walker), small (Arbutus and Mission Point Press) publishers, along with an eBook original for Belgrave House. The three novels that comprise *Mysteries of Colonial Times*, published by Berkley, were set in the 17th century. *Murder on Old Mission*, published by Arbutus, was a finalist in the historical fiction category of Foreword Magazine's 2005 book of the year competition. Its sequel, *Murder Undone,* came out in 2016 from Mission Point Press, located where he now lives in northern Lower Michigan. He has also published six college textbooks and numerous poems and short stories.

Dedicated in loving memory to my wife, Carolyn Johnson Lewis, my support and best critic.

Stephen Lewis

FROM INFAMY TO HOPE

"In Rama was there a voice heard, Lamentation, and weeping, and great mourning, Rachel weeping for her children, And not be comforted, because they are not,"

– Matthew, 2:18

AUSTIN MACAULEY PUBLISHERS™

LONDON * CAMBRIDGE * NEW YORK * SHARJAH

Ordering Information
Quantity sales: Special discounts are available on quantity purchases by corporations, associations, and others. For details, contact the publisher at the address below.

Publisher's Cataloging-in-Publication data
Lewis, Stephen
From Infamy to Hope

ISBN 9781685624804 (Paperback)
ISBN 9781685629106 (ePub e-book)

Library of Congress Control Number: 2023912402

www.austinmacauley.com/us

First Published 2023
Austin Macauley Publishers LLC
40 Wall Street, 33rd Floor, Suite 3302
New York, NY 10005
USA

mail-usa@austinmacauley.com
+1 (646) 5125767

I did my doctoral thesis on Edward Taylor, a minister and poet in 17th century New England. My research included reading religious tracts written at that time with which Taylor would have been familiar. I used that background as the basis for the religious views expressed in the novel. For my understanding of Puritan New England, I am indebted to the pioneering work of historian Edmund Morgan. My specific source material includes Francis J. Bremer's biography of John Winthrop, Winthrop's Journal, and Alfred A. Cave's book on the Pequot War of 1637. And a nod to Nathaniel Hawthorne from whom I borrowed the idea of a letter stitched on the gown of a woman convicted of a sexual offense.

For want of a better alternative, I have made up two Pequot names—Nanawag and Malawala—to go along with the historically correct Mohegan Uncas.

Chapter One

I don't know how long I have been lying on this straw. I shift away from the spot that is wet and warm. I settle myself on the one place that remains dry, and the pain cuts me so hard that I do not feel it for a moment. I think I am going to pass out and I hold my breath until the pain goes away. But then it comes back. It reminds me that my penance is not done yet.

That's what he calls it, my penance, as though I be a cross kissing papist working off my sin like those monks in one of Master Winthrop's books that I saw the pictures of, whipping their backs with goads and pressing thorns into their foreheads. They had only a strip of cloth around their middles, too, and that could make you think what was happening beneath that cloth, but it's thoughts such as those that he says got me into my present state anyway. He may be right. He's a man, after all, and they're supposed to know better than us poor things. My God, I think I could laugh if it didn't hurt so bad, there down between my legs where my troubles began, and where he says they will end, one way or another.

He sits there on that stool by the table with his rum dribbling down his chin, muttering about the mother I didn't know because as he has told me a thousand times she went up to heaven after she dropped me, an ungrateful and unwanted bundle on his doorstep, and now he wants me to remember her. He doesn't make any sense when he's like this, and for that matter not much more when he's sober. If I had known this is what he had in mind for me when he said I could come home when my time came, I would have found a place to lie down in the snow, or maybe I would have looked for a barn someplace like Mary did with our Lord.

If he doesn't talk reasonable about my mother and me, his hands are skilled enough when it comes to tying things together. He thatched this poor hut so not even a breath of air can come in and the smoke from the fireplace settles a while before it finds its way up the chimney. Yes, he can tie, and he's got this leather strap around my knees tight as you please, so tight that when I can't squat proper to pee into this stinking straw, my piss dribbles down my thighs where it dries a crusty brownish yellow on my skin. I feel something, maybe the head, pushing my thighs apart but I can't open them against the pressure of this strap, and each hip bone has said goodbye to the other just like some poor criminal being drawn apart by horses. He's got me just like he said he would.

"Hey," I cry, "for God's love."

He doesn't turn. Maybe he can't. Maybe he's asleep. Or dead.

"Come on," I try again, raising my voice to a scream above the howl of the wind driven snow outside the hut. This time he glances at me, and then gets slowly to his feet. He staggers to the door that the wind has blown open since the leather now binding my legs used to hold the door shut. That idea tickles me somehow, as I look at his powerful, stooped figure in the doorway. The sky is black, whitened only by the falling snow. I have had a feeling something or somebody has been outside waiting for that door to blow open, or for him to go out to shit, and now I see them, and I don't know whether to laugh or to cry, to say my prayers to save my poor soul or to beg pity for my body and for what's pushing out of my belly. I see him coming back pulling up his breeches, his hose down around his feet, and reaching for the door. Whoever is out there has faded back into the snow. I can't blame them for being afeard of a thing such as him. Maybe next time I will invite the devils in for tea before they beat my brains out.

He stumbles back in and leans over me. His breath is rum rich.

"You could give me a sniff," I say.

He doesn't answer, but runs his thick fingers over my legs. For a moment I think he has taken pity on me. He forces his thumbs under the leather strap. I have worked it down almost past my knees so I can spread my thighs just a little when the pains come. The bastard must have noticed, for now he pushes up and my legs are clamped shut again.

"She'll be here soon enough," he says. "I've sent for her. And when she comes, she'll ask you the same thing I been doing and if you speak true to her I can cut this strap." He opens his mouth as though to smile and his spittle drips down his chin. "If I feel like it, I can," he says.

"You could do it now and save us the wait."

He stands up and walks over to the table. He is rocking back and forth on the balls of his feet as though trying to steady himself, and I remember how he held me when I was a little girl and the ship was rolling on the waves. Even then his breath was always smelling of some kind of drink, but his eyes were kind, and his voice soothed my fears when I thought we was going to be washed overboard with the next mountain of water coming down on us. I feel a sudden warmth in the memory of how he took care of me then, but now my belly starts to tighten again and the pain clenches my spine and travels down my thighs. I wait for it to find my center, there between my thighs like it always does like a fist pushing, pounding to get out, and I try so hard to open my legs until they go numb against the strap, and all I can taste is the blood dripping from the lips my teeth have torn open once again. And when the pain subsides and I can open my eyes, I see him sitting there at the table, cup in his hand, just staring at me like he has never seen me before.

I look at him, and I think I see a smile, like he is enjoying this, and I don't doubt that he is. He used to like to tell me stories, which I never knew the truth of, like the one of how his father took him to a witch burning when he was a little boy. He said sometimes they were merciful and broke the poor woman's neck first, but other times when they were angry because they knew she had been lying with the Black Man himself, they would drive a stake up into her belly through her arsehole and then they would light the faggot, so they could watch her turn like she was a pig on a spit, and the smell of her roasted flesh, he said, made his mouth water. What he didn't say, but I would dare to believe, is that the sounds of her screams caused him to rise in his breeches, just like my breasts swinging naked in the breeze at the whipping post excited bulges that had nothing to do with the stern glances on the faces of these men.

He can't stand that I won't tell him what devil lay with me, because he says I must have invited him to my bed. I can't convince him that this human devil was all hands going up my coats, again and again, and what was I to do, scream out? And who would believe me, me who had already been tied to the post and whipped until my back was raw because they said I was unclean before I even knew what that could mean, just that some boy took me out into a field and lay on top of me, him sweating and grunting and me wondering what he was doing until they pulled him off me and said I lured him there. He was going to be whipped too, but his father paid a fine, while this one at the table only asked how many lashes I was going to get, and thought it should be double what they said. And so they had me unbutton myself and pull down my shift and then they laid into me with the lash, and I could not stop the tears. This time I knew what it was all about. They would call it fornication, but I was fucked, good and proper. When he threw me down with his hands pulling my legs apart, I still tried to push him off but then he gave me reason to lie there, and I did. One whipping is enough for me, I thought, and so I have come to this, waiting for it to be over, but I don't know what the *it* will be, death or life, mine or my babe's, and it hurts so bad I don't care anymore.

I think I can fall asleep if I hurry before the pain comes and then maybe I won't wake up again. The fire has burned down, almost out, and I have nothing to cover myself with against the cold. There's a stump of a candle on the table. Its wax is only a lump of drips and the flame will be out soon. If I look at it long enough, it seems to move with my own breaths, getting bigger and smaller as I breathe in and out.

He is snoring on his pallet in the corner near the fireplace. I shut my eyes, and I breathe slowly, just like the candle's flame rises and falls in the cold air coming in through the door frame. I am almost asleep but I will not make it. The pressure has begun again, pushing my spine back and my hip bones into twin knots of pain. I do not think I can stand it one more time, and an idea has jumped into my mind amazingly clear. If I am a witch like some say I am, but nothing happens.

Well, then I'll do it without the devil's help. Maybe if I do, the black man will come and help me out of my pain. All I have to do is pull myself across the floor and push the table over before the candle dies.

I've got my hand around the table leg and I am pushing and pulling it, but I can't get it off the floor, and meantime my belly has tightened so hard I think it is going to just split open. The candle is only one poor drip now, the flame almost out. The straw I've dragged with me is so dry it would make a marvelous fire. I heave again against the table leg and it lifts from the floor. I roll into it and it rises higher and the candle starts to slide. I imagine we are burning together, but then I have to close my eyes against the pain between my legs. I open them to darkness. The candle is out and there is no fire, and I feel a strong hand on my shoulder. I can't see him, but I sense that he is still in his corner by the fireplace, and then I hear his snoring coming from there.

I expect the hand to lift from my shoulder and then come down again to split my skull. But it moves to my forehead in a caress and then I hear a voice, a woman's voice, whisper.

"You will be all right. Just wait a little longer."

The hand moves between my thighs and I sense her leaning over me.

"I'll have to wake him, but I won't let him hurt you anymore."

"Can you…?" I begin. Her hand is on my forehead again.

"Soon," she says.

There is a crash from his corner and a stream of mumbled curses. He is on his feet, righting the chair he knocked over. His arm reaches into the fireplace and pokes the embers until they glow. He lifts a stick out of the ashes and blows on its red end until it starts to flame. He finds the taper where I have left it hanging in the fireplace and he lights it. He stares hard at the woman whose hand is still on my forehead.

"We're very glad you have come," he says, and his voice carries a respect I seldom hear in it.

"Do you have a knife about you?" she says, and her voice is as commanding as his is humble.

"Sure," he says, "but I'm not going to use it until she tells me who the father of her bastard is. So I can have him before the magistrates, if you please, and see that he pays for it, which is more than I can, or would, do."

"If you don't use it soon," she says, "you won't have to worry about that. All you'll have to do is dig a hole in the ground to put her in."

He is in the shadows, so I can't see more than the outline of his shape, but I sense his movement, and I know him well enough to see the shrug of his shoulders.

"That's the way her mother died. It seems to be what God has in store for me, to see women dying for their ways."

"I don't think that is so at all," she answers, and her tone now is both warm and hard. "But I didn't come here to argue theology with you."

"No," he sputters, "I'm not one of those women who come to your house on a Tuesday to hear you explain what Master Cotton or Master Wilson really meant to say on Sunday, if only he had your wits to say it."

The pain comes again, and although I clench my teeth, I cannot stop the moan.

"Child," she says, "it would be best if you told us who the man is."

"Why?" I manage to say. "So's he can deny it, or his master can pay his fine while I'm whipped again?"

"Just put the saddle on the right horse," he says, "and then Master Winthrop will make things right."

13

This time the pain takes what strength I have left and turns it into a scream.

"You'd better leave," she says to him, "so I can see what I can do."

He reels toward the door.

"That babe will not be born in this house, less she gives it a father."

"Leave," she says, and he does.

"Do not be afraid of what happens next," she says, and then I hear a dull thud followed by a louder one as his body collapses in the snow just outside our door.

"Is he dead?" I ask, but she does not answer. She squeezes my hands and leaves.

The snow is coming down so hard and fast that I can hardly see him where he lies almost motionless. Almost it is, for I see his chest move and I don't know whether the rush of warmth I feel is relief or anger. I don't have time to worry about that, now, anyway, not with three or four savages about to carry me off, and my mysterious savior, Mistress Hutchinson, I am sure, gone like a visitor in my dreams.

The pain has stopped for the moment. Maybe it is my fear, waiting to feel the blow to my head that has made me insensible to the other. I do not know. But I do see that I am about to be pulled along through the snow lying on a deer skin stretched between two poles. My captors, for that is what I must take them to be, all are covered in snow so I can only make out their dark eyes as they check to see that I am settled. One of them finds the leather binding my legs, pulls on it and then shrugs.

"Cut it off, please," I say, although I do not know if he can understand.

The one whose hand touched me smiles. I can see the whiteness of his teeth even against the white of the snow. He is missing one front tooth, but he seems to be grinning.

"Later," his voice says. "We cut you open later." He laughs and then he waves a knife in front of my belly, and his companions laugh. I would stop breathing if I could, but I know I can't since I have already tried that, and it is not likely this group is going to be kind enough to lead me to a bridge someplace that I could jump off.

"Cut it."

So she has not disappeared into a dream after all. And the knife drops between my legs and then I feel the strap press against the back of thighs for a moment, and then its pressure is gone. I raise my head to thank her, but she is not there.

One of them lays a skin over me, covering my face. I do not know if the act is intended as a mercy or to prevent me from seeing who they are, but I am grateful for the warmth. I smell the rank scent of the deer that used to wear this skin. I push it down to my nose so I can see, as we start out. I breathe in the animal smell and think that I have crawled into the living beast's belly. There's a savage in front, and another walking behind, which is the direction I am facing. I can tell that we are heading toward the marshes, and as the snow lets up just a little I see over their shoulders the three summits of Trimountain, and beyond the windmill sitting atop Copp's Hill, its huge sails somehow making me think of a giant cross, only they are turning slowly in the wind and if Christ was nailed to this one he would be now upside down and now right side up, and that idea almost forces a smile to my face.

I hear a grunt and I turn my eyes to the one walking right by my feet. He has positioned himself between the poles, and leaning forward, so that he is very close to my face. He throws open his mouth as though he is going to howl, but I hear nothing. I do smell his foul breath, and then with a push on the poles he heaves his body away from me. The snow thickens again, and the wind howls, and I pull my face fully under the skin, which smells of musky life and dead flesh, all mingled, and I, too, balance between life and death, with new life pulsing between my thighs while I feel my own breath and heart weaken from pain and exhaustion.

I wake to the deer smell, only I am no longer covered by a skin. At first, I think I am back in the hut my father built, only now I realize that this one was put up by the savages. Its walls are covered with woven mats made from the reeds that grow in the marshes, colored red and orange with dark lines running through them that seem to form figures whose significance I do not understand. The mats move as the wind from outside pushes against the walls. Instead of a chimney, there is only a hole in the top, through which the snow falls onto the ashes of a dying fire, and I am frozen to the bone.

My feet hurt, and I remember that I haven't felt them for hours and hours. I look down at them and I realize that they are separated, and that my legs are akimbo, and I can cry for the relief, and then the familiar clenching pain begins, only this time I can raise my legs and push with it. The pain builds, mostly in my back now, where I can swear my spine is being bent up to my neck, and I try to push out this thing that is splitting my belly, but I cannot and as the cramping dies I think I will lose consciousness.

I feel a hand between my thighs, and I think of Henry, but I know he can't be here. He wouldn't dare. This hand, though is not like his when it forced my legs apart. This one is gentle, and it is followed by a voice, the same one I heard in my own house, only now that it does not have to compete with my father, it is only comforting, and I can fall into its rhythm even before I understand the words it says.

"It is coming down wrong," the voice says. "Here you can feel it yourself." A hand takes my hand and leads it down over my swollen belly until I can feel what is almost out of me down there. The hand on my hand forces me to press on this thing.

"Do you feel what is there?" the voice says.

I nod, for I surely do. My hand is on top of a tiny foot. I can count the toes, and there are five. I am flooded with a sensation I could never have imagined feeling.

"We don't have much time," the voice says. "Your father saw to that. And your babe cannot come out this way one foot first, without killing you. I am going to have to turn it, and you will have to bear it, or you will both die, and then what will all of this have been about?"

The hand pushing mine now lifts it away, and then returns. I feel it between my thighs and I can imagine it on the tiny foot. I think she is going to pull it down, and at the thought I begin to protest, but that is not what the hand intends. It pushes up, and I think I am going to break open, now, and finally. I reach down to stop the hand, to stop her, to stop the pain, but my hand is brushed away. The pressure increases upward and then I feel the strange hand forcing itself inside of me. I can sense it turning now, and as it turns I understand my babe is being turned, and then the hand retreats, and its pressure is replaced by something hard.

"We have a chance now," the voice says, "if it is still alive. You must push it out when the next pain comes."

It comes almost immediately and this time it intensifies at my opening like it never had before and I feel myself expanding as though my body would fill the space of the miserable hut where I lie. I push and I feel movement between my legs and with a whoosh it slides out. The pressure vanishes, but the pain remains, and I close my eyes.

I have been asleep, and as I awake I see that Mistress Hutchinson is sitting on the ground next to me, holding a small bundle. A pink arm reaches out from the swaddling.

"A girl," she says.

I reach toward it, but I have no strength to lift my arms. I feel something wet between and down my legs, and I look to my shift wadded there. There is not much light from the small fire, but it is enough for me to see that my white shift is now red.

"Just lie quiet," Anne says.

"I don't think I can do otherwise," I reply.

She extends the tiny bundle toward me and places it as my side. I pull the cloth away from the baby and examine it from its tiny toes to its almost bald head, from which sprout three golden hairs, like three yellow wild flowers that have escaped the scythe clearing a planting field. Her eyes open, and I see that they are blue. She stirs, and I am frightened. Still I have to look to see if there are any marks. I see nothing on her front and I turn her over. Her backside, too, is clear. She stretches her legs sleepily.

"He said there would be signs on her," I say.

"What kind of signs? She is perfect."

"Signs of the sin that made her. But I don't see anything."

She covers my babe back up, but leaves it lying at my side. I feel a new pressure growing, this one in my breasts, and it is pleasurable.

"There are no marks on her," Anne says, "but it would be well if you told me who the father is."

"Why? I want nothing to do with him. He forced me."

She leans over so that I can see her face in the half light of the fire. It is both gentle and yet hard with a defiance I am unused to seeing on a woman's face.

"They will not believe that is true."

"I know they will not. Still, it is the truth."

"I can try to help you," she says.

"You already have."

"This is just the beginning."

"Right, then," I say, "for what it is worth. Henry Watkins. He is a servant, just like me, in Master Winthrop's house, and I am not the first he has had, but I may be the first to bear him a bastard."

I can see that she is waiting for me to tell her more, but I am so suddenly so tired I cannot speak.

"It can wait," she says. "But not for too long. And you must rest, since we can only stay here for a little while."

I want to ask her, but she seems to know the question before I find the strength to utter it.

"We are in a special hut. Where the Indian women come every month. Those who took us here will be back soon so that I can pay them for their service. And," she lowers her voice to a whisper, "your father is all right. They did not hit him very hard, and he was very drunk."

"That is too bad," I say as I remember staring down at his chest, hoping that it would not move, and recalling the disappointment when the snow lifted with his breath.

"Hush," she says, and I feel my eyes close as though pressed down by her finger tips although she has not touched me.

I feel a tug. I am warm. I open my eyes to a decent fire and my babe lying next to my side nursing at my breast, which filled as it is with milk has swollen these past weeks so now I almost look like a grown woman. For a moment I can feel joy, but then I remember where I am. And how I got here. And at the thought of what I will do, now, my head begins to ache giving me a new pain to mark against my new pleasure. My babe takes its lips off my breast, and I cannot believe how strongly she can suck until the pressure of her tiny mouth is gone and I can again feel the air stirring in this hut. I see that she is screwing up her eyes as though to cry, and I roll over to give her my other breast. She fastens onto it, and I am happy.

Happy, until, as I drift off to sleep, I remember, and I start to push the babe away. Her face reddens, as though to reflect the dyed reeds on the wall, or the embers in the fire, and I do not want to hear her cry, and I do not want to feed her, not while I remember how it is she came to grow inside of me. I am too tired to hold her away as she strains to my breast. I let her suck and I close my eyes to bring back that afternoon so that I can begin to forget.

I feel Henry's hands as he threw me down in the chamber where Elizabeth sleeps and where I was that Sunday because I was too weak to go to meeting. Master Winthrop, listening to his wife Margaret, had put his big, soft hand on my forehead, felt my fever and said I could stay abed. I remember how surprised I was at that hand's warmth and its delicate touch, and how it was so different from his cold eyes and his lips so often pressed together like a shut book. He stroked my forehead while Margaret watched, and he agreed that it would be better for me to sleep, since the snow was falling and the meeting house was cold this time of year, all this he said, and seemed to be taking an interest in my well-being, and yet he did not consider the most important thing and that was Henry who was supposed to be still in Salem village where he had been sent to get the quire of paper that Master Winthrop was waiting on so he could continue his scratching that I hear him do every evening, only he had crept back Saturday night, with his face grinning away, and told us all not to say a word. And then he had put his hands all over Elizabeth while his eyes were on me, as though to say without the words that he wished Elizabeth who is, truth be told, not very pretty, what with her flat nose like a pig's snout in the middle of her fat face, and her hands always red from the washing she does, that he wished I was Elizabeth, and that soon I would take her place beneath him. I didn't pay them any mind, when he crawled into bed with her, didn't listen to his grunting or her moaning, but just went to sleep in the soft warmth of my fever.

When I woke up with my head on fire, everybody else was dressed for church and I didn't see him. Yet I could sense him lurking about somewhere. So Master Winthrop did not know Henry was back, and if he did he would not have said he could stay with me, this same Henry Watkins, whose back still bore the stripes for not going to church like everybody is supposed to.

She is stirring and I cannot go to sleep, and somehow I know that before she seeks my breast again I must make myself remember what happened that day so that I do not smother her, remember how he crawled into my bed and whispered in my ear, words that through my fever I could not tell the meaning of, only the hum of his voice and then the feel of his hands on these same breasts that my daughter will want very soon, and how I just said for him to go away to find Elizabeth or someone else that would be more agreeable to him than me, and how he said he wanted no one else and he would have me, sick or not, willing or not, and that I would not say anything about it because Master Winthrop would not believe me, me who had myself spent time at the whipping post and was adjudged to be a whore already for inviting that boy to lie on me. So he said I'd better just be still unless I wanted another whipping or worse, this time.

But I would not lie still and I got up and I surprised him, and myself, with my strength, and yet I was not strong enough. He threw me down as though we were playing a game, and then when I could not rise one more time he reached his hands, those hard farm working hands, cow milking hands, wood splitting hands, under my coats and pushed my legs apart. And then he knelt between my thighs and pulled down his breeches. He showed me his member, red and angry looking and said wasn't it a thing I wanted to touch, and then he grabbed my hands and placed them on it, and it jumped at my touch, like a startled animal, and I was, for a moment surprised, and then I thought I would squeeze its life out of it, but he saw my mind. He pulled my hands off and threw himself on me, and pushed and pushed until he could push no more. I felt the sharp pain of his coming inside me where nobody had ever been before, not even that silly boy in the field, and then for a bit he labored above me while I could only push against his chest. When I could push no more, I let my arms drop, and I waited for him to be done, and for the pain to stop.

When he was finished, he stood and reached his hand between my legs and then examined my blood on his fingers, and he said, "Well, maybe you're now the whore I thought you was anyway. You'd better clean yourself up before they come home." He laughed to himself as he walked away, and that is the laugh I still hear, and with a start I understand that in her blue eyes I see his, for mine are brown.

She is awake now, and I give her suck until she wants no more, and I can doze once again.

I hear men's voices reaching me from outside, grunting in a language I have heard but do not know, the same as that spoken by the men who brought me here. Then I hear her, calm and commanding, just like when she spoke to my father. I still don't know if I can trust her. The thought comes into my mind that she is trading me for something, or maybe it is my babe they want. I have heard that sometimes they take women and make them wives or they steal children to raise as their own. I do not know what I will do if they come in here to take me away. But they will not have my child.

She crawls into the hut. Snow is plastered on her cloak, and on the mantle she has wrapped around her head. She glances at me, and offers a quick smile as though to calm my fears and then she walks into the shadows of the hut where I see for the first time bolts of cloth, and as she drags them into the light I can note they are brightly colored in reds and greens and yellows.

"Russell worsted. They like the colors," she says, "and the warmth. Will won't miss them."

It takes me a moment to realize she is talking about her husband, a man Master Winthrop despises for making too much money and leaving his wife too much opportunity to get into mischief.

"They are the price we agreed on," she says.

So they were hired hands, after all, and the thought occurs to me that maybe Mistress Anne could have thrown in another bolt of pretty cloth so that they would have hit my father just a little bit harder. Then as though my evil thought has summoned him, I hear his voice raised in anger outside the hut.

"You're not going anywhere just yet," he says.

"What is it you want?" she says.

"I have business with them, not with you, Mistress," he says.

"They work for me."

"Begging your pardon," he replies, and his tone is mockingly respectful of her position as the wife of a very rich man, both of them and all their brood church members as well while we, well, let's say we don't breathe the same air as those folks and our noses are the better for it. I catch myself taking his side, but then it's only natural sometimes for a child to forget what a monster her parent is when he is made to be not much better than a pile of dung, for if that is what he is, what am I? His tone, though is what I'm thinking about, and it has lost some of its deference, because he thinks he now has her in the wrong. And as the power shifts a little toward him, by so much is my hateful distrust of him returned.

"Inside," he says, "I have had enough of the snow and cold for one night."

I feel the rush of cold air as the mat that covers the opening to the hut is pushed back, and then I hear the tread of heavy feet and rough clothing rubbing against the bent saplings that form the arch of the doorway. I hear and feel all these things, for I will not open my eyes to look. I clutch my babe closer to me. I know my father is going to do something with her, or to her, and I will not be able to stop him. Nor will Mistress Hutchinson.

The worst is I do not know what I want. Or to be clearer, I want two things that have nothing to do with each other.

He, or they, or anybody can have *his* baby.

But nobody can take *mine*.

I hold her closer to me, and I understand that she is the only thing in this world that will love me when she gets old enough to know I am her mother. I would never use that word to describe how my father feels toward me, and 'love' has nothing to do with what Henry was thinking about that day. But this babe that grew under my heart and is now pressed against my breast is going to love me, like I would have my own mother if she had lived. Henry, my father, those savages, they can all go to hell, and I will be happy to meet them there if that's the only way I can keep her with me.

I pull my blanket over my head and drag my babe under it to hide with me. The voices are now muffled. My father is saying something, and Mistress Anne responds and then the savages speak what sounds like English words. I find myself surprised that they know our tongue. The conversation goes on, and I huddle deeper under the blanket. I am again exhausted, and I know that as hard as I hug my babe to me I am too weak, and they are too strong.

The voices have stopped. I pull the blanket slowly down to uncover my eyes. Before I can see, I can smell the strong and unmistakable odor of animal skins. In a second, I recognize them from the last time my father traded with the savages. He gave them a bottle of rum that he had watered down by half, and they gave him skins, beaver skins, and that is what I smell now. That time they came back after a couple of hours and threw the empty bottle at him, and then two of them held him down, for he is a powerful man, and the third held a knife to his throat. But, as he told me later, they were only interested in doing business, not killing, and when he offered them a fresh, good bottle, they let him up, with his promise that he would make up for this insult at a later time when the opportunity presented itself.

I edge the blanket a little further down so I can see. There are the skins. And next to them on the floor is a small pile of polished beads that glow red in the light of the fire.

So now I know what the price of an unwanted babe is. I feel rough hands tugging the blanket off me. I pull back on it as hard as I can, and for a moment or two, I hold it over me and my babe. Then I feel the cold air. A hand grabs my arm. I sink my teeth into that hand, and it pulls away. Other hands grab my hips, where I cannot bite, and I am lifted up. I wrap my babe in my arms, but she is wrenched from me.

And I do not even look up.

Chapter Two

Yesterday afternoon, as soon as the snow let up for an hour, Constable George Middleton pushed open our door. I was lying on my bed of straw in the corner where my father has had me since I came back without my babe. He hasn't changed that straw in all this time, and it stinks even worse than it did before. And sometimes I swear it moves, what with all the creatures that now live in it. He says he won't be able to get any fresh straw until spring, and I should just close my nose to it. The other night when he was drunk he got to wondering if he would ever have a little grandchild to hold on his knee, and then he looked over at me and he cursed into his rum, the spittle running down his chin that he had not shaved in a week or two. Constable Middleton stared at me and then he said to my father, "Bring her before the magistrates tomorrow at noon."

So today we are on our way to the meeting house. The sun is out and the snow is beginning to melt in places. Our road takes us past the harbor, where a small ship is tied up at the new dock. The black water is now visible between chunks of ice, and the sailors on board are moving about. My father sees where I am looking.

"It's a thought," he says. "Maybe the two of us, if I had some coin in my pocket."

"But you don't."

"No, not even enough for myself."

He shrugs and walks on. I can hardly straighten my back, and I bleed when I stand, but I struggle to keep up with his long stride through the snow that is up to my knees where it has formed drifts. He does not wait for me, nor does he offer a hand. I trip over something, and tumble face down. I lift my face up and see that I am staring at the snoot of a hog that is sprawled where the wind has blown most of the snow away. I don't say anything, but wait for him to notice that I am not with him. After a while he does, and mumbling under his breath he comes back to where I lie. I stand up and he is about to pull me along when he sees the hog, and he smiles. I look at the animal's beady black eyes which are open like it is looking up at us, but its thin ribs are not moving.

"It's dead," I say, "starved and then frozen."

He nods.

"Like we are like to be," he says. He bends down and inspects the carcass, finding somebody's mark on the beast's flank. He walks away a few paces, and gathers up some snow from a drift and piles it on the hog. He does this until he has it almost covered, although its snout and one hoof still stick out.

"Come on, now," he says, "we don't want to keep them waiting." And he is off ahead of me. I do not try to overtake him. I know where I must go. It is no use to think of hiding or running away. So I put one foot in front of another, reaching to step into the tracks he leaves in the snow. For a moment, I am again a little girl with nothing to do but play. The warm blood dripping down my thighs brings me back to the present. As we reach the common, I feel something brush by my side and look to see a woman hurry by. She is carrying something bundled in a blanket. She does not seem to know that she has bumped into me. She continues toward the western edge of the common and stops by the rough planking atop the town well. She stops and clutches her bundle.

I hear the sound of banging and I see that it is coming from right in front of the meeting house. I turn my eyes from the woman to my father who has stopped next to the whipping post and the stocks, where the snow has been cleared away. He is looking at some men who are sawing planks and others who are hammering them across the top of a scaffold. He motions to one of the workers who puts down his saw to talk to him. They exchange a few words, but as I approach, my father waves the man away and he returns to his work. When I reach my father, he points to the whipping post, which is covered in ice.

"They won't be using that for you," he says. "They think they need something more to get your attention."

"And just what is that?" I ask, but I know he will not answer. He strides ahead of me into the meeting house. I watch the men work for a moment. A small crowd of people is also watching. They keep their eyes on the laborers and will not look at me. Out of the corner of my eye, I see that the woman with the bundle has sat down in the snow next to the well. I follow my father through the door and into the meeting house. It is gloomy inside and at first I cannot see. Then my eyes find my father on a bench in the front. I go to join him and sit down. Before us is a table. Behind it sit Master Winthrop, our governor, and Master Dudley, our assistant governor. They were talking to each other, and now they nod at my father.

"He should be here presently," Master Winthrop says, and I guess they must mean Henry. "We beg your patience," the governor says in a tone of voice that means he really would never beg anything from the likes of my father.

I try to shut my ears to the sound of banging that is coming in from outside. I look around at the empty building, and I remember how it was other times when we came here. The benches would be filled, and we would sit way at the back, me on one side with the other women and girls of our class, and he with men like himself on the very last seat on the very last bench where he tried not to nod off, like once he did, when his snoring cost him a few shillings. Mr. Wilson, or Mr. Cotton, would be talking away up there about the meaning of the Word, and me wishing I knew how to read so I could see for myself what they was talking about. The words of the minister would come floating over them to me where my back was almost pressed against the packed mud that they made the walls out of, and when it was raining on a hot summer day those walls would stink like the swamp they came from. I would listen, though, to the way the minister's voice would sound like music playing a melody to a song whose words I did not know.

I remember seeing Master Cotton baptize a baby once. His face is usually as stern as stone but when he looked down at the babe, there was a twinkle in his eye, and I recall thinking that if I ever joined the church, which would have to happen after my father died, and when I had a baby, I would want to have it baptized, just like this one, being held out by its mother as Master Cotton said some words and sprinkled some water on the babe's head, and it howled, and nobody seemed to care. Why I think there were even a few smiles among the people sitting on the benches, but the biggest smile was on Master Cotton's face. That was when I made up my mind that he would baptize my baby when I had one.

Well, I had one. And Master Cotton is not going to baptize it. He is not even here. Nor of course is my babe. Who is here is Master Winthrop and Master Dudley, and I know they will be sending me out onto that scaffold before long. The table they are sitting behind is in front of the pulpit. The table

25

is lower than the pulpit, but it is higher than our bench. At the end of the table is a man with close set eyes, and one shoulder higher than the other. He has pen, ink and paper in front of him. All of them are wearing heavy cloaks and do not seem as cold as I am. I can see the white of Master Winthrop's ruff beneath the cloak. He has a pointed beard that gives a hard line to his soft face. He is stroking it like I have seen him do a thousand times when he is impatient, waiting for somebody to do something that should have been done. I know he has a temper but he keeps it in check by stroking that beard. Right now, he is pulling on it as though he might yank out a few hairs.

A shouted curse comes rolling in from outside, and it is followed by laughter of the other men out there building, and I can imagine that one of them must have hit his hand with the hammer, which his friends find very amusing. The curses and laughter stop and there is just the hammering and crash of heavy boards as they are laid down. I want them to stop building soon. I have figured out that I can't be hanged on a scaffold. They would have to build something higher to drop me down from, so if they stop hammering, I won't be hanged. But I suppose that it wouldn't take much banging to fasten a stake to the scaffold. I cannot help thinking of those stories my father used to tell me about how the witches were burned, and I try to remember if there is any kindling lying about where the men out there are working. I can imagine the fire rising from my feet to my face, turning my skin to ashes. I think I'd rather hang than burn.

"Which is it going to be, then?" I say, but they don't seem to hear me. "The rope or the fire?" I say, louder. I figure once I know what they intend, I can plan how to talk them out of it.

Master Winthrop puts his hand down, clears his throat to speak, and looks at my father.

"Quiet your child," he says. "For she is making a mockery of what we intend."

"She is afraid," my father says, and for a moment I think he is going to defend me. "But then she has a right to be, don't she?" he adds. Then he turns to me, and he says in a soothing voice like when I was a little girl. "Hush," he says, "you know it is too wet outside for there to be any dry kindling to light a fire." And then he snorts a half-swallowed laugh like he hoped the others would share the joke with him, but if they don't he can be pretending to be coughing in the frigid air. His breath, which I know is heavy with rum, leaves a cloud in front of his face. I look at the six or seven places his razor has missed his beard, and the others where he has gouged his skin. He don't have nothing in our house to use for a mirror and even if we did his hand is never very steady.

Master Winthrop raises his eyebrows like he is peeking past a door and into a room he has never seen before, and then he lowers them like he don't like what he sees. He glances at the man with the pen and ink sitting at the end of the table as though he has just remembered he is there. I have not heard the scratch of his quill. This is most unlike the governor, and I wonder if he is that upset that he would forget to do things in their proper order and in the right way. He is always telling us servants how we should clean this, or cook that, or mend this other thing. And he is a lawyer and here he has forgotten the formalities.

"You are Rachel Moore, are you not?" he asks.

"I am," I say, and I hear the pen scratching now.

"And you are a servant in the governor's house?"

"Yes."

"And you are fourteen years old?"

"Yes."

"And that is Jonathan Moore, your father sitting at your side."

"Yes."

"And you have borne a babe, within the fortnight?"

Yes, yes, and yes. I answer these questions that everybody knows the answer to, and I hear the pen scratch, scratch, scratching. In between scratches, I hear my father's yawn, just like he does when he is in the meeting house.

"Tell us who the father is."

I look at him.

"I think you know, sir," I say. "He is the one we are waiting for."

"Excuse her impudence," my father says. He is paying some attention after all. I think I would prefer it if he was snoring.

I stare hard at Master Winthrop. I want him to respond to me. All the time I worked for him, he never looked at me except that one time he put his soft hand on my forehead and said I could stay abed. Today, I want him to see me.

"I think you know," I repeat. "It's not for me to have to tell you what happened under your own roof."

Master Winthrop strokes his beard hard. I know he is trying to be patient.

"I am here today as your magistrate, not as master of the house where you are a servant. What I may or may not know as master means nothing to me as magistrate. Do you understand this difference?"

I want to say that I understand that whether he's master or magistrate, he's a man like my father, only with more money and power, but I don't think he would fancy being put in the same pot with my father. He would pull his beard our hair by hair, no doubt. I have seen him in his temper.

"I am a poor, uneducated girl," I say. "I know that you are Master Winthrop whose house I work in, and that you are governor of this plantation. That I truly do, know, sir."

I watch Dudley's expression sour as I say that Winthrop is governor. And I can also see that he is not going to be moved by me declaring my ignorance. That will only confirm the idea he has of servant girls, as fit only to empty chamber pots, or such like work. He has a pinched face, he does, in keeping with his bilious personality, and now he turns to the Governor.

"Indeed," he says as though that one word places me a hundred feet beneath his boots where I must lie still so he can step on me or over me as he listed.

I hear a shuffling of feet behind me. I turn and here comes Henry himself, sliding in as quiet as he can, like a rat coming out of its hole in the wall, and behind him is Constable Middleton. He is a big man, with a bushy mustache and a smile that comes easy to his mouth. He has his large hand on the back of Henry's neck, and it is clear that Henry has no choice but to go where the constable directs. Henry looks over his shoulder at the constable, and then lets himself be pushed down onto a bench across from where we are sitting.

"He was about to take a little voyage when I caught up to him. Had his foot on the gangplank, he did," Middleton says. I stare hard at Henry. He offers me a shrug and a smile as if to say that we should have thought about fleeing together. I shake my head.

"And where were you going, Henry?" Winthrop asks.

"Wherever that ship was going," Henry replies.

"Indeed," Dudley says. For a man so fond of words, he seems to use the same one, as thought it might cost him some coins to employ others.

"There may be time for that later," Winthrop says, and his lips almost curl into a smile, or maybe a sneer. It is hard to tell with him. "But first we need to hear what you have to say about Rachel sitting at the bench with her father, and about the baby she says is yours. Is it?"

I wonder how he is going to answer. I have no doubt that he will have something to say. He is like the rest of them, and even without their education he can make words hop or skip to his tune.

"Why sure," he says. "And Rachel there is my wife, by the laws and customs of England."

I think Winthrop's face is going to explode from the heat that turns it from pasty white to red.

"Do you mean to instruct us in the law?" Winthrop asks.

"Begging your pardon," Henry replies. "I thought only to answer your question."

"If you are married," Winthrop says, "who else knows of it? What father gave you permission or her?" He pauses and his color starts to lower from red through deep pink and back to pasty white. "I am your father, as yours is dead, and I certainly did not." He turns to my father.

"I know nothing of what he intends," my father says. He looks at me. "Nor her neither."

"Well, we had words between us, and then we lay together, and so we are married, I think," Henry says.

"The only words we had," I say, "is when I told you no and to get off me."

"Fornication," Dudley says, using another word. "They are not betrothed in the eyes of God, or man. And the child she carried is therefore a bastard."

"And so says I," my father adds.

"She invited me into her bed, and said we would be man and wife," Henry replies.

I start to rise to my feet, but I remember what Mistress Hutchinson told me that night my poor babe was born. I remember it through all the pain. That they would not believe me, that they would not even listen to me, and I understand that she is right. My only question is how they will twist what happened to their liking.

"Child," Winthrop says, and his tone suggests he is trying to be another father to me, seeing as how my own did such a miserable job, "you say he forced you?"

"Yes," I say. I will use only a few and very simple words.

"But the babe?" Winthrop says. He looks genuinely puzzled. Dudley though has the answer.

"It is not possible," he says. "Many learned doctors have said that, well, what you claim cannot be." He seems embarrassed, but he continues. "For if a woman conceives, she must have found pleasure in the act." He is warming to his theory. Maybe he remembers how it was, a long time ago, when he was young. "If she does not have pleasure, as when a man forces himself upon her, she cannot conceive. It is as simple as that."

"That is simply wrong," I reply.

"And you, too, wish to instruct us?" Winthrop says. His voice is cool, disbelieving.

"Did you invite Henry Watkins to lie with you?"

"No," I say.

Winthrop starts to turn toward Henry. It looks as though his head has become too heavy, and he stops. He takes a breath and then he is looking at Henry. He waits.

"She did," Henry says. "After everybody went to church. I came back from the errand you sent me on too late and only she was there. She was in the bed in Elizabeth's room. She said she fooled you into thinking she was sick. And she pulled down the cover on her bed and said I should come lie with her. I know I should not have. But I am a young man, and when she pulled down the covers I could see her naked body, and I could not resist the temptation she offered me. No more than Samson could say no to Delilah." A smile starts on his lips and he cannot stop it though he wipes his hand across his mouth. Still, he says all this without blushing, and I can only wonder. For a second I almost believe him, thinking maybe I was so feverish I did what he said. But then I can recall the pressure of his hard fingers on my legs, and the sour smell of his clothes and even the dung caked on his boots as he climbed on top of me, and I would spit in his lying face if I thought anybody would believe me.

Winthrop's eyes have turned angry.

"Are you then Samson?" he says. "Are we then the Philistines?"

Henry looks confused. I guess he figures he should have come to meeting more often, and that he has stepped too far.

"I don't take your meaning, sir," he says.

30

"Never mind," the Governor replies. Dudley, though, has not taken his eyes off me. He seems to have no interest in what Henry says or doesn't say, what he knows, or doesn't know.

"This is how it stands with *you*." He says the word hard so I can be sure to understand that he is talking only to me. "I remember we had you before us once before for playing the whore, and now you have shown us the proof with the babe you have borne. The only question is how it is between you and the lad. If he is telling the truth, you are both guilty of fornication. If you say that you had an understanding, you have still fornicated but we can be a little more understanding, since you expected to marry, even without your fathers' permission. If you insist that he forced you, we must conclude that you are not being truthful, as the learned doctors I mentioned before would have us believe. By saying that he forced you, anyway, you deny an understanding, and that puts us back at fornication with no intent to wed."

It is though the stop to his river of his words had been removed and out they flow in a dizzying current that moves down and around into an eddy that makes my head spin. All I hear is his word *fornication*, as though he liked the sound of it.

"I can only tell you what happened," I insist.

"Then we will have to decide," Winthrop says, "with God's help."

You'll need more help than God can give you, I think, but I know better than to say such a thing aloud. But, still, what am I to do with such as these to make myself understood? They use a word to describe an act. And the word they use comes from the Bible, which tells them what punishment should be applied to a person, such as myself, who does such a terrible thing. But the word they use means nothing to me. That word has intentions I never had, at least not with Henry sitting over there. It seems to mean just what he said, that I wanted him in my bed. Or what Master Dudley said, as another choice, that it describes an act leading to marriage, still filthy but one that could be washed a little cleaner by a wedding, so it would be dark gray instead of black, and maybe after a few years it might even leave me almost white again if I didn't do anything else naughty. The wonder of this all is that everything seems to be heaped on my head while Henry sits there with a silly little smile on his face. Now what word can I use to describe him? One comes to mind, but it is not one I should say to these grave gentlemen. I look at the man at the end of the

31

table, and he is not writing anything. Perhaps he does not like these words. Or maybe he already knows how this play is going to end.

"Where is the babe?" Winthrop says. "We have questioned Mistress Hutchinson, and she does not deny that she was with you in your travail, and that you were delivered of a baby girl."

I am too stunned to answer. He is, of course, asking my very question, as though he did not already know the answer.

"Stolen from me," I say.

"You do know the punishment for infanticide, do you not?" Dudley asks, his voice a cackle and his eyes bright. "Did you bury it, or perhaps with the ground frozen you threw it into the ocean one dark night?" He tries to soften his voice to tell me he is on my side, but the effect is hideous, as though he was a filthy toad trying to talk like a man. "Come, now," he says, "you can tell us. You would not be the first girl to try to hide her sin in such a manner."

I cannot bring myself to answer.

"You do know what the word means, the killing of an unwanted babe?" he presses.

I must remain mute. I look at my father. He is attentive now.

"It was taken from her," he says, "with my blessing."

"Taken?" Winthrop asks. "Taken by whom?"

"It was a bastard," my father replies. "Who was going to pay to feed and house it?"

"By whom?" Winthrop repeats.

"By them what owns the hut she was lying in," he says.

"The savages?" Winthrop asks, and my father nods.

"They will raise it," he says.

"Are they praying Indians, then?" Dudley asks.

My father's lips start to curl but he stops them into a small twitch.

"I didn't ask them," he replies. "I have done business with them before. But we don't talk much about religion. Mine or theirs. Just the price of things."

"Indeed," Dudley says.

My father picks up on the assistant governor's favorite word.

"Indeed," he repeats. "I do what I can to put bread on my poor table. Times is hard as your honors know, with nobody having the money to build a house, that I might put a roof on."

"We are sorry for that," Winthrop says without compassion. "But God teaches us to suffer our difficulties so as to better understand our help is only in Him."

I can see my father's eyes brighten with the thought that Master Winthrop and Mistress Hutchinson, and Master Dudley, all of them in their fine houses, do not look like they are suffering too many difficulties, but he does not say anything. He is a stubborn, willful man, but he is not stupid.

"Since I can't thatch, I trade," he says.

"Your daughter's babe?" Winthrop asks as though he is shocked.

My father shrugs.

"We had some old business to fix, and this was part of the fixing. I owed them a debt, a favor, if it please you. One of them I had traded with before had just lost a child to sickness. You should talk to your neighbor anyway. She's the one who interfered."

"I take it you mean Mistress Hutchinson."

"I do." He rubs his head. "She thought she was getting the better of me, but she did not know I had already had dealings with those she sent to rob me of my property."

"Explain yourself," Dudley insists.

He starts to tell the story of the rum, but I do not listen. I already know it. As he speaks, I look at the man at the end of the table. His pen is quiet. When my father is done with his lies, Winthrop leans over to whisper in Dudley's ear. Dudley nods. Winthrop motions to the man at the end of the table, and he comes over with a paper filled with writing he did not do while I was watching him. Winthrop motions my father forward and shows him the paper.

"Do you understand?" the Governor asks.

"I can read a word to two what is printed on a real page, but not this in this man's hand," he says.

Winthrop pulls back the paper.

"But you do understand, do you not?"

"I do," my father says. He looks at the paper. "I can see the numbers written here, that tell me how much my purse is going to be lighter because of her lust and disobedience."

"You are her governor," Dudley says, "as every man knows that he must take care that his children walk the right path."

Winthrop starts talking. As he does, I feel warmer and warmer, as though my face is too near a fire, but there is no fire. I hear him say *fornication, abomination, unclean,* and other such, which are supposed to describe what happened between Henry and me, and then words with amounts of money, which are the costs for the first set of words, and then where he says I am going, which is Hell, and now I know why I am feeling so warm, for wasn't it Master Cotton who talked about Hell being inside of us even while we are alive and maybe that is why I am burning up inside as I sit here in this meeting house. Still, I wonder if I will hear certain words like *hanging, or burning,* or *lashes* or *babe*. Especially, the last, but everybody seems to have forgotten about her. I do not care about the rest of it. Master Winthrop raises his voice to show he is coming to an end of what he has to say. He turns to Dudley.

"You will tell the girl her punishment. It is only fit, since you argued for it so hotly."

Dudley looks at the man at the end of the table, and nods. The man again comes forward and this time he hands a piece of paper to Dudley. The assistant governor clears his throat. He reads. I hear my name.

"Rachel Moore," he says in his dry, flat voice. "Stand up."

I do. There has been no thumping coming from outside for some time now. I am hopeful.

Dudley stares down at the paper.

"Master Winthrop exaggerates my responsibility. I would have had you at the end of a rope on the gallows instead of this mockery. But since you are so young yourself, and since some here do not fully believe the lad's story, we have been merciful in not applying the full measure of God's law."

"I am to live, then," I say.

"Yes," he answers.

"Well, then," I say before I can halt my tongue, "I can only thank you for your mercy."

He stares hard at me.

"And what about him?" I say, gesturing toward Henry. "Is he too young or innocent for the rope as well?"

"We have not forgotten him," Winthrop says. "He will stand beside you." He nods at Dudley, who reads from the paper.

A drop of water splashes on the back of my neck, and I look up to see that the snow is melting through my father's thatched roof. Maybe Hell has come inside this meeting house. Or maybe it means the sun is shining. I wonder how I am going to endure my shame. Is it worse to just stand there in front of a crowd of people who see you as something foul that must be cleansed than it is to receive the lash as I have done once before, for then there is the pain to take your mind off the way they look at you with such loathing? They will stare at me like I was a worm eating into an apple, and then they will go home afterward thinking they are now free to do whatever nasty business they have a mind to, just so long as they are not stupid enough, or clumsy enough, to get caught. But I will be looking into the eyes of the women, for at least some of them will understand how I come to be standing in front of them.

The constable raises me from my seat on the bench. His hold is not unkind, but it is very firm. He has two pieces of rope in his hand. He pulls my arms behind my back and ties them there with one piece. The other is already knotted into a hangman's noose, and this he slides over my head. He tightens it just enough so that I can feel it against my neck. Then he takes the other end and with it he leads me out, just as though I was a dog that had soiled the Governor's house. I turn back for a moment to see my father digging into his purse and dropping coins on the table in front of Dudley. The coins clunk against the wood on the table, and for some reason I think of the plop of melted ice dripping from our roof in a spring I now think might never come. Henry is still sitting where he had been. After the constable passes him, and as I approach at the end of my rope, Henry stretches his legs out so I have to step over them. He manages to bring his leg up between my knees for a moment. He looks at Winthrop and the others behind their table and they are shuffling through their papers. The constable is still looking toward the door, not aware that I have been stopped. Henry nudges his leg up higher. The constable now sees that I have stopped, and he pulls on the noose. It tightens and my head is yanked toward the constable. Henry relents and drops his leg. I step over it and stumble toward the door.

The first person I see when the constable pushes me through the door is Elizabeth. She is standing right by the steps that lead up to the scaffold. She is shading her eyes from the sun, so at first I do not understand the direction of her glance. I think that she will nod at me, to show her sympathy although I know she must be careful in what she does. Right after my belly began to swell to the point I could not hide it anymore, on the day when Master Winthrop knew what the women in his household had known for weeks, and so he had sent me home to be taken proper care of by my father, on that day Elizabeth came to talk to me to say how sorry she was, and that Henry had many times put her in danger of filling her own belly with a babe she would have no way of taking care of.

And so I look into her eyes now for a sign of our friendship, and if not that, at least an understanding that was set that day. But I see that she is looking past me, looking for her lover, for that same Henry she uttered curses about when she placed her hand gently on the swell of my stomach. When she does not see him, her eyes focus on me. She has powdered her cheeks, but can do nothing to give a more pleasing shape to her flat nose with its wide nostrils. And her red hands are in thin cloth gloves that somebody must have given her, for they are far too small and do not nearly reach her wrists. She raises her gloved right hand, and something shines in the sunlight, and then it is coming at my head.

I am too shocked to move out of the way, until the last moment, so that all I can do is close my eyes as it crashes against my cheek.

"Whore," she shouts. "We were going to be married, and now he is being taken away from me."

I am lying on the ground, and my face throbs where the chunk of ice struck me. It is next to me, and I reach to pick it up before I remember my arms are tied behind me. Constable Middleton's large hand comes down and swallows the chunk.

"You could throw it back at her," I say, and for a moment something in his eyes tells me that he might do that, but he tosses it behind us.

"Can you stand?" he says. But he does not wait for an answer. He takes my arms in his hands and lifts me right up.

"Whore!" The shout starts with Elizabeth, but then it is picked up by the others standing around, for there is a goodly crowd, and the word seems to be on everybody's lips, *Whore, Whore, Whore,* in all tones, high and low, but most from the women and above them all from Elizabeth who puffs out her fat cheeks before exploding with the words again and again in a high wail of a shout, half of mourning and half of righteousness.

Constable Middleton motions toward the steps that lead up to the scaffold.

"Aren't you going to lead the way, then?" I ask. "It's the least you can do."

He shoves me hard toward the steps and then he heads back to the meeting house. I expect he has to fetch Henry. I stumble into the snow that has been shoveled aside. I mount the steps and stand in the bright sun looking out at the crowd come to yell their curses at me, and the word *Whore* howls louder and louder, and I turn my face hard to face their scorn. I study their faces, one by one, until I come to one whose mouth is closed and whose eyes are cast down, as though ashamed of them, not me, and I feel a little comfort. At least, she has not given me up.

The shouting stops, and I look around to see why. Winthrop and Dudley have come out, and they take their place in front of the scaffold. My father joins them. And now Henry is led out by the constable. He has a rope around his neck, and his hands are tied behind his back, and his step is not so jaunty as I am used to seeing it, though a trace of a smirk remains on his lips as though to say that he is not touched by this shame.

He fairly bounds up the steps and stands next to me. I move away. I see that the Reverend Wilson has now joined the proceedings. He is a burly, short man, wearing a beaver hat that is pulled down almost to his eyes. I know that under that hat he is bald, for I have seen him in Master Winthrop's house when he was not wearing that wig he preaches in. He mounts the scaffold and stands behind us. I feel his bony hand on my shoulder, pushing me toward Henry. I shake my head hard against the noose on my neck. He can say what he wants, but he cannot force me a step closer to Henry. He seems to understand and takes his hand from me, but does not remove his hard stare until I feel forced to look down at the planks beneath my feet.

"Aye," he says in his high-pitched voice, loud enough for everyone in the crowd to hear, "that is where your eyes should be looking, down to Hell that awaits you. What a dreadful thing to think of. Will you confess to save your soul?"

I lift my eyes and shake my head.

"Child, think of your soul," he says.

"I am," I reply, "and I will not lie to satisfy you or them. If God is just, He knows what happened to me, and that I have no sin to repent of."

I see the smile on Wilson's face. He is happy with my stubbornness. But the smile is only for me. When he turns again to the crowd, his expression is as black as the Hell he loves to picture. I am surprised at my boldness, but even if I wanted to confess I would not know the words to use. I stare down at the planks of the scaffold to see if they will open up and drop me down into the flames. Nothing happens. Wilson waits, and then he turns to Henry.

"And you lad? Is your heart still stubbornly turned away from our Lord?"

Henry has been waiting for an opportunity, as he always is. He lowers his eyes for a moment, and when he lifts them his face is bright with new knowledge.

"I pray God forgive me for my abominable sin," he says.

Wilson looks like he would like to hear more, but Henry offers nothing. The minister starts to address the crowd. Again, I shut my ears, as his voice drones. What more can he say? Except to explain what he has clenched in his other hand, and for the answer for that I will have to wait. For some reason, I glance over at Henry. He has his head bowed as though he is listening to Reverend Wilson describe how he is a youth who cannot subdue his carnal disposition. I have heard that description before for what he does with girls, although like all the other words these learned men have used it seems to have little to do with how he threw me down on that bed and climbed on top of me. The crowd is silent, listening, and Henry is playing his part as though he truly wants to be forgiven, as though he intends to walk with righteousness from now on. Henry lifts his head for just a second so I can see that he is looking at me while he pushes his tongue in and out of his mouth fast and I feel a sickness grab my insides. Then he bows his head again as the minister says how he will be sent to a good Christian family in Salem, where he is originally from, with his instructions to them to govern him hard so he can grow straight. A howl lifts from the crowd. It is Elizabeth. In her hand is another chunk of ice. My father notices it, and holds her arm hard until she drops it.

"He cannot be taken from me," she shouts.

Minister Wilson goes on as though he has not heard anything, and Constable Middleton is at Elizabeth's side pulling her away. As she is turned to the side, I see her belly. She is still plump, but no more than that, and so now I cannot explain her anger away that way. Henry does not lift his head to look at her. I watch as she and Middleton make their way through the crowd and then onto the broad street that leads to the square. The way is covered in snow trampled by hundreds of feet. When the snow melts in spring, it will run to mud before the sun hardens it back to dirt. As Elizabeth and the constable reach the edge of the crowd, and the people standing there part to let them by without taking their eyes off me and Henry, I see the frozen hooves of the hog sticking up black and stark against the melting white snow. I sense that Wilson's eyes have followed Elizabeth just as I have, and he too sees the hooves and the trampled snow still covering the animal.

"A portent," he says, and now everybody looks at the feet of the dead animal. "Lo, the cloven hoof of the hog, the devil, covered by the whiteness betokening the purity of our community's heart, and see how it has been trampled under our feet as we have come here to show Satan how we will not suffer sin to grow among us."

"And now," he goes on, his voice rising even higher, "another sign to remind us, and these grievously erring young people." He lifts the hand that he has been holding clenched all this time, and in it he has a piece of black cloth. His fingers are red and numb from the cold, and he has trouble running a pin through the cloth. He almost drops it, and as he clutches at it, his thumb closes on the pin drawing a bright drop of red blood. I am surprised that he can be made to bleed. He steps to me and pulls back the thin blanket I still have bunched around my shoulders, and he fastens the cloth to my gown. I look down on it, and I see that it has four lines that form what I recognize as a letter, but I do not know which.

Elizabeth is gone, but another voice raises the cry of "Whore! Whore!" and I can only guess that the letter has something to do with that word. I look at Henry and then at the minister, but the hand that held my piece of cloth is empty. I fasten my eyes on one young man standing off to the side. He, too, is mouthing the word although I cannot hear his voice in the general din. I do not know why I have chosen to look at him. Mayhap it is the huge mole on the side of his nose. Even from this distance, I can see the coarse, reddish hairs growing from it. If I look at it hard enough, I do not see anybody else. But I cannot shut my ears. They insist on admitting the words that flow from Master Wilson.

"You will wear that on your garment whenever you go out, until we judge you have had its lesson seared into your soul, for you will not be instructed with gentler means," Wilson says.

And then the minister steps down and nods at Constable Middleton, who has returned. The constable takes up a position in front of the scaffold, and the crowd starts to drift away. We are to stand here all afternoon until sundown, with the ropes around our necks, and me with the new decoration on my gown. Almost everybody has now left, except for a group of boys a little younger than me, and the young man with the mole. He approaches the platform, his eyes only on me, as though I am standing alone. His eyes run up and down my body, and I feel them like they were his hands. His gaze stops at the letter on my gown. His face is twisted into a look that is difficult to describe. It looks something like Henry's expression when he was on top of me. I can almost hear him pant, as Henry did, and for the moment I am confused as to whether I am back in my bed, or standing here in the freezing cold before this strange young man. Then his expression changes into an ugly sneer, and he brings his hand up to the mole on his nose. He swipes at it as though it is causing him pain, and then he bends down and picks up a handful of snow, forms it, and throws it at me. I do not move, and it bounces off my shoulder. I hardly feel it, and concentrate on returning his gaze. The other, smaller, boys follow his lead, and soon Henry and me are pelted. Henry turns his back, but I stand firm. I do not feel the hurt as I am hit, and the cold snow seems only to douse the fire of my rage and humiliation. Constable Middleton watches and then he motions them away and the boys run off laughing. I hear "Whore" in their high voices floating back to me. The constable remains standing on the ground in front of us. Mole face stands with his eyes locked onto mine until an older man in a fine cloak and hat comes to his side and takes his arm to lead him away.

The sun has slid behind a cloud, and a chill wind blows across the common. We are shivering, and I almost think I could press myself against Henry for his heat. Almost. But I do not think I will ever be that cold.

"They're all gone. You could let us go, and find a warm fire for yourself," Henry says.

"I will go when my relief comes," Middleton replies, "but you two will stay here."

But not everybody has gone. I see her standing by herself near her house, which is across the common from the meeting house, and also right across from Master Winthrop's. I do not know how long she will stand there. She beckons to somebody, and I see it is the governor. She approaches him and they talk. She nods and waves at me, and then goes into her house as the governor does his.

I have been watching the sun as it comes out from behind the clouds and starts to slide behind a high tree near the well. A figure bends over to lift the planking. Whoever it is must be very thirsty for it is bitter cold. I cannot see the person for I am looking into the setting sun. I cannot feel my feet or my hands. My cheek throbs where the ice hit me. Henry has already been taken away so he can be put in a wagon to start his trip to Salem. Our other constable, Samuel Grover, now stands in front of the scaffold. He shifts his weight from foot to foot, and blows his breath on his gloved hands.

40

She arrives now, and says something to Grover I cannot hear. He climbs the stairs and comes up behind me with a knife and cuts my hands loose. I try to move my fingers but I cannot. He takes the noose off my neck, and then he is gone. She comes up as he leaves.

"Come," she says, "I have a fire waiting, and some warm rum for you to drink."

I try to walk, but I cannot feel the planks beneath my feet. She puts her arm around me and helps me down the steps.

I look down at the letter.

"Do you know its significance?" she asks.

I shake my head.

"It is the letter *w*. They think it stands for 'whore', but we will teach them that it is the beginning of wisdom."

We approach the hog, now almost fully exposed from the afternoon sun melting the snow that had covered it. Two men are talking near it. One is my father. I do not know who the other one is. Their voices rise in anger, and my father leans down to grab the rear legs. The other man tries to stop him, and points at the mark on the animal's flank. My father shoves the other man away, and walks off dragging the hog. The man looks for Constable Grover, but he has gone off.

"It was my hog," the man says. "That thieving Moore took it."

We pass my father who is breathing hard as he drags the hog. He only glances at us, and then continues walking. I look at the animal.

It is just that, a dead animal, too thin to yield even a decent slab of bacon. I start to call out to him, but I know he will not answer. Instead, I follow her. We are heading across the common where their two houses stare at each other. The Governor's is on the left, and hers on the right, and we are walking right toward both of them. One of them, I figure, as I turn once more to gaze at my father's back as he heads in the opposite direction, is my new home.

Chapter Three

I am sharing a feather bed with Bridget, who is a year older. All of the beds in this room are filled with children, girls on one side, and the boys on the other. I have not had a chance to count the lot of them yet but there must be about a dozen. Having shared one room with my father for my whole life, I find all this company overwhelming. They seem to be kindly disposed toward me, or at least they are being so at their mother's urging. Still, I am not comfortable among them. I miss my father's drunken snorting.

Bridget tosses in her sleep and her elbow pushes into my poor back, still aching from my travail. I cannot sleep. There is too much to learn, and too little time. The candle burns low, but I can see the page. "These are the letters," she said. "Learn them and you will see how they form words. You will practice by saying the words out loud after you know the letters." She did not know how she made my heart beat with excitement as she handed me the book. How could she? For her, and her children, reading is as ordinary as breathing. They all can read, except for the two very little ones, and even the boy, Samuel, who is only three already can say his letters.

I run my finger down the letters on the page. I stop at the same one that is now sewn to my gown. I trace the lines on the page with my fingernail, down, up, down, up, and then the same on the letter on my gown, down, up, down, up. I know one word that begins with that letter. And Mistress Anne told me another. *Whore*, they shouted again and again until I would have cut my ears off gladly to shut the sound out. It is not the act I am ashamed of, even if I had wanted it, for it is like the letter in its movements, just as I am tracing these lines faster and faster. No that is not what caused my face to burn. It was something in the way their voices lifted with the word, curled into it and then burst out in anger and mockery such as I have never seen before. That other word that Mistress Anne told me about, *wisdom*, seems very far away from me, and I am sure it will be very hard to learn.

I move to the top of the page to the first letter. Bridget told me that it is an *A*. I trace its lines. Then I count all the letters on the page, and the last one takes me to twenty-six. I flip through the pages and I see how the letters are put together in different ways, and these are the words I must learn to read. My head begins to ache. But the bed is softer than anything I have ever lain in before, and a smile forms on my face as I snuff the candle. Tomorrow, I must go across the way back to Master Winthrop, but each night I will return here, and that idea is enough to keep me grinning into sleep.

I feel the sun full on my face, and I sit up. I do not know where I am. My breasts ache. I bring my hands up slowly to them, and touch my nipples. They are full to bursting, and they are leaking. I lick my milk off my fingers, and I remember how it felt when she sucked. I almost think that I hear her angry little cry, that she is still lying on the bed next to me, waiting for me to give her my breast. But she is not there, and I look to my left where I know Bridget should be. She is gone, and I run my fingers over the mattress where she had been sleeping. It is no longer warm. The house is alive with voices rising up to me through the floor boards. I look down at the side of my bed and through a crack I can see down into the kitchen where the voices are coming from. I hear the floorboard creak and I feel as though I should hide beneath my blanket.

"Do not worry child," she says. "You are safe now."

Her voice is gentle, as I remember it being when first I heard it that night in my father's hut. I catch myself. I no longer view that hovel as my home, and maybe that is why I am afraid that somebody will see me here where I do not belong, lying on this soft mattress in a room made warm by the breakfast cooking in the fireplace in the kitchen below. The rich smell of baking bread is coming up through the floorboards. She seems to understand.

"Are you hungry, then?" she asks.

"Yes. But I will get up in a moment and help the other servants."

Her face broadens into a smile. She is not a pretty woman, now that I have the opportunity to look at her closely. Her face is plain, and her brown hair is graying. Her nose is a little too large, and her cheeks rounded. She is short, and a little plump as befits a woman who has given birth fifteen times. Yet there is a brightness in her eyes, that can dance between anger and a twinkle of laughter. I have seen both those moods. Now, she seems amused.

"My husband's cousins are taking care of the cooking, leaving me free to tend to you."

I cannot respond. It is as if she is not speaking English, although I understand the words.

"How are you then?" she asks. She does not wait for me to answer, but pulls up the thick woolen blanket that has warmed me to the point where I felt I was feverish. She sees my naked breasts and swollen nipples. She takes one between her fingers and tugs as though it was the teat of a cow. My milk squirts out and we both smile. She does the same for the other breast.

"This will stop before long," she says. "It is just that God intended for you to be giving suck now." Her voice has its sharp edge.

"Do you not think I can get her back? Before I am dry?"

She shakes her head.

"We can try. Will," she pauses. I try to wipe the question from my face by forcing my eyebrows down but they rise again. She waits, a smile playing on her lips. "Will," she repeats, "Master Hutchinson, my husband." My brows relax and she continues. "Will knows some of them that he has traded with, and he has asked them to find out what they can."

She pulls the blanket down past my hips. Her forehead wrinkles and she tightens her mouth into a frown. I follow her eyes to where she is looking at the bed beneath my thighs. I am bleeding again.

"You cannot afford to lose much more," she says. She has a small cloth folded into a triangular shape. "This will not hurt," she says. "It will stop it." She pries my legs apart. I start to resist, but then I let her move them. Her fingers place the cloth where the blood is flowing, and then inside. The cloth is warm.

"Is it a kind of plug, then?" I ask, "Like you would put in the bung hole of a cask."

She cannot help but smile, but I did not intend a joke.

"No," she says. "It is what I soaked the rag in that will stop the blood. Sit up, if you can."

I do, and she hands me a cup to drink from.

"It may taste a little bitter, though I have sweetened it with honey. It will relax you, so you can sleep again."

I sip the beverage, and it is sweet.

"I only taste the honey," I say.

"Good. Are you feeling a little better?"

I manage a nod. I find my hand moving to the table next to my bed where the primer lies. It is still open to the page with all the letters on it, just as I left it next to the candle. I run my finger up and down the letters.

"If they had put a letter on Henry, which would it have been?"

The smile on her face disappears, and I am afraid that I have offended her. But she places her warm hand over mine and guides my finger down the page a short distance. She recites the letters, one by one, "*A, B, C, D, E, F,*" and then she stops. I count along with her as she says the names of the letters, so I know that the one called *F* is the sixth one. She has watched my mouth as I count.

"Yes, that is right," she says. "But they didn't put that letter on him, did they? No, they sent him off to Salem instead."

"It's a good thing for him that somebody cares enough to look out for him."

She nods.

"And now you have me. Come down to get something to eat when you feel well enough."

She leaves and I study the primer. I say the letters as she had said them, and each time I stop on the sixth one, and I imagine stitching it onto his back. I push my needle through the cloth of the letter, which is as long as my forearm, and then into his skin. He twists as the needle pricks his flesh, but I continue, in and out, drawing the needle through first the fabric and then his skin. He bleeds a little more with each stitch until my hand is covered with his blood. It is warm. I finish stitching and wipe my bloody hands off on his cheeks. I feel tired, again, and I fall asleep with a smile on my face.

I wake up a second time this morning to an almost quiet house. I hear only the murmur of female voices coming up from the kitchen. My stomach now aches, and I cannot remember when last I ate something. I stand up and reach for my gown. As I draw it to me, I see my letter, and it spins before me. I pull the gown over my head and feel my face redden. My shame is arguing with my hunger, but my stomach wins, and I go down the stairs, hoping that I will not be remarked by the two women whose voices I still hear.

The kitchen is twice the size of my old hovel. The fireplace looks big enough to put a bed or two into. In front of it is a short, very plump woman with a red face beneath a white cap that hides all but a few wisps of gray hair. Her eyes are set wide apart, and she has a long thin nose that is strangely at odds with her fat cheeks. She is pulling a loaf of bread out of the oven on the side of the fireplace, and does not look up. On the other side of the kitchen is a tall, angular woman, also wearing a white cap, but hers does not hide the striking black hair that falls over her forehead. Both women are wearing coarse, gray cotton gowns and dark blue aprons. I do not know if they are servants like me. They are talking in excited tones as I enter.

"Into the well, they said," the one at the oven says.

"That is the very truth of it."

"And the babe?" the other asks.

"It lives," the tall one replies.

At the same time, they become aware of me, and they stop talking.

The one at the oven motions to me.

"Well, come on over here, and give us a hand," she says. Her tone tells me that she is one of Master Hutchinson's spinster cousins, who is paying off her room and board by doing chores that she feels she was not bred up to do. It might seem like a lot of information to get from a simple sentence, one that could have been uttered by a woman of my own class, but I have learned how to tell these things. There is something in the manner, in the quality of the voice that has a downward movement to it, and the look in the eyes that goes with it, a look that says I see you from up here, like you are at the bottom of a foul, stinking cistern with toads and other slimy creatures, and that is where you belong. I can hear and see that attitude in this woman, and I am sure she is no servant even if she is doing a servant's job right now.

The tall one stops what she is doing at the table at the far end of the room. She turns to face us, holding the carcass of a large fowl, probably a turkey, in her hand, and a long knife in the other. Her voice is hardly more than a whisper.

"Give the child a chance, Patience," she says. "Remember what Anne told us about what she has suffered."

"Indeed, I do remember, Mabel," the one called Patience says, and the way she looks at me and the sound of her voice cause my hand to cover the letter on my chest. "And because I do, I am trying to help the child by giving her some meaningful work to do."

"Yes," Mabel replies as she approaches, "but look how pale she is."

I am tired of them discussing me as though I am a broom waiting to be used, and the question is whether I still have enough straws left to do a decent job of sweeping. So, although I do feel a little faint, I go over to Patience, whose red face and quivering lip seem to have nothing to do with her name, and I grab hold of the board holding the fresh baked bread. I pull it the rest of the way out of the oven, and turn around, looking for a place to rest it. Mabel points to the hearth, and I set it down.

"There," I say, but the next moment my head starts to whirl and I sit down next to the bread.

"I told you," I hear Mabel says.

"Aye," Patience replies. "She's an artful one, she is."

The room is spinning. I stare at Mabel, and there are six or seven of her, each one holding the same carcass and the same knife rotating in front of my eyes, and for a moment it looks like the knife is moving in and out of the carcass, and Mabel's mouth is opening without any sound coming out. She slows her motion, and now she looks like she is dancing with the carcass. Once when I was a little girl, back in old England, my father took me to a grand house where he had some business, and while he was talking and laughing with this man in a pantry in the back of the house, I heard music playing, and I stole away down a hall through a door into a darkened room. The door on the other side of the room was open a crack, and I saw light coming through the opening, and the music was very loud. I crept to the door, got down on my knees to press my eye against the frame so I could peek in and there I saw these musicians playing in front of people dancing, moving very slowly and elegantly. The whole scene just about took my breath away, as I had never heard music like that before, nor seen dancing, but then I felt my father's heavy hand on my neck. He lifted me up, and I waited for that hand to come down hard on my face, as it usually did, but his breath was heavy with whatever he had been drinking with that other man, and he had a smile on his face. All he did was pick me up and carry me back through the darkened room and through the pantry and out in the night air, the music still playing in my mind, and the dancers still dancing in my eyes, and that is how Mabel now looks until the memory of the music stops, and so does she.

"I'm better now," I say.

"Then sit down at the table," Mabel says, "and eat something."

She puts the carcass and knife down and walks over to the fireplace. Patience does not, at first, get out of her way.

"Can she not fetch her own?" she says.

For answer, Mabel puts her hand on Patience's shoulder and turns her aside.

"No, she cannot," Mabel says.

She takes a large pot out of the fireplace and ladles something steaming into a wooden trencher, which she sets on the long table that fills one side of the kitchen. This is where the family eats, and Mabel beckons me to sit down.

The soup is rich, with pieces of meat floating in it. I try not to eat it too fast, but in a few seconds the bowl is empty. Mabel smiles and fills it up again. This time I do eat slowly, and enjoy the flavor and the warmth until again not a drop is left. I hear someone coming in to the kitchen, and I know without looking that it must be Mistress Anne.

"Back into bed with you, now," she says. "Tomorrow, you must at least go over to Master Winthrop's and do what you can. He thinks I will spoil you here, and that what you need is to be back at work."

"I do not think Master Winthrop knows what I need."

"Hush, child," Anne says. "Even if that is true, it is not for you to say."

I look past Anne to the other two. Patience is busying herself with stirring something in a kettle hanging in the fireplace. Mabel is rubbing something onto the skin of the fowl. I remember how she was dancing and I start to smile.

"What is it?" Anne asks.

"A minute ago I was dizzy, and when I looked at Mabel it looked like she was dancing round and round with that fowl."

Her face turns serious.

"And have you seen much dancing?"

"I remember once. In a big house when I was a little girl."

Her eyes turn inward for a moment, as though she too is remembering something.

"I don't think you or I will see many dancers here in Boston."

"The ones I saw looked so happy."

"Yes," Anne replies, "I have seen them like that myself."

And something in her voice tells me that maybe she, too, once moved her feet to the rhythms of the musicians.

I have slept most of the day and through supper. I find another bowl of broth on the table next to my bed. It is still steaming, but I do not care about that. I search about for the primer, as that is now more important to me than food. It is on the pillow where Bridget's head usually lies. I pick it up and hold it to my chest. Now, I can eat.

The other children come wandering up to bed as I finish the broth. Each looks at me, but in different ways. The little ones come right up and stare at me, and when I smile, they smile back at me. The ones closer to my age are a little shy, and they pretend, at first, that they do not notice I am here among them. None of them talks to me, and that is how I like it for now. I would not know what to say to them. Bridget, being older, is still downstairs among the adults.

I hear voices coming up from the first floor of the house, many voices. It is Tuesday evening, and I remember hearing about all the people that come to Mistress Anne's house every week on this day. I know they come to hear Mistress Anne, and I want to listen with them too. My father says they are just a bunch of women gossiping about things they would do better to leave alone. But I think he is wrong, like he usually is. I hear a number of men's voices mixed in with those of the women. I cannot hear the words. They are gathered in the great room on the other side of the house, and only because there are so many can I hear anything at all.

I put one foot onto the floor, but a little head bobs up from across the room. It is Samuel. He smiles at me and puts his head back on his pillow. I wait until his chest moves up and down with his sleep. The breaths of the children float toward me, a ragged melody, but each by itself even. They are all asleep. I slide out of bed. The floor boards are cold beneath my feet. I walk slowly to the door, stopping after every step to make sure none of them has wakened.

This room is on the top of the house and runs two thirds across its width. There is a hall outside where the back stairway comes up, and beyond that a door to another, much smaller room that was the nursery for Samuel. I push that door open and drop down to my knees. I crawl along the floor. I am over the great room downstairs. I can hear the voices clearly now. A woman is speaking. Her words come haltingly as though she would not say them. Light streams up through a crack an inch wide in the floor board. I stare through the space and see the woman's face. I pull back, sure that she has seen me, but her words continue. I look again through the crack and see that her eyes are downcast. She stops talking.

"Go on Goody Hett," Mistress Anne says, her tone gentle but insistent.

Goody Hett shakes her head, but then she nods.

"I was in black despair. I knew not what to do. I felt on the rack. I could not convince myself I was saved, or I was damned. I did not care which it was, if only I could be certain."

"Then what did you?" Mistress Anne asks.

"We know what Goody Hett did," a male voice says. "We want to know why."

I remember the conversation I interrupted that morning in the kitchen, and I recall the woman at the well the day of my punishment. I am ashamed. To be sure I was being humbled, but that woman was floundering in the blackness of a hell she had created in her own mind. I press my face against the crack. If someone was to look up I would be discovered, but I do not care. I turn my head so my right eye can peer through the crack. I study the woman's face. I see it change from white to red in anger.

"You must hear then," she says, spitting her words out through her clenched teeth. "I told myself I must make myself certain about my soul's estate, and as Master Wilson teaches, as we act, so are we justified or not, so I acted."

"Indeed, you did," the male voice says again, and I strain to make out who it is, but the crack closes so I can see to the space in front of Goody Hett, but not to the people I imagine are sitting beyond. "But the voice you heard was from the devil himself, and not good Master Wilson."

I find myself agreeing with this invisible man. I remember my own babe at my breast, and I want to hear this woman explain herself.

"I bundled my babe," she continues without answering the man. "I thought she must be warm, for the water would surely be cold. Then I placed her on the ground and lifted the cover of the well. I thought I might kiss her good-bye, but I did not have the courage to unwrap the blanket about her. If she opened her eyes to look at me I would have to take her back home, and I knew I could not do that. So I dropped her into the well. I heard her splash. My heart leapt in the joy of the sure knowledge that if I can kill my babe I must be damned to hell everlasting."

She stops and begins to weep. Mistress Anne embraces her and leads her away. The room below is silent. I am afraid to breathe. Mistress Anne is now standing beneath me. She looks up, and I think she has seen me, but she starts talking to the people.

"Damned you surely are," the man says, and I hear murmurs of agreement. I am not so sure. I hear her confusion, how she worried about keeping her babe warm even as she sought to end its life. It is, I think, not so different from the way I thought of mine own when I remembered who planted it in my belly and how. The murmuring continues for a few moments, and then Mistress Anne's strong voice rises above the whisperings.

"This poor woman's tale is what happens when we are taught the Covenant of Works." She pauses. "The babe was saved by the grace of God by Robert Parish who was on the watch that night and saw Goody Hett drop her babe into the opened well. God did not intend to have His holy Word lead to such a terrible end."

Somehow I feel that eyes are spying me through the crack in the floor. I am sure the floor will now open up and send me tumbling down into a crowd that will remember who I am and how I stood on the platform just a little while ago. I crawl backward out of the room before the floor gives way beneath me.

Back in my bed, I light the candle again. I know I cannot sleep. I must carry my thoughts away from Goody Hett and her mad act of drowning her babe to convince herself that she is damned. I pick up my primer and study my letters, forcing myself to concentrate on their form. At first, all I see is the face of the babe peering over its blanket, its mouth opened in wonder. It does not know what is happening. It reaches its arms as though to seek its mother, and then it feels the cold water seeping through the wool of the blanket and it shakes its tiny, clenched fingers. Its mouth now opens and closes in a noiseless howl as it sinks into the water. My breasts ache.

I put the primer down and rub my eyes until the vision of the drowning babe disappears and I can again see the letters on the page, although my breasts remain so full I believe they will burst. Bridget has promised to teach me what sound the letters make, but she has not had time to do so yet. I only know the names of the one that is stitched on my gown, and the one that should have been branded on Henry, and the first one, that Bridget did name for me. She called it *A*.

I hear the breathing of the children settled into sleep, and my eyes ache from looking at the letters. The door opens and I hear Bridget's steps. She slides into bed next to me.

It is cold now in the room and she presses her body against mine for the warmth. I feel her breath. I know she wants to talk.

"Tell me how it was with you and Henry."

She seems so young to me, even though she is a year older. Still, I do not want to talk with her about what happened between Henry and me.

"Please," she says. "Just a little."

She is too earnest, and I am too tired, and at least it is not Goody Hett that she is interested in.

"Well, I say. What do you want to know?"

She is too ashamed to say.

"You know."

"What?" I am going to make her pay for her answer.

"What was it like?"

I turn to face her.

"You mean when Henry held me down, forced his way between my legs, and shoved himself into me? Is that what you want to know about?"

Her eyes are bright, but she cannot hold mine.

"Yes," she says, in a whisper just audible above the breathing of her brothers and sister. "Yes, about that. Not all of it. Just the last bit. When he was, you know…"

"When he was inside of me?"

She does not say anything, but she manages to nod her head.

"It hurt like nothing you can imagine," I say, and then I turn away. I don't know what answer she wanted, but this is the one I want her to take into her dreams, for her own sake. I do like her after all, and hope we can be friends.

I have breakfast with the children, after the adults have eaten. I am still somewhere between servant, guest, and member of the family. Nobody tells me to do anything, and so I just sit down next to Bridget. I notice that she keeps glancing at me, but she does not seem to have any other questions. Mabel and Patience serve us gruel and bread. Nobody has ever served me a meal before I arrived at this house, and I am beginning to see that the food tastes a lot better when somebody else's hands set it in front of you. Patience places the trencher in front of Bridget and says good morning to her. She slides mine onto the table in silence and moves on. I do not care.

I walk across to Master Winthrop's house right after breakfast. Bridget has gone to help her father in the shop which is built onto the side of the house. I glance through its windows and see bolts of material on shelves on the far wall, just like those that Mistress Anne paid the savages that night. I am trying to

52

train myself to forget that night, but I am not having much success. My breasts still ache almost all the time, and I can feel my milk begin to run. I clench my arms across my chest for a moment to still the pain, and then I go on.

Eleanor, a sturdy middle-aged servant woman, with wide shoulders and hips to match, and a face marked by the pox, opens the door. She does not say anything but just looks at me. I understand. I open my cloak so she can see the letter. She lifts her head away as though her nose has been assaulted by something foul, and then she steps aside with a gesture to the woman who is standing a few feet behind her.

"About your business, Eleanor," the woman says. Margaret Winthrop is tall and elegant, with gray streaks in her brown hair, and kindly blue eyes. In this house, though, I know my place as a servant. And Mistress Margaret, as kindly as she is, never lets me forget who I am.

"My husband wants to see you," she says, and I nod. I know Master Winthrop will be waiting for me at his desk in the parlor. He is reading a book when I walk in, and I wait for him to look up. This he does after a few moments. That is the way with these people. They are always doing something else when you come to see what they want you to do. He motions me into the room without taking his eyes from his book until I am standing right in front of him.

"How are you child?" he asks.

"On the mend, sir," I reply.

He looks through a window at the Hutchinson house.

"Are you being treated well?"

"Yes." I could say something more, but I do not think his are the ears to hear my feelings on Mistress Anne and how she has dealt so warmly with me.

He waits for me to go on, and when I don't he looks down at the page of the book on his desk.

"God always makes Himself known to us," he says, "even at the time of sorest trial."

I imagine it is my sore trial he is after, but I do not know exactly which of my troubles he has in mind, so I just wait for him to continue.

"Is that in that book?" I point to the one in front of him.

"No child. What I said is from Scripture. This," he holds up the book, "is one that tells stories of remarkable instances of God's showing us the way. Here is the one I was reading." He hands me the book with his finger pressed to a place on the open page.

"I cannot read."

He pulls the book back, and places it flat on the desk.

"Well, then I will tell you this story. And perhaps I can arrange to have you instructed so you can read the Scriptures yourself. It would be well for you to learn." His eye catches the letter on my gown. "As I am sure you now understand."

"That I do, sir," I say, but I will not tell him that Bridget is teaching me my letters. "What does the story say?"

He smiles and strokes his beard, gently, with pleasure. It seems he likes to explain things.

"It tells of a man named James Andreas, in Germany in the last century, and how he did God's will by causing a most marvelous conversion of a criminal, a thief and a Jew, who was being hanged by his heels while two dogs chewed on his flesh. The Jew was calling to God in Hebrew, but he did not understand that God would not heed such words coming from such a one as he. So this Andreas bent over him and taught him about our Lord, how he died for our sins, and even such a heathen as him could be saved if God chose him and if he would accept our Lord Jesus as savior. And while Andreas spoke, God caused the dogs to fall quiet, and to leave off chewing the man's flesh wherein they had been making a feast. The Jew thanked Andreas for his instruction and asked that he might be first baptized and then hanged so as to meet this Christian God sooner, and all this was done accordingly."

This is truly an amazing story. My mind fills with the picture of this man hanging upside down, his face all red and just off the ground, and the dogs with their fangs covered with ribbons of flesh running blood. And while the dogs are feeding on this man, another comes by and talks to him about Christ as savior, and the hanging man is taken with this instruction and so is saved to hang with head pointing toward heaven. This is what I can take out of the story, but I see that Master Winthrop is waiting for me to say something in response to the telling, but I do not know what I am supposed to gather from it. I have learned that it is better not to say anything than the wrong thing with gentlemen such as Master Winthrop, so I stand there, hoping my face does not give away my thoughts.

"Do you see, my child?"

I nod.

"Good. Then you do understand how you are like that poor wretch in the story whom God chose to scourge and then save."

"Then the dogs, sir," I begin. "The dogs, sir, what am I to make of them, for I see how I could be the man, and maybe yourself could be the man who taught the other about our Lord, and the tearing of my flesh is like the punishment I have just endured to show me that God cares for me, but the dogs, sir, confuse me."

He seems genuinely pleased that I learn so quickly.

"Why, just so," he says, "they are His scourges."

"Yes, I see that," I reply, but in my mind I see the curs skulking about the backs of houses looking for whatever they can find to eat.

Master Winthrop now starts to stroke his beard more forcefully, and I know that he is going to ask me something I do not want to hear. He does not disappoint me.

"Last night was Tuesday night, I believe?"

From remarks I remember my father making, I think I see where Master Winthrop wants to take me, and I must go along as best I can.

"Indeed, it was," I say, and Master Dudley's word comes strangely to my lips. Master Winthrop appears not to care or to notice.

"I saw a large number of guests arriving at Mistress Hutchinson's house."

"Yes," I reply, "I heard them through the floorboards. I was too weak to go downstairs."

He seems disappointed with this answer, as I hoped he would be.

"Then you did not see the people arrive?"

"No, I heard them."

"And what did you hear?"

"Their voices?"

"And?"

He yanks on his beard.

"What sort of people did you hear?"

"A goodly number of women. One woman I heard. I think her name was Goody Hett."

His eyes brighten.

"She told about throwing her babe in the well."

"Yes. But I did not want to hear any more. I put my blanket over my head. I had fearful dreams that night."

"Is that all you can tell me?"

"Yes."

He sits quiet for a while.

"You know," he says, "it is no accident that you are living in that house while you still work in this one."

"No sir, I imagine I am here because you want me to be."

"Yes, for two reasons. First to give me another opportunity to prove that I can be a better governor for you than I was before, for I am responsible for your transgressions, as much or more than you yourself."

"And the second?"

His brows contract, and his eyes harden to where his face now appears ugly.

"Because you can be of use to me in her house."

"Yes sir," I say.

He motions me toward the door.

"About your chores, then," he says. "And the next time we talk, perhaps you will have more to tell me."

Mistress Margaret is waiting for me as soon as I leave the room. Standing beside her is Elizabeth.

"You are to assist Elizabeth," Mistress Margaret says, "until you are able to work on your own again."

What she doesn't say, but what I understand, is my being able has nothing to do with how well recovered I am in body. It is my soul they want to straighten out, and somehow they think that Elizabeth is the one to help me do that. I guess she is like the dogs in the story Master Winthrop just told me, for I feel her beady little pig eyes burning through the letter on my chest and into my heart. My breathing quickens and the color rises to my face, but I have no choice but to endure my portion. I do not know if God is chastening me, but I am sure that the governor is doing his best. Elizabeth cannot stop the grin that is forming on her lips, even when Mistress Margaret turns to her with a stern look.

"I hope," Mistress Margaret says to Elizabeth, "that you can remember what we spoke about before." The grin dies from Elizabeth's lips, and I am grateful.

"Yes," Elizabeth says, "I surely do remember." She beckons to me. "Come, we are to work the spinning wheel."

She leads me into the small room behind the kitchen where the wheel sits beneath dried venison meat. The odor reminds me of the night under the deer hides being pulled through the snow. That seems like a long time ago, but I am sure Elizabeth will want to remind me. She sits behind the wheel and motions to a basket filled with raw wool.

"Do you know how to card?" she asks, and hands me the carding comb.

"No," I say. "I know nothing about any of this."

Her face forms into a sneer.

"Comes from being raised by your father, I expect. Brought you up all delicate, like. That must have been what Henry saw in you, for otherwise I have no understanding."

I cannot begin to tell her how wrong she is, and so I just shrug.

"My father bought cloth and sewed our clothes. He has very nimble fingers."

"That is a fact," she sneers.

"Look," I reply, "you know as well as I that I did not take Henry from you. I never wanted him."

"Oh, I do not care about him. It is true that he tried to force his way with me, but I would have none of it. I pushed him away, not like some people."

I remember Henry and Elizabeth sweating and bouncing in the bed next to me every night for weeks before he tired of her and began looking at me, and I recall how she grunted with him on her, more like a squeal of pleasure, and I guess that is what she means by pushing. Also, I hear her screaming *whore* at me, so I suppose she does feel she is my better.

"Master Winthrop knows all about how I resisted Henry, and he has told me to be your teacher."

"Yes," I say, "but what did Mistress Margaret tell you?"

I know that Mistress Margaret governs the servants in the governor's house. And I also know that she is just more aware of what goes on under his roof than is her husband. So I cannot think that she has been taken in by Elizabeth. Elizabeth's expression tells me that I am right.

"I am just doing what I must," she says.

"Well, then, do it well."

She picks up the carding comb and runs it through the wool, separating the strands. Her hands work fast and well. She hands the comb to me.

"Try," she says.

I start to pull the fibers through the teeth, but then I let the comb fall to the floor. If she is going to be my teacher, I do not see any profit in being too apt a scholar.

She picks up the comb. "Clumsy you are," she says. "Try again."

And I do.

My hands ache and yet they are softened from the oil that flowed from the wool. I spent the day being taught by Elizabeth how to card, and how to hold the fiber just tight enough so that it will spin properly. After our first conversation, we did not say much, just words necessary for the work. As I left, she said, "Maybe you can practice in your new home. I am sure there is work for you to do there." I began to remind her that I was living with a cloth merchant, but again I just shrugged. I imagine I will be doing a lot of that in Master Winthrop's house.

Now, I await Bridget coming to bed. As I walked across the garden on the side of the house, I saw her talking to the young man who clerks in her father's shop. They were standing among the frozen stalks of Indian corn, and their heads were so close that their breaths mingled. I know that she will want to talk to me about him, and I do not know what I can possibly tell her. I hear her steps approach the door, and I snuff out the candle by which I had been studying my letters, as I do every night. She is out of breath as she undresses in the dark and slides in next to me. I do not see the flush on her face, but I feel that her body glows with warmth. I do not know why, but I am irritated by her youthful foolishness. Reminding myself that she is my elder does not convince me that she is not playing the wanton with that young man, and doing so in perfect ignorance. I turn my breathing into a loud snore, but she is not to be so easily put off.

"You were looking at the doorway when you heard me come in," she says. "And you put out the candle as though you did not want to be troubled by me."

I face her. It is the way she sees things only through her own eyes, I realize, that is annoying. I shrug, so as not to agree or argue.

"I also saw you looking at me and Tom in the garden," she says. "Don't deny it."

"I was just wondering what you were doing out there with no corn to pick, and ice forming on your nose," I reply.

"Well, then, what do you think?"

"I think you would do better to be inside where it is warm."

"That's not what I mean, and you know it."

"You are right. You are already much too warm, and you need to cool down. Alone. Or in prayer."

This last surprises me, but then it is what Elizabeth said to me just before I left, that she had turned to prayer after Henry left, and that God was showing her how to walk.

"You mock me," Bridget replies. "I am my mother's daughter, but I am not my mother." I cannot see her face, but I would wager she is pouting as she says this. Still, she is too excited to remain peevish. "Tell, me," she insists, "what do you think of him?"

"I think he is dangerous."

I can feel her glow.

"Yes," she replies. "I think so too." And she rolls onto her back to dream.

I am tired, but my mind is now awake. Bridget begins to snore gently and happily. I am thinking about the dogs in Master Winthrop's story, and how it would feel to be hanging by my heels with my face staring at fangs dripping with my blood and pieces of my flesh, and how my blood would flow while I was upside down, and what would I do if somebody came to talk to me about Our Lord. I imagine I would listen to that person for as long as the dogs stopped chewing on me. I do not know if I would ask to be hanged right side up, with or without benefit of baptism. I think that as long as I could draw breath I would try to leave. I have to wonder what kind of God this is that Master Winthrop is presenting to me, who would use snarling dogs rending flesh to bring one to an acceptance of His Mercy. That one is too much for me. I am sure I need to be better instructed on this mystery.

In the meantime, I can only try to sleep. Bridget is breathing hard in some dream, and that is good. As long as I listen to her, I will not hear the growling of the dogs, nor feel their sharp teeth ripping my flesh.

Chapter Four

It is Tuesday morning again. Elizabeth is waiting for me in the pantry, but the spinning wheel has been shoved into a corner, and in its place is a tub of steaming water. Next to the tub is a basket filled with hanks of wool.

"It's time for a bath," Elizabeth says. "We need to get the smell and the dirt of the animal out of it so it is fit for people to wear."

I hear what she says, but I know that her words are not innocent. They mean to say that I am also unclean. I do not know how she manages to add that idea to her simple words, but she does.

She picks up a hank of dirty, gray wool.

"See," she says. I note the color and the smell of the wool, but also how her hands are cracked and red. She follows my eyes, and reaches for my own hands. "These are much too soft," she says. "Why, they feel delicate, like a lady's hands. But we can fix that." She guides my hands into the tub of water. I resist, but she is very strong. The water is pleasantly warm. She releases my hands and I take them out.

"That wasn't too bad, now was it? Oh, but I forgot. We have to add the lye." She reaches behind her for a bucket of lye and pours a generous amount into the tub. She tests the mixture of warm water and lye with her own red hand. "Ah," she says. "Not enough. For the wool, or you." She empties the bucket of lye into the tub, and then dumps several hanks of dirty wool into it. "Go ahead," she says. "Wash it."

"Don't you want to test the water?" I ask.

She grins, and I see a bubble of saliva captured in the gap between her widely spaced front teeth.

"No," she replies. "I am sure it is just the way we want it."

My hands burn as soon as I put them in the water and I begin to lift them out, but Elizabeth has hold of my wrists.

"No, no," she says, "you will get used to it. It always hurts a little the first time. Don't you remember how it is?"

My hands feel as though they are being held in fire and I push up against her but it is no use. Instead I find a hank with my fingers and scrub it between my fingers.

"That is right," she says, "scrub it well."

I finish with this piece and lift it from the tub. It is white and smells of lye. Elizabeth brings over another basket, and I put the clean wool in it. The air stings my reddened hands. She gestures toward the tub and I force myself to put my hands back in. The water feels like it is peeling my skin off.

"They say you did away with your babe," she whispers. Her words whistle through the space between her gapped teeth.

I jerk my hands out of the tub, but she is waiting for me to do that, and she grabs both of my wrists and pushes down.

"That is a lie, and you know it," I say, but I am finding it hard to think or speak against the burning in my hands.

"I know what I hear. They say that story about your father trading the babe to the savages was just that, a story. They say your father was protecting you from being hanged."

I try to laugh, but I can only manage to gasp.

"Well, it must be so, if they all say so."

"That is what they say. And Master Winthrop, he chose to believe the story because he did not want to see you at the end of the rope, not just yet. He wanted you back in his house while you were living over there. With her."

This has the ring of truth, and Elizabeth sees that I recognize it. Her eyes betray her. She has told me too much. I struggle to raise my hands from the tub. As I do, she smiles.

"Did Henry like your hands?" she says. "He always thought mine was too rough on his skin. He is very particular about how he is touched. But I expect you know that better than I do." She relaxes her grip enough for me to pull my hands up. I look at my skin. It is redder than blood, like meat before it is cooked. I have to turn my eyes away and my stomach begins to churn.

"Why look at them now. They are red enough." She holds her own hands next to mine. "Mine look nicer than yours."

"Yes," I mutter. "It is only too bad that your Henry won't be feeling them."

61

I see her hand come toward my face, but I cannot move away fast enough, and her hard palm crashes against my cheek.

"Whore!" she snarls.

"Slut!" I scream. And then we hear a hurrying of footsteps.

"Here now, what is the matter?"

Mistress Margaret is at the door, her hand to her mouth, and her eyes on my hands.

"Elizabeth? Rachel?" she demands.

"I guess I put too much lye in the water," Elizabeth says. "I was just going to dump some out and put in more water."

Mistress Margaret holds my shoulders and studies my face. I feel that I am sweating and pale.

"May I go home?" I say. I have never used that word before to refer to my new home across the way.

"Yes, surely. But let me wrap your hands."

I do not protest, and she reaches for a jar on a shelf. She dips a piece of cloth in it and then wraps my hand. The cloth is soft and smells like my hands did yesterday from something in the wool. She wraps my other hand. The effect is soothing. She picks up the washed hank of wool. She tugs the fibers and they snap.

"Elizabeth, you should know better. I don't care about the wool, but this child's hands. What were you thinking?"

"We were talking, and I guess I didn't mind," Elizabeth says. She looks at me to see if I am going to contradict her. I know better, and so when Mistress Margaret's eyes find mine, I nod. Just then the floor boards creak beneath a heavy tread, and Master Winthrop appears. He glances at my hands and at the spoiled wool his wife is still holding.

"It is Tuesday," he says to me. "Tomorrow, when you come here, I will be waiting to speak with you. And you better have Elizabeth show you how to take better care."

"She already has," I reply.

He nods, strokes his beard, and leaves.

"This cloth is not doing you much good," Mistress Anne says, as she starts to pull it off. A sharp pain shoots up my arms, and she stops.

"You are going to lose a little skin," she says. "Can you bear it?"

"Yes," I begin to say, but before the word is out of my mouth, the cloth is off my hand, and I almost fall down as my head spins. I feel her hand cool against my forehead. She holds it there until I can open my eyes without feeling sick.

"These burns need stronger medicine than what can be worked out of a sheep's wool." She cuts off a piece of a plant stalk and squeezes it until a white cream comes out, and this she spreads over my hands. Immediately, they feel cooler.

"You don't have to tell me how this happened," she says. "I can imagine."

That is just as well, for I do not have the strength to talk. My face feels hot and clammy, and I can just stumble up the stairs to my bed.

I awake to the noise of many people greeting each other, and I remember that it is Tuesday night. I feel a little better. Bridget is not in our bed, and the other children are asleep. I am still in my clothes, except for my shoes, and I remember that it was too painful for me to undress. Mistress Anne had contented herself with taking off my shoes. The floor feels unusually rough beneath my bare feet. I think about putting on my shoes, but I do not want to make any noise on the stairs. Besides, I am having a little trouble standing, and I fear that if I stoop down, I will fall onto the floor and have to remain there until Bridget comes to bed. I cannot afford to miss the meeting. Master Winthrop will want me to tell him something, and I don't think I can make up anything good enough to satisfy his hunger.

The back stairway is dark, and my feet do not yet know it very well. I make my way slowly, pressing my shoulder against the wall as it curves away from me. But then the wall is not there, and my foot does not land on a step. I reach out for the wall and find it with my hands. The pain is startling, and I begin to sweat. I regain my balance and again lean against the wall until I find the bottom of the stairs. I stand still and breathe until my heart quiets. I see a shape making its way slowly toward me. It is Bridget.

"Rachel," she says. "Is that you?"

"Yes."

She steps forward and I feel the cold she has carried in from the outside.

"I heard what happened to you."

"It is nothing." I do not want her sympathy. "How is Tom?" I cannot see her face, but I sense it is red, and not from the cold night air.

"Why how should I know?"

"Wasn't it him you were just with?"

"I'm just going to Mother's meeting."

"Do you think I might come?" I say. "I was just on my way, but I am not sure it is well for me to come in."

"Come in with me, then. Mother likes people to listen to her."

"Yes," I reply. "But does that include such as me?"

I do not know if she understands my question, but she takes my shoulder with one hand, while with the other she hangs her cloak on a peg, and then she guides me through the kitchen, which is still half lit from the fire. She glances down at my feet. I shrug and hold up my bandaged hands. She takes a sharp breath, and then guides me through a hallway that leads to the parlor. As we approach, I hear Mistress Anne's voice, and only hers. All else is quiet as we walk in. Most of the people are standing, for there are only a few chairs. One of these, though, is empty as though intended for Bridget, and she sits down on it. I find a place at the edge of the crowd of those standing, with my back against the wall, and for a moment I think I am with my father slipping onto the last bench at the rear of the meeting house.

Mistress Anne nods first at her daughter, and then at me. She does not say anything, but she stares across the room. I feel her eyes on the letter on my chest, and then it is as though all the eyes in the room are looking there. I try to steady myself by looking at Bridget, but my vision blurs and I cannot find her. In the silence, I hear my own heart beating loud, and I wonder why others do not remark the sound. Mistress Anne raises her hand and gestures toward me. I think she wants me to leave, and I take a step toward the door through which we entered. Mistress Anne shakes her head.

"No, Rachel. Come to me."

I do not want to. I wonder how many of these people whose eyes I now feel on me were there on the common not so long ago. And I think of the story Elizabeth told about me killing my babe, and I look for hatred in their eyes. An old crone stands in front of me. She is stooped and wrinkled, and she offers a toothless smile. I scan the faces of the other, younger women, not much older than me, and a few men scattered among them. I cannot read the expressions I see in all these faces. They are probably waiting for guidance from Mistress Anne as to whether they should seek stones to hurl at me, or extend their arms in sympathy. The silence in the room now weighs on my chest, and I find it difficult to breathe. I recall how Mistress Anne huddled with Master Winthrop on the day of my shame, and I am sure that she is going to betray me now. Yet, I must do as she says, and so I step to her, quickening my pace as I imagine I might go to my execution, to get it over with.

She embraces me, and then turns me back toward the crowd. She points at the letter on my chest.

"This," she says, "shall be our text this evening."

I turn to escape, but she has hold of my arm. Her eyes say I should trust her, but I do not. Why should I? I have had no experience being rewarded for such trust.

"The men who put this letter on this child's chest," she says, "are God-fearing men. They fear the word they find in God's book. And that word says that this child should be punished for knowing a man and bearing his child without sanctity of marriage."

Everyone in the room seems to be nodding in rhythm with the flow of her words. I feel the rhythm myself like the waves rolling in on a beach. But I want to know if this ocean of words will take me to safety, or leave me abandoned to the unkind contempt I see in the old crone's eyes. Her expression has not changed, and I figure I will watch her so as to know the worst right away.

"And so they call this child a *whore*, and they say she must be punished for violating the *Law* of Moses. They dangle a rope around her neck, and they sew a letter on her gown, so that she can become a living sermon, a constant reminder of what there is to fear about God, for truly it is written that whosoever commits an unclean act shall be unclean in God's eyes, and God shall turn his face from that man and from that woman."

There is now a murmur of assent, and I find myself wondrously agreeing with the Law that has so marked me. If this is a betrayal, it is sweet. The old crone nods her head so vigorously that she almost loses her cap. She fumbles with crooked fingers to straighten it again on her head.

"But," Mistress Anne now says, lowering her voice so that everyone must strain to hear her, "God's love is truly illiterate. It knows not how to read. It knows only how to be, and to grow." She places her hand on my chest, and I feel myself stir beneath her touch. "It knows not such instruction as placing a letter that signifies a word that calls to mind a law, as this letter on the chest of this child, who for all we know has done no wrong in the pure eye of God, and who has been cruelly branded by men who know only how to fear and not to love, or labor under the abandoned Covenant of Works of Abraham, fit only for reprobates, and know not the Covenant of Grace, which gathers us into Christ's bosom, where there are no letters, no symbols, only His love itself."

As Mistress Anne speaks, I note a man occupying one of the few chairs, a little to the right of Bridget. I have seen him before, of course. For at his side is the young man with the mole on his nose. When I was standing on the platform with the rope about my neck, and my mind numbed by the cold, not only of the wind but of the hatred I felt coming from the crowd screaming at me, I did not recall Master Stanton's name, but now I do, and that of course must be his son Oswald. Master Stanton is a large man, more of fat than of brawn, with his eyes set back into folds of skin. His eyes, though, seem to be bulging forward as though to escape their walls of flesh, and they are focused right on the letter on my gown. They do not move from that spot as Mistress Anne's voice rises and falls. Only he and his son, among the listeners, appear not to be caught up in the rhythm of sound. Everyplace else I look in the room, though, I see heads nodding, and I, too, listen.

"I have a dream to share with you this evening," Mistress Anne says. "I know not if it comes from God, but I feel that it does." Some in the room shuffle uncomfortably. Master Stanton looks like he has just bitten into a rancid piece of beef. I wonder if Mistress Anne sees him, but her eyes are shut. I close my eyes too. I would crawl into her skin if I could.

"In my dream," Mistress Anne resumes, and I feel my lips mouthing her words, "I see a long line of people outside of our meetinghouse. One by one, they enter the meeting house. Inside behind a table sit all but one of the ministers of the churches in New England. As each person approaches the table, the ministers turn the leaf of a large book that they have on the table. On the top of the new page is the person's name, and beneath the name, like entries in a merchant's ledger book, are the deeds of this person's life. On one side of the ledger is a place to record the deeds wherein the person has walked in accordance with God's law, and on the other, those times where he did not."

"This is indeed a marvelous keeping of books. What price do we place on a man coming to the meetinghouse on the Lord's Day to hear the Word of God. Is that worth a shilling, do you think? And if he sit there with his mind not on the Word but on his neighbor's wife, how much do we subtract from that shilling? And what about the wife, who may be sitting there not attending to the Word, but her mind calculating how she will sew a new dress for her babe? Does she get the full shilling?"

"On the bottom of the page is a balance. The ministers read it out. If it is a negative number, a trap door opens beneath the feet of the person who then falls head first into the fires of hell. Those with a positive balance ascend at once to heaven."

The room is quiet. Mistress Anne leans forward.

"Do you think that God is no more than a clerk in a counting house? Or that Heaven is for sale to those who have full purses of deeds that others think are righteous? I cannot think so."

"All but one, say you?" Master Stanton has risen to his feet. He is dressed elegantly in a wide ruff, looking like the prosperous merchant I expect he is.

"All but one, I declare," Mistress Anne says.

"The one?" Master Stanton demands. "I suppose you mean Master Cotton."

"I do."

"Master Cotton is a fine minister, as is Master Wilson. They do not say they speak with God, nor he with them," he says. "Nor do I. I read His book. I do not dream such dreams."

I see that the old crone who had been nodding in assent to what Mistress Anne said, has continued moving her head up and down without stop as Master Stanton speaks. He looks hard at me.

"I saw that child not so long ago on the platform of shame, along with the man she had seduced and ruined. And I have heard the story about what happened to her babe, and I am only left to wonder at the truth. Maybe she did away with the babe as some say. And if she did not, I still wonder what lesson we are to be taught by her this evening. Or by you."

"As for teaching, sir, you know I do not profess so to do. I speak only what I am moved to say. If others find instruction in my words I am gratified, but I take no credit, more than the conduit should puff itself up for permitting the water to flow through it."

Master Stanton just shakes his head.

"I feel compelled to tell you, Mistress, that I needs must report what I have heard to the magistrates."

"I am content that you do so, for is not that why you came?"

"And if it was, it was a good purpose. I can tell you that." He waves his hand as though he is dismissing us from his thoughts and he walks out of the room. People step back more than is necessary to give him passage. Oswald rises, too, but does not leave until he satisfies his eyes by staring at me. Then, he follows his father out.

I want to tell Mistress Anne that Master Stanton is not the only spy in her house tonight, but I am afraid. She puts her hand on my shoulder.

"This child is but a lamb. Master Stanton and the magistrates would drive her away from the flock. I do not think that we should do that. And that is why she has come to live in my house." She places her hand on my letter. "They have placed their brand on her as far as they could reach, but they cannot claim to know her heart." She leans down to whisper in my ear. "Rachel, do you want to witness what has been done to you?"

Her breath is warm against my ear, but I feel a cold fist clench my heart. Still, I can try.

"The word," I start, and I see that the people in the room are leaning toward me, some with their hands cupped over their ears. The old crone's mouth is moving too, but whether to coach or mock me, I know not. I try again, only this time I take a deep breath and I aim my voice to the far reaches of the room. I move my lips and in my mind I hear me say, "The word signified by the letter on my gown has nothing to do with me or what Henry did to me." I think these words, but I am unable to say them, and the people at first nod encouragement at me as I mouth my thoughts, but when they cannot hear me, they lean more and more toward me, and it is as though they will fall upon me. I close my mouth. Sweat runs down my forehead and into my eyes. I have been standing still, only moving my lips in a hopeless effort to explain what I do not understand, and yet I am out of breath as though I have been walking up a steep hill.

"Is the child dumb, then?" a voice cries out from the crowd. It is not an unfriendly voice, but it causes me to shake. There is now a murmuring and a shaking of heads.

"Her silence speaks louder than any word she might utter," Mistress Anne says, and she embraces me. "Go, child," she says so only I can hear, and I am only too happy to do just that. I start to leave. My bare feet feel every crack in the floor planks, and my back burns under the eyes of the people who I know are staring at me as I walk through the door and back into the dark. I look over my shoulder at Mistress Anne. No doubt, she will continue to talk about me after I leave the room. I realize that I have been on a platform for a second time. Whether Governor Winthrop put me there, or Mistress Anne, I figure it amounts to the same thing. I am a tool to teach with, although nobody has bothered to explain to me what the lesson is.

I make my way into the darkened passage, and I hear steps behind me. It is Bridget.

"Mother says I should go up with you." She smiles. "I thank you for that."

"Is Tom waiting for you, then?" I ask.

She does not try to deny it this time.

"Yes," she says.

"Well, go to him, if you must. I can go up by myself."

"Are you sure?"

"Yes," I reply, and I am, for all I want now is to sleep. But she takes my hand, and I almost scream out from the pain. She drops my hand, but steps so close that I can feel her breath on my cheek.

"You must tell me," she says. "About your babe. What they are saying you did."

"I am surprised that you would ask," I say.

"I cannot help it."

"If that is what you think, I will share your bed no more. I will find a place on the floor."

She takes my wrist, gently, and it does not hurt.

"Of course, I believe you. I just had to hear the words."

"But you have not, and you won't."

"Yet, I know." She steps back. "I am truly sorry."

"Good night, Bridget. Remember how I looked on that platform when you go to Tom."

Unaccountably, she giggles.

"I see him, and I forget all else."

"Then God give you luck, if He cannot give you wisdom."

I see Goody Hett walking to the well. She is carrying her babe in her arms. The babe is asleep. It stirs, and the woman gives it her breast to nurse, and as she does my breasts, which have almost forgotten my babe, begin to ache. The babe sucks hard and my nipples feel its toothless gums. Goody Hett is at the well now, her eyes sad beyond tears. She pulls the babe away from her breasts, leans over the well, and drops the babe. I hear the splash, and I see the startled eyes of the babe as it lands in the water. In my dream, I reach for the babe, but it slips from my fingers just as I am about to grab its hand. I see it sink ever so slowly.

And there is nothing I can do.

I remember that Goody Hett sought to end her babe's life because she had so despaired of her own. I think I am beginning to understand how a woman can feel that way for many reasons.

Goody Hett saw only blackness where her babe was. I see only emptiness where mine should be. Who is to say whose despair is deeper?

I am weary from lack of sleep as I make my way to the governor's house. It snowed last night, and the holes in the bottom of my shoes quickly fill, turning my feet to ice. My hands, though, burn as though they were soaking in lye. My body is both cold and hot, and my mind seems to share the confusion. I am sure Reverend Wilson would be able to find a message in my condition, just as he did in the dead hog that my father stole. As for me, I cannot discover such sentiments in these facts, and so I do what I can. I cannot warm my feet until I reach the Governor's house, but I can cool my hands with the very same snow that is torturing my feet. This I stoop to do, and as I kneel, I see Master Stanton walking toward me from the Governor's house.

I want him to see me, and so I stand up. I roll the snow in my hands as he approaches, and it does cool the fire on my flesh. He strides right up to me and then passes by without a sign of recognition. He did not see me, though I was no more than an arm's length away from him. Maybe I need to be standing on a platform, or next to Mistress Anne, or the governor, or some such, to become visible for Master Stanton. By myself, I am no more meaningful to him than the snow darkening beneath the soles of his fine leather boots.

I expect the governor to be standing by the door when I come in, but he is not. The hallway is empty, and so I make my way to the parlor. The door is shut, and I hear voices from inside. A moment later, the door opens and Mistress Margaret and Elizabeth come out. Mistress Margaret nods at me and indicates that I should go in to see the governor. Elizabeth, though, offers a big smile and then throws her arms around me in an embrace.

"Truly, I will miss you," she says, and then she is gone. I watch her back as she leaves, and it is as though, big as she is, she has wings on her feet since they seem barely to touch the floor. I prepare myself for the worst. If she is so happy, something very untoward must be waiting for me inside that room. The governor, though, seems not to want to talk about Elizabeth.

"What can you tell me?" he asks.

"Sir?"

His hand reaches toward his beard, but stops itself just at his shoulder as though he has instructed himself to be patient.

"Did you not attend Mistress Hutchinson's meeting last night?"

I am sure that Master Stanton must have reported the occurrences of the previous evening to him, so I can see no benefit in lying.

"Yes sir, I did. But I was feeling unwell and I did not stay until the end."

He waves his hand in front of him as though he is not interested in what I have to say.

"I did see Master Stanton," I say. "Last night, and again this morning as I came here. I do not think he was pleased to see me at the meeting."

"He was not, but his displeasure falls not on you, child. As does not mine."

"What is it you would have me tell you?"

"Just what you remember." He dips his pen into his ink well and holds it over a piece of paper. I remember the dream that Mistress Anne recounted and I see how Master Winthrop fits. I must give him something to write on his paper.

"She talked about salvation," I say, figuring that is a safe thing to mention. Salvation is a very common topic of discussion. The governor seems aware of its ordinariness.

"Yes, child, but what about it? What did she teach about salvation?"

"Just how it is God's free gift to us who are with Him."

He starts to write a word or two, but stops.

"Nothing more?"

"Oh, sir, a great deal more, but not that I can repeat, for I am afraid her words flew above my poor head, and then I retired with a fever."

He puts down his pen.

"That is all, then. I will trust that you can do better when you are better instructed. And feeling recovered from your illness."

"Thank you," I say and leave.

Mistress Margaret is waiting for me outside the parlor.

"Did he tell you?" she asks, and her eyes glance at my hands. I take her meaning, and I shake my head.

71

"Well, then, I suppose there is no harm if I do. Elizabeth is leaving us. To go to Salem where she will marry Henry. It has all been arranged."

I can find no words to express my relief.

"Hush," Mistress Margaret says. "I understand."

Chapter Five

I am learning my letters very well now. Mistress Anne says I have an aptitude
for them, but I know it is more that I am working so hard. Every night I
study them, and mouth their sounds silently so as not to disturb Bridget and
the others, but as for that, Bridget's mind is so much taken with her dreams of
Tom that I don't think she would stir if I sang a song in her ear.

The candle is starting to sputter and I have only a few more minutes before
I will be in darkness. I think it is a terrible extravagance to be burning these
candles down the way I do. When I lived with my father, I was the one who
dipped the candles, and we never had enough, so most nights, the only light
we had, came from the glow of the fire. But here nobody seems to count how
many candles I use. Mistress Anne stops by almost every evening to help me
with my lessons, and she encourages me to work as hard as I am able to learn
them. She has even told me how her own father taught her when she was a
little girl. She seems to want to make up to me for my father's neglect. She
says soon I will be able to begin reading the Bible. But for now I have this
book.

I know the first page, the one with all twenty six letters on it. The next page
has the same letters at the beginning of words, and I am learning how to say
them. 'A' starts 'Adam'. That makes sense. 'B' starts 'Babel', and I now know
that is the name of a tower that people in their arrogance built to try to reach
God in His heaven many years ago. But I do not know why that letter and its
words come after 'A'. I thought it would have been 'E' for 'Eve', just as we
have all come from our first father and first mother, so I thought all words
should come for the letters that start their names. Mistress Anne said I was
probably right.

Bridget has taught me how to sign my name, 'Rachel Moore', and she has
complimented me on my hand, which she says is just like that of a lady born.
I do not pay any attention to such idle flattery. But I do take pains forming the

letters that make my name. There is something about the 'M' that is familiar. I run my finger up the leg, down, up, down. I turn the page upside down, and now the 'M' is the same as the 'W' they pinned on me, only my finger now moves down, up, down, and up. I frown at that revelation.

I am studying the letter turning it one way and then another, and I do not hear her come into the room. This is not the first time she has surprised me this way. She can walk as silently as any cat.

I show her how the 'M' becomes a 'W' when I turn the page.

She pulls her mouth into a quick smile.

"Tush," she says. "It is only a simple letter, an invention of man. The Holy Ghost does not speak in letters and words."

I fear she might begin one of her more lengthy explanations, but she has more pressing matters to contend with.

"Get dressed," she says. "Mary Dyer's travail has begun two months before her time, and I want you to help me."

"But…" I begin to protest. Once or twice she has mentioned that it would be well for me to learn midwifery, as I do not seem to have many good prospects for making my way, but I am not prepared to start tonight.

"Come, now," she insists. "The babe is not going to wait for you to make up your mind."

I follow her into the street with care. It snowed heavily yesterday, but it is very late in the season, and the snow has been melting, turning the street into white mud. Mistress Anne is hurrying, and if I do not keep pace I will lose sight of her. I quicken my step and feel myself losing my balance. I reach out for her arm, but instead grab the little sack she is carrying. I hold onto that and slide along behind her. She does not stop walking.

Half sliding and half stepping, I follow her as we turn down a narrow lane. A full moon shines over my left shoulder, lighting the small houses on either side. We make our way on the right hand side of the lane, walking through a pool of yellow light at the edge of the shadows cast by the house across from us. I sense the way dipping a little and I smell a taste of salt water in a breeze that reaches us from some place up ahead. We must be nearing the harbor. Finally, at the end of the lane is a house bigger than those we have been passing by. A window in the front is open, and a man's face flickers in the light of the candle in his hand. The yellow light of the candle stretches to meet the pool of moonlight on the ground in front of the house. The man's other hand emerges and reaches from the candle light into the blackness and toward the moonlit street where we stand. His hand beckons us to hurry.

"Praise be to God," the man says, "that you have arrived, and not a moment too soon. Hurry, please. She has been calling. She says she knows something is not right." He ushers us in through the front door to a small room just off to the right of the entrance way. The room is only large enough to hold a bed, and next to it on the floor a cradle and a stool. The man puts the candle on the stool. A little boy, old enough to walk is standing next to the cradle, rocking it. He gives it a push and it tips so far that he loses his balance and falls down. He struggles to his feet with a big smile on his face. His father picks him up and squeezes by us out of the room.

"I will be in the kitchen," he says. He looks down at his son. "I do not think he will go back to sleep. He used to sleep in that cradle."

Mistress Dyer's face is aglow with perspiration although the room is quite chill from the window being open. Her eyes are closed, but she reaches her hand out.

"Anne," she says. "I am so tired. It has been so many hours. It is before time."

Seeing her there takes me back. I feel faint for a moment. I do not want to be reminded. Mistress Anne reaches beneath the bed clothes to run her hand over Mistress Dyer's belly and then lower. She pushes her hand there, and it is as though she was again pressing her fingers into me. She stays stooped over for several minutes, probing. When she stands up, I can read the concern in her eyes. She reaches into her sack and brings out a cloth.

"Go outside, and wet this in the snow."

When I return, she motions for me to stand by the head of the bed.

"Try to cool her," she says.

I place the cold cloth on Mistress Dyer's forehead. Her eyes are still closed. She reaches her hand on top of mine. It feels very warm.

"And who is this?" she asks.

"Rachel," I say.

"Oh, yes, Rachel," she replies, and her voice tells me that she knows who I am. This is not surprising. I do not think there is anyone in Boston who does not know my name. My hand seeks the letter on my gown. Mistress Dyer senses my motion and opens her eyes. She shakes her head slowly from side to side.

"No, child," she says.

I drop my hand, and her lips pull back in a quick smile.

"Better," she says, but then the pain comes to her, just as I remember it coming to me, and she utters a little moan. It is as though she does not want to cry out too loud, but cannot stop herself completely. Meanwhile, Mistress Anne is working.

"It will come soon," she says. "But it is coming feet first, and I cannot turn it."

I keep the cloth pressed to Mistress Dyer's head while I try to see over the mound of her belly. Her stomach is not so large as I thought it would be, certainly not as big as mine was.

"Give a good push, Mary," Mistress Anne says.

The poor woman nods weakly and lifts herself off the bed. Her heels dig into the thin, string mattress, and her thighs strain away from each other. She grunts and pushes. I see something coming out between her legs, but I cannot tell what it is. Mistress Anne takes hold of it and moves it so far to one side that I think she will tear Mistress Dyer apart. But a moment later something else comes out, and it looks like the first. I drop the cloth.

"Pick it up," Mistress Anne says. "Everything is going to be over soon."

I lean down to pick up the cloth, and as I stand up again, I get a better look at the two things, which I now see are feet at the end of skinny legs. But the feet are stumps without toes. Mistress Dyer raises her head to look, but Mistress Anne shields her view with the bed clothes.

"It is fine," she says. "Just push one more time, and we will be done."

Mistress Dyer again lifts off the bed and contracts. The rest of the babe now slides out faster than I could imagine. After the feet and legs come the body and neck. And then there is something that should be a head but it is not like anything I have ever seen before. Mistress Anne places her fingers to her lips, and I understand. She reaches into her sack once again for another cloth, this one prepared with the same medicine that she had used on me, and she places it between Mistress Dyer's legs to staunch the blood which is now beginning to flow. She has been holding the babe with one hand, and now she swaddles it. Mistress Dyer reaches for it, but Mistress Anne just shakes her head.

"No, Mary," is all she says, and after a moment Mistress Dyer drops her arms and collapses back onto the bed.

"I knew it was not right," she says.

"It wasn't."

"Is it alive?"

"It will not live."

Mistress Anne lifts up the swaddled babe and hands it to me.

"You do not have to look, if you do not want to," she says. "But I still have to attend to Mary."

I take the small bundle. It is amazingly light, so much so that as I first hold it I think it must be falling. But it is not. Mistress Dyer groans and again lifts herself wearily from the bed. A bloody lump issues from between her legs. Mistress Anne gathers it up into a small sack and then takes the snow dampened cloth from Mistress Dyer's forehead and uses it to clean the blood from her thighs.

I stand there amazed, thinking that not so long ago I must have had such a double birth, first a babe and then the rest of it which seems to be no more than garbage to be disposed of. Only my babe was not like this one. Mine was perfect while this one makes me quake where I stand, wondering what it is. I am terrified, but also curious, and I must look.

I pick up the corner of the swaddling. I cannot stop the gasp that forces itself out of my mouth. Mistress Anne looks sternly at me and then at Mistress Dyer, but the exhausted woman seems to have fallen asleep for the moment. I nod that I understand, and I make my eyes look down again.

There is a huge, starting face. There is no top of the head, only wrinkled skin over what seems to be a hole as though the head had been smashed flat by some heavy stone. The eyes are bulging out of the tiny face. I feel them looking at me, into my very soul. Above the eyes are four little horns. Beneath them is a hook of nose pointing down to its mouth, which is larger than it should be for the size of the face. It is breathing, and I feel my own breath being sucked into it.

It has arms and legs like other babes, and its hands have fingers. I count them to five on each. But where the toes should be are claws like I remember seeing on the turkey Mabel was cleaning. I see them move toward my arms as though they would clutch me. I almost drop the bundle in my fright. Instead, I place it on the edge of the bed, next to Mistress Dyer's foot. It starts to roll over as though it will fall to the floor. I make myself stop it just before it reaches the edge. It is on its belly, and bony lumps stick through the skin of its back. It shudders and then it stops moving.

It has gone from whence it came, I think, and I believe it has taken some part of me with it.

Mistress Anne now turns to see what I have been doing. She picks up the babe and studies its monstrous face. Then she presses her fingers over those starting eyes and forces the lids down over them.

"She is dead."

I am startled by the word. I had not thought this devil child has a sex.

"It is an imp," I say. "And when it stopped breathing, I felt it take my breath with it. I fear."

"Hush," Mistress Anne says.

"Is it not from Satan?" I demand.

"No, I think not. All is from God. Now, go and find Master Dyer."

"What shall I tell him?"

"That his wife has survived."

"And?"

"That the babe did not."

"But…"

"Tell him that. No more. Then, go to Master Cotton's house. You know where it is."

"Yes."

"Hurry there and wake him. We need his advice and comfort."

The street is now darker than it had been. I look up to the full moon, and see that it has been blackened by a cloud. The cloud has covered the center of the moon's face, leaving just an outline of yellow around the black shadow. And the shadow has two arms and two legs, and a misshaped head. It is breathing deep in and out, and I feel myself panting along with it. I mistrust Mistress Anne. She does not want to see this babe for the devil child that it is. The shadow gets larger and larger until the moon disappears behind it, and I force myself to hurry away in the darkness. At least I am going to Master Cotton's house, for he will be able to protect me. But first I must get there.

I start to run and my feet slide out from underneath me, and I am in the mud. I struggle to get up, and fall again, this time onto my face. Mud clogs my nose, my eyes, and my mouth. I raise myself up and spit the mud from my mouth and take deep gagging breaths. I swipe the mud off my eyes, and I look up at the moon. The shadow is gone and the moon again shines brightly down.

There is no sense in trying to run. I will only fall again. I put one foot in front of the other with care. I feel the cold mud hardening on my face, and I can taste it on my tongue. I walk on the side of the way lit by the moon. I have had enough shadows for one night. I do not think I will ever be comfortable in them again.

I have remarked Master Cotton's house many times in the daylight, but never before have I sought it in the dark. It is just down the way from Master Winthrop's. It is not quite so grand, but it is big enough so that I can recognize its outline. I breathe a deep sigh when I see that it is on the bright side of the street. I quicken my pace just a little and knock on the door.

Of course nobody answers for a while, but sooner than I would have thought I hear a shuffling from inside. I suppose men in Master Cotton's business must learn to sleep light because they will, from time to time, find people in need at the door in the deep of the night. There is a window next to the door, and its shutters are thrown open. A head leans out. Two horns sit on top of it. I fight the tremor in my legs which want to carry me away. I make myself stand still to deliver my message. He blinks at me.

"Yes? What is it?"

"I have come from Mistress Hutchinson, sir," I reply.

"At this time of the night?"

"She is at Mistress Dyer's house, and she says she must talk to you."

He leans out further and seems to be examining my face.

"What happened to you child?"

The head comes more fully out of the window, and the hand cups the flame so that it burns steadily. The horns are gone. They have been marvelously replaced by two thick curls of gray hair that stand out from the round and red cheeks of Master Cotton.

"Is that truly you, sir?"

The head moves up and down slowly, and then disappears. I hear footsteps behind the door, and then it opens. Out steps Master Cotton, brushing his hair out of his eyes. He reaches a hand toward me, and I cringe, but do not run. His fingers are gentle as they peel off some of the mud on my face.

"I thought you were Master Stanton's Negro maid," he says, "and I feared that he had suffered some accident that you were coming to tell me about."

"No, sir. It is just the mud I have fallen into. I am Rachel Moore."

He holds the candle toward me and peers at my face, and then his eyes travel down my body. I know what he is looking for. I open my cloak and push my chest out toward him so he can see the letter. He turns his face away. I close the cloak.

"You say Mistress Hutchinson has sent you to me."

"She is at Mistress Dyer's house, and she says she must talk to you."

"Is not Mistress Dyer with child?"

"She was."

"I see," he says. "I will dress and then you can take me there. I am not sure I can find the way in the dark."

He steps back into the doorway, and the dark of the night falls over us. I am afraid again, and I must be sure.

"Sir," I cry out, loudly, so he will turn of a sudden and not have time to change himself back. As I hope, he is startled and spins toward me, holding the candle up so that he can see me. And I, too, can see him, and the tufts of hair still on his forehead.

"I will wait here for you," I say.

He looks at me strangely, and then closes the door behind him.

I look up at the moon. It is bright yellow, and I feel safe for the moment.

We push open the door of the Dyer house and follow the light of the fire into the kitchen. There we find Master Dyer sitting on the bench at his table, talking with great heat to Mistress Hutchinson. I think I see a leaf caught in her bonnet, as though she is fresh from the forest. I wonder if she has blood smeared on her forehead.

"I tell you, Anne," he says in a harsh whisper, "the child is a sign from God. I have tried to warn Mary that she is following you too far into places neither of you should wander. The babe is proof of my fears."

I have never heard anyone speak so harshly to Mistress Anne, but she does not seem to be angry. She only reaches her hand to Master Dyer's shoulder.

"No, Charles. If she has traveled too far, it is she who is leading the way. But do not fear it. God's truth cannot lead us astray."

Master Dyer pulls back from her hand.

"I fear for us," he says.

"As do I," Master Cotton who has been standing in the shadows now says. He starts to walk toward them, and I grab his arm. I do not think he should approach too close to them.

"What is it?" he asks. "I must speak with Mistress Hutchinson, and Master Dyer. Go see if you can comfort Mistress Dyer."

I let go his arm. He must know what he is doing, or he will soon find out his mistake. I make my way into the room where Mistress Dyer lies asleep. I do not see the devil child. I am not surprised. It must be in the woods. Mistress Dyer is breathing deep, and I do not think it would do her any good to rouse her. Above her breathing, though, I hear a creaking noise, and I feel a gust of wind as though we have left the front door open. I gather my cloak about me, but the noise gets louder.

I feel something nudge my foot, and I look down at the cradle. It is rocking back and forth faster and faster. Lying in it is the shrouded body of the imp. I am sure of it. I expect any moment that it will rise up and fly to my face. I am too terrified to move. Mistress Dyer stirs in her bed, and I wonder if she is rousing herself to give her child suck on her hidden teat. I hear a giggle coming from behind the rocking cradle, and then I see a tiny hand. The little boy stands up and looks at me, his face full of mischief. He gives the cradle another push, and then he toddles off toward the kitchen.

I hear a flow of sounds with now and then a bubble of a word that I can recognize. The little boy has come back, and he has climbed into my lap. The thought of his sister in the cradle makes me wary of him, but his warm brown eyes, dancing with fun, are more than I can resist. I hold him to my chest, and we both listen. Master Cotton's voice rises above the others. It commands silence and respect from the others.

"It is the best thing to do," Master Cotton's voice says. "No good will be served by anything else."

"But is it right and proper?" asks Master Dyer.

"Would you invite the community to witness?" Master Cotton asks. "I tell you I do not see the point. There will be talk coming from those who do not know any better. The babe's deformities are grave. I believe that God sent them to you for your private instruction, and you should learn from them what you can." His voice rises. "But the lesson is not for anybody but you. Look within yourselves, and ask how you have displeased the Lord that he would send you this poor misshaped thing to you."

"Truly, it is for the best." Mistress Anne's tone is sweetly insistent.

"I do not want to look at it," Master Dyer says.

"But you must, of course," Master Cotton says. "You must see what the Lord has sent to you. Else will you be most arrogantly denying God, and you will bring further curses down on your head, until you are left like Job sitting in ashes, scraping at your running sores with broken pieces of potsherds. And remember the lesson of Job. Do not question God's will. Attend only to His power while you pray for His mercy."

There is silence and then footsteps. A moment later, Mistress Anne is at my side.

"I see you have found a friend in Peter," she says.

"Yes. He chose my lap for his bed."

"We must rouse Mistress Dyer." She casts her eyes for a moment on the cradle. "And then we will take that unfortunate to its rest."

Master Dyer stands in the doorway holding a shovel, and now I know what terrible business they have been discussing. He stares hard at Peter and then the cradle.

"Peter was born before," he says to Mistress Anne. His voice is a sharp hiss, and it wakes his wife.

"Charles?"

He starts to walk toward her, but he is stopped by the cradle. He will not step over it.

"Charles?"

He does not answer, but stands there, looking down at his monster child. Mistress Anne pushes him aside and pulls the cradle out of his way.

"Talk to your wife, Charles," she says. "And then bring her outside. Don't be long." She picks up the babe and wraps the swaddling tighter about it. Master Dyer turns his eyes from it. I do not blame him. I hold my breath as Mistress Anne and her terrible bundle walk by me and out the door.

We stand next to a lone tree, on a rise behind the house. The moon again shines brightly, and I can see the fields below us mostly covered in snow, but here and there the muddy earth looks like filthy slashes of dark brown against the white. Soon the snow will be gone, and there will be only the mud, and it will melt into softness.

But now only the very top of the mud gives beneath Master Dyer's shovel. I look up through the bare branches of the tree at the moon and listen to the clang of the shovel against the frozen earth. He starts to mutter and I know that if he was alone that muttering would grow into a full curse, but he dare not do that with Master Cotton standing not five feet away from him. Mistress Anne has one arm around Mistress Dyer. The other holds the terrible bundle. Nobody else has the courage to touch the dead babe, but Mistress Anne seems unafraid. She is holding it, gently, as though it is alive. The wind picks up suddenly, and I pull my cloak tighter around me. The clanging continues. Clang, clang, and then every once in a while, a sloppy thud, as the shovel finally bites through the frozen crust and Master Dyer is able to force a small pile of dirt out of the grave he is digging.

The breeze carries the feel and the smell of the cold waves of the ocean to where we are standing. The smell is like that of rotting fish washed up on a beach. I sniff to locate the source. It is not on the breeze but coming from the babe in Mistress Anne's arms. I wonder that she can stand it. It is getting stronger. I can see Master Dyer raising the shovel high over his head to drive it into the frozen mud. He brings it down and then screams out in pain. The shovel has bounced off a stone into his leg. He collapses onto the ground. Master Cotton offers him his hand, but Master Dyer struggles to his feet himself.

"No, sir," he says. "I can manage. If you want to help, there's a lantern by the door of the house."

"I will get it," I say.

"Fine, then, hurry," Master Dyer says. He has the shovel under the rock now and he heaves it out. It leaves a deep impression in the earth, and he goes at it with his shovel.

I find the lantern where he said it would be, and hurry back up the hill. The mud is now flying off Master Dyer's shovel at a good pace. I hand the lantern to Master Cotton. He fumbles in his pocket for a match, and then lights the lantern. It casts a pale-yellow glow on the shallow grave Master Dyer has managed to carve in the stubborn ground. Master Dyer moves the lantern closer and places his shovel into the grave. He puts one hand on the bottom of the grave and the other on its top. He shows Master Cotton the distance. Master Cotton shrugs.

"Bring it over here, then," Master Dyer says to Mistress Anne. She steps closer to him and holds out the babe. He hasn't moved his hands and he holds them, still apart, against the babe. There is a little space, as wide as one of his fingers, top and bottom between his hands and the babe.

"A little more," he says, "and it will be enough."

He lays into his shovel again and brings out dirt mixed with stones of various sizes. The larger stones thud and splash against mud and snow. He leans down and places both hands into the grave. Then without standing up, he reaches his arms toward Mistress Anne.

"Give it here," he says, his voice a growl.

She bends down and hands him the bundle. I am standing under the tree now and they are in the light of the moon. I see them from the side as the white shrouded figure passes one to the other. Just as he receives it into his arm, they disappear. The lantern has gone out, and the moon is covered again by a black shadow. I turn to the grave, and it is as though shadows are dancing there, and then one of the shadows swings its arms away from the grave and into the dirt at its side. The shadow shovel moves quickly to replace the dirt that has been removed. When it stops its motions, and the grave is covered, the moon starts to emerge from behind its black cloud.

"A confirmation," Master Cotton says, casting his eyes heavenward, "that this act was intended to be performed in the mercy of darkness, just as the babe's poor soul is hastened to its eternal oblivion."

Master Dyer stretches full to smooth the cricks in his back, and then he lets his shovel drop.

"Aye," he says, "dark it is as it should be. May the merciful Lord lead us again into the light."

He and Master Cotton start down the hill, talking to each other. Mistress Anne helps Mistress Dyer to follow. She stops to look for me where I stand, still, in the shelter of the tree.

"Can you find your way home?" she asks. "I must stay here."

"Yes," I reply quickly before she has to explain that there is no place for me in this sad company. I watch the women follow the men down the hill. I pick up the lantern. It is still warm, but provides no light for my way down. I put it back onto the ground and turn my back to the grave and the Dyer house. I am in a hurry to put the hill between me and it.

At the bottom of the hill, I come out into a street I do not recognize. I have lost my way. I am sure the devil child, laughing in its freshly dug grave, has spun me around and left me in a strange place. I see one building with lights in its window, and the sound of loud voices coming from inside. As I approach it, a man and a woman stagger out into the street. The man seems to be holding the woman as she struggles to free herself. The man is tall, wearing a white ruff very visible in the moonlight. It is Master Stanton. The woman stops straining to get away and collapses against him. She laughs loudly.

"But where do you want to take me?" she says.

Master Stanton staggers against her, and she seems to be holding him up. Her hand reaches inside his cloak and between his legs. I forget my fear of the shadows and move into them so as to see better what is going on. Her hand is busy now and Master Stanton has spread his legs. His eyes are half closed, but then they snap open. I fear that he has seen me, but they are looking back into the tavern. He takes hold of her hand and removes it from his cloak. She strains her face upward to kiss him but he turns away. Instead, he takes her by her shoulders and steers her into a narrow passage beside the building. They disappear into the darkness.

I creep along the edge of the tavern, but I am not bold enough to follow them. I hear her laugh, a kind of moist, slurping giggle, and then a murmur in a deeper voice, his voice. "Yes," that voice says, "that's a good whore." She laughs even louder, but this time there is a harsh edge to it, and a moment later there is a thud and then curses in male voices. I can recognize Master Stanton's voice, but not the other. The woman continues to laugh. I sense somebody running toward me from the darkness, and for some reason I step forward. A man comes hurtling at me.

"Out of my road," he screams.

I step back but he crashes into me anyway, and we both go down in the mud. A second later Master Stanton comes out. He is trying to run while holding up his breeches with one hand. He stumbles toward us, and starts to fall. He lets go his breeches, and I have a brief, unwanted view of his nakedness before he lands in the mud. The man next to me tries to rise, but I kick at his leg, and he falls down again. I look into the darkness for the woman, but she is gone.

Master Stanton struggles to his knees and falls toward us. He is a large man, and when he lands he splatters mud. He succeeds in grabbing the other man's arm. We have been making a lot of noise and finally it has aroused the watch. He comes running toward us. The man struggles to free himself.

"Help me," Master Stanton says, and I grab the man's other arm.

"Here, what is the matter?" the man approaching us says.

"Are you the watch, then?" Master Stanton asks.

"Aye." He leans down. "Excuse me, sir, I didn't recognize you at first in the dark."

"Hold this one," Master Stanton says.

The watchman grabs hold of my wrist.

"Not that one, the other."

"Right," the watchman says, and releases my wrist. He seizes the other, now sitting quietly.

"There was a woman." Master Stanton points to the passage next to the tavern.

"She is away by now," the watchman says.

"After her, nonetheless."

"And let this one go?"

"Yes."

The man lurches forward, breaking free. I reach for him and he swipes at my arm. He loses his balance and falls, knocking me to the ground. He lands on top of me, his face directly above mine. I breathe in his breath, and suddenly I remember. The watchman and Master Stanton have his arms again, and he does not struggle as they roll him off me. Somebody now comes from the tavern with a candle.

I do not need to use its light to recognize the face of my father. He does not seem to know me. If he does, he does not care to say. Instead, he turns to his captors.

"You're holding an innocent man," he says. "I was just in the alley pissing a night's drink into the mud."

"Yes," Master Stanton replies, "while your friend, a lady who asked my assistance to take her home, lured me into that self-same alley so that you and she relieve me of my purse."

"A damnable lie," my father says.

"The magistrates will deal with you. We know you as a thief, and your daughter as whore."

I roll away into the mud and shadows. Master Stanton sees me.

"Young man," he says, "let me give you something for your trouble." He seems to be reaching beneath his cloak for his purse.

I pull my cloak about my face, reach out my hand for the coin he drops into it. I strain my voice to a lower pitch.

"Thank you, sir," I say, and then I am gone. I hear him call "Wait," after me, but I run and slide through the mud and the darkness until I am sure that nobody is following me. I stop to take a breath, but then do not stop until I find Mistress Anne's house in front of me. The house is dark except for a slight glow from window upstairs. I count from the side of the house. It is the third window, my window, the one not five feet from my bed. Somebody has a candle lit and is waiting for me.

I am shivering from my repeated falls, and I feel my skin cracking under layers of caked mud. I stumble up the stairs and follow the path of light that spills out from beneath the door to the bedroom. I push open the door. Two figures are on my bed.

Mistress Anne turns when she hears the door open. She glances at me and nods.

"Rachel, please wait outside a moment while I finish talking to Bridget."

I step back into the hall. I want only to take off my wet clothes and crawl into my warm bed. I still have the coin clutched in my hand, so hard that it is going to mark my skin. The door opens and Mistress Anne comes out. She closes the door behind her. I hold out the coin.

"What is that?" she asks.

"Master Stanton gave it to me."

Her eyebrows shoot up.

"Explain yourself, child."

"I got a little lost coming home, and I met Master Stanton outside the tavern." I pause seeking the words. "I fetched him his hat which he had left on the table inside."

"I see," she says, but I do not think she believes my tale. She places her hands on my face, and then moves them down to my shoulders and arms. I am still shivering.

"Well, then," she says, "you had better get into bed and tell me the rest of your story tomorrow." She lets me go and looks back toward the bedroom as though she can see through the door. Then she leaves.

I open the door. As I walk toward the bed, I hear Bridget sobbing quietly. She looks up as I climb into the bed.

"She has told me I cannot see Tom anymore," she says.

I start to shrug, but I see how her shoulders are still shaking beneath the blanket.

"That is too bad," I say.

"The worst part is I couldn't tell her."

"Yes?"

"That I should have listened to her when she warned me away from him before."

"Oh, then, is that the way it is?"

"Yes," she says. "Will you help me?"

I reach for her and hold her until she stops shaking.

"I will do what I can."

Bridget pokes me in the ribs after we have both tossed without finding sleep for what seems hours but might only have been minutes.

"Swear," she says, "that you won't tell anybody."

"I have already done so."

"I'm sorry. I forgot."

We fall into a weary silence, and then Bridget against starts to sob.

"I don't know if I can bear it," she says.

"Of course, you can. Let me tell you why you are luckier than you think you are, if I can be so bold to say so."

"Bold indeed. Explain yourself."

"It is very simple. You could have been me this evening, and for all the evenings and years before."

"Then tell me. I need to think of something else."

"I know that."

I do not care that she is so self-centered and unable to offer me any comfort. I tell her about Mistress Dyer, about the devil child and the moon going dark and about me helping the watch catch my father. It is a great deal, and I am happy to tell Bridget who is so full of her own problems that she can only listen to mine without comment, and that is exactly what I want. I need to hear all that has happened in words so that I can try to understand. I say the words slowly and watch them bounce off Bridget's uncomprehending eyes, and then they return to my own ears. But somehow these words, these sounds floating in the air between us seem too weak to carry what I would have them bear.

After a while, Bridget no longer even pretends to be listening. She curls herself up, her knees pressed tight against her chest and her back to me.

"Good night," she murmurs.

I continue talking even as her breathing turns to her usual, quiet snores. I say the word 'father', and then 'thief' to see if I can make them hold on to each other. Then I try 'babe', and I see my own in the arms of the savage who carried it away, and the one brought to the baptism in the meeting house, and the one that was rescued from the well, all of these babes leaving me with an ache in my breasts reminding me of my failed motherhood. But then as though to chase those away comes the one from tonight, its horrible deformities and the black clouds and shadows that accompanied both its birth and its burial.

And Master Cotton, I am sure, would see God's providence in all of these events. I, in my ignorance, see only pain, suffering, and evil.

I don't think I have ever been so tired, or so distant from sleep.

Chapter Six

I am not very skilled with my needle, and I am nervous this morning, so I have trouble guiding the thread through the eye. With the needle now threaded, I go to work. I push the needle through the material at the top of the letter, and then bring it back through. My stitches are uneven, but I like the effect I am getting outlining the letter. The needle pricks my fingers and I suck the blood from the tip. I do not have the time to wait for the bleeding to stop and I do not want to spoil my work with a blood stain. I rip a piece of cloth off the hem of my shift with my teeth and wrap it around my finger. I stitch all the way around the letter, and then again to thicken the outline. Now, I am ready to face them.

Bridget stands on one side of me, and Mistress Anne on the other. It is only the second day after my father's arrest, and he has already been tried, convicted and sentenced. He now stands next to the pillory, just a few steps from the platform where I faced these same people not so very long ago. Master Cotton and Constable Middleton are on the other side of the pillory. My father's face is unshaven and his eyes are bloodshot. He is wearing only a shirt and breeches, both still coated with mud, and he is shivering. The ground is covered with a thin layer of fresh snow. But I have taken my cloak off. Mistress Anne remarks my handiwork.

"'Tis too cold this morning not to have your cloak on," she says, and tries to lift it back onto my shoulders. I stay her hand.

"I feel quite warm."

"Are you sure you want to do this?"

"You thought it well to have me stand in front of the people in your house when first I put on this letter."

"That was then, and this is different. You may excite the crowd."

"I do hope so."

I turn to look at them. A few feet to my right are Governor Winthrop and Assistant Governor Dudley. Standing behind them is Master Stanton. I see people whose faces I have seen staring back at me either when I was on the platform or when I was in Mistress Anne's parlor. Behind the crowd are some Indians. Maybe they have come to learn the white man's method of punishment so they can improve upon their own.

Governor Winthrop is staring hard at me. I puff my chest out as far as I can. His expression hardens.

"Mistress," he says, to Mistress Anne, "do you see what that child has done?"

"Surely."

Dudley, who had been talking to Stanton, now looks at me. He squints to focus on the letter.

"Why the brazen thing has turned it upside down," he says.

Winthrop steps toward me.

"So this is the use you put to learning your letters?"

"It is the letter my father's last name begins with," I say. "And mine."

"I see that well enough, but it is not the letter you were commanded to wear." He looks at Mistress Anne. "What say you?" he asks her.

"That it is enough that she is here to see her father punished," Mistress Anne replied.

"That man is her father no more," Winthrop snaps. "Have her put on her cloak."

Others nearby now look at me, and a murmur rises from them. But just then, Master Cotton motions for silence so that he can be heard as he questions my father. Mistress Anne motions me to pull my cloak about me, and I do. I am suddenly very cold.

"Do you want to confess your sins before punishment is imposed on you?"

My father is trying to stand straight, but age, too much rum, and a hard life have bent his spine. He opens his mouth to speak, and I see that he has lost his front teeth. He shrugs and closes his mouth.

"Come, man, for the benefit of your soul and the improvement of those who stand here to witness your shame."

"It is not my soul that you will be abusing," my father replies. "I am just a poor man that has not enough coin to put food on his table."

91

Master Stanton steps forward. He pauses as he comes next to me, and then continues until he is in front of my father.

"And so you decided to correct that lack by stealing my purse, did you?"

"Yours or somebody of your kind," my father replies. "Don't feel that you are chosen. It was nothing personal. You just came to hand."

Master Stanton draws in his breath and his face reddens.

"That is right," my father repeats, "came to hand. Or was it in somebody's hand?"

Master Stanton raises his arm as though to strike my father, and then he drops it to his side.

"Can we get on with it, Master Cotton?"

"You have nothing to say?" Master Cotton tries one more time. He turns to me. "For your daughter's sake, then." My father just shakes his head.

"Then here you will stand, mute as you are, to testify in your shame that thievery brings you to such a place as this."

Governor Winthrop steps forward.

"Jonathan Moore, you have been found guilty of thievery for the third time. The Court therefore has sentenced you to lose your ear and then to forever leave this town. We will not have you live among us to continue to contaminate our community, nor will we send you abroad, unmarked to unsuspecting people in other communities. Constable, proceed."

Constable Middleton, who is standing close by, lifts up the top board of the pillory with one hand, and grabs my father's hair with the other. He yanks on the hair to pull my father's head into the device, and then still holding the hair so tight my father can hardly breathe, he pulls his hands into place. He drops the board, so my father stands there now, hands and head in their wooden embrace. The crowd murmurs. "Good," says one. "It will be better ere long," says another. "Thief," cries out a third. I turn and see that the last is the man from whom my father stole the hog on the day of my shame.

I remember the darkness of the night with the shadow crossing the moon when Master Cotton presided over an act of secret shame, choosing to hide the birth of that terrible babe because God, he said, intended only the babe's parents to be instructed by its deformities. Now, the same Master Cotton is standing next to my father in the pillory declaring that his punishment must instruct the community. I wonder if he is remembering that night as he stands there with a little, forced smile on his lips. My father, though, does not complain about his punishment. He is not a good man. He never said he was. And now I feel closer to him than I have since we both stood on the deck of that ship as it rolled on the waves of the mighty ocean so long ago.

I walk up to the pillory. The crowd increases its murmur again after it had almost quieted down. I stand in front of my father, pull back my cloak, and offer the letter on my chest to them. Some snicker, and some just shake their heads. I do not care. If there is a sermon to be made today, it is right that I be part of it.

"Be gone," my father mutters just loud enough for me to hear him.

"Yes," Master Stanton says, "look at the child that this man has raised. She has turned her letter upside down to tell us that *Moore* and *Whore* are two ways of saying the same thing, and there she stands without shame, just like her father. But let us not think all our children are such as she. There is in this town a lad so modest that he will not come forward. But it is he we have to thank for capturing this terrible man, for this lad threw his own body into the path of this thief as he attempted to flee."

I have Master Stanton's coin pressed into my palm. I open my hand so my father can see it. He struggles against the pillory to shake his head.

"No," he says. "Be gone, I tell you."

I close my hand around the coin, but remain standing in front of my father as though to shield him from the eyes of the crowd. Mistress Anne and Bridget now come to me, each taking an arm and they pull me away from the pillory. I do not struggle.

"Constable, proceed," Master Stanton says.

Constable Middleton steps to my father. He has a big iron nail in one hand, and a hammer in the other.

"Do your worst," my father says. "It is no matter."

Constable Middleton places the point of the nail into my father's ear and presses it against the wood of the pillory.

"Be careful you don't knock him in the head," says one in the crowd.

"Yes," says another, "we want him sensible to his punishment."

Constable Middleton raises his hammer and brings it down on the head of the nail, driving it through my father's flesh and into the wood of the pillory. Blood spurts from the wound. The constable raises his hammer again and drives the nail further, and more blood spurts out of the mangled ear. One more hard blow and the nail is well into the wood. Through all this, my father has been silent. His eyes now follow the constable as he walks away. The blood oozes around the head of the nail and drips down the wood of the pillory onto the ground, reddening the white snow.

"Because you have been a stubborn man, unwilling or unable to take our instruction," Master Stanton now declares, "we are going to mark you for all to see, for know you that since you have not listened to God or magistrate, you no longer need your ear. Constable, he is yours."

Constable Middleton holds up a long, sharp knife, its blade bright in the sun. I can feel the excitement run through the crowd. Mistress Anne takes my shoulder and tries to turn me away.

"No," I say. "I must see it all."

She relaxes her hold and instead caresses my arms as I force myself to keep my eyes fastened on that bright blade. Constable Middleton places his left hand flat against my father's cheek, and holds the knife in his other hand on top of my father's ear, which is fastened by the nail to the pillory. He pushes my father's head so that the ear is pulled away from the side of his head. More blood spills from around the nail. Then with deliberation he places the blade on the top of the ear. With a sawing motion, he hacks away at the ear.

He is not a surgeon. Something is stopping the progress of the blade. He saws away with renewed vigor and the blood now flows freely splashing onto the sleeve of the constable's great coat. He looks at my father's bright red blood and mutters something. He draws the knife back and down and suddenly there is a space between the ear nailed to the pillory and the side of my father's head. A loud cheer rises from the crowd.

I break free from Mistress Anne and run to my father. I stare for a moment at the hole where his ear used to be and see that it is filling with his blood. I lift my hand to his, which is trapped in the pillory, and I press Master Stanton's coin into it. He does not refuse it. Then I dip my fingers into the hole on the side of his face and bring back my fingers dripping with his blood. I run my fingers over the new white border on my upside-down letter until the white thread is completely red.

Constable Middleton now pushes me aside. I stumble back to Mistress Anne and Bridget. My fingers still drip blood, and Bridget steps back from me. Mistress Anne though throws my cloak about my shoulders. The constable unfastens the pillory and lifts the top board. My father staggers back, but he does not reach for his wound. Instead he grabs his ear, still nailed to the pillory, and he pulls it off, ripping the flesh.

"Master Stanton," he calls, and then he tosses the severed ear at the feet of the gentleman.

"You can have the other one for a shilling or two," my father says, and then he laughs loudly. Master Stanton glares at him and then walks away. I take a step toward my father, but then stop. Governor Winthrop, Dudley, and Master Cotton follow behind Master Stanton. The governor pauses as he passes by me.

"You will come to work, directly," he says. "As soon as you affix your letter properly."

"Yes," I reply.

He gestures toward my father.

"That man has renounced his rights to you as a daughter." He runs his finger over the blood, still wet, on my gown. "Even if his blood runs through your body, I am your master now. Remember that."

"Yes," I say again.

The rest of the people now start to leave. My father holds up the coin for me to see and then he walks away in the opposite direction from the way taken by Master Stanton and the others.

Bridget tries to embrace me, but I pull away. She holds my arms fast and looks earnestly into my eyes.

"How terrible for you this must be," she says.

I can see that she is moved by what has just happened, moved enough to be pulled out of her usual concentration on Thomas and her own concerns. She seems to want to console me, but how can she? She lives on the mountain of comfort and ease built by her father's money and her mother's powerful reputation while I live in the valley of my father's degraded life which has just reached its bottom. We sleep in the same bed, and we talk girlish things to each other, but in this respect I am a hundred years old, and she no more than a babe still crawling on her hands and knees. And that difference has nothing to do with the fact that she is, indeed, older than I am. Until she dies she will be like a baby sister to me.

"Yes," I say in response. "It is very terrible, indeed."

I find a small knife in the kitchen and climb the stairs to my room. I remove my gown, sit on my bed and slice through the stitches I had sewn that morning.

I turn the letter right side up and lay it on my gown. My father's blood on it is cold and sticky. I sew the letter back on as it was intended to be worn. If the governor can make me an orphan, I suppose he can call me whore.

Eleanor is waiting for me when I return to Master Winthrop's house. She wants to see my letter without appearing to look at it. She glances sideways once or twice. I point at it and she stares and nods.

Pewter plates are stacked high on the table. Next to them are the spoons. Eleanor hands me a rag.

"I heard about your disgraceful behavior," she says. She points to the plates. "Rub them until your arm cannot move, and then use your other arm."

For a moment, her face shows something that I could almost think was tenderness for me, but then she just shrugs and leaves me alone with my pile of plates. And in truth, I am not unhappy with a chore such as this. My poor mind is overwhelmed as it is with the picture of the hole on the side of my father's head and I feel his blood on my chest as though it is fire running over the thread that outlines the letter.

I attack the first plate with my rag, rubbing it as hard as I can. It is blotched with purplish stains that I know are in the metal and no amount of rubbing will remove them, but I go after them just the same. I move my hand round and round, faster and faster, and the stain gets brighter and brighter instead of fading until it is blood red. I put the plate down and examine the dull stain that almost blends into the dark silver color of the finish.

I take up another plate, and then another. In between, I try the spoons. I go at them all as though they were Master Stanton's plump, arrogant face. I want to erase his sneer. I want him to feel pain. I want him to know how I hate him. I do not hear the steps behind me, but I do feel the hand on my shoulder.

"Good," Eleanor says. "I see you are asweat with good honest labor, enough maybe to stop that foolish tongue of yours."

I do feel the sweat in the corners of my eyes and dripping off the tip of my nose. I lick it off my lips. I am compelled to silence.

Eleanor picks up one of the plates and stares hard at it. She puckers her mouth as though she could see herself in it. I wonder why she should want to, but I hold my peace, as she said I should. She puts the plate back down.

"The governor wants to talk to you. You know where to find him."

He is sitting behind his desk, writing. He looks up as I walk in and then back down at the paper. He crumples it up and tosses it onto the desk.

"Rachel," he says in a tone that tells me he is trying to be kind, but he is not sure that he can manage it. His hand goes to his beard.

"Rachel, I am sure you know that what you did today was very wrong, and that it shamed me, as your master. You mocked the letter on your breast while your father was being punished. Is it true that you have learned nothing all this time?"

"He is still my father, whatever he has done, and he has done his worst with me, God knows."

"Silence," the governor says, his voice now barely containing his anger. "He is no longer your father. You must understand. He will leave Boston. We have marked him, just as God marked Cain, so all will know him for what he is, a thief."

"And me, sir?"

He does not hesitate.

"A whore." He reaches across his desk to press his finger against my letter. "Jonathan Moore's ear cannot be reattached, but this can be removed, in time."

"If I do as I am told?"

He relaxes.

"Yes. But know the only reason you are still here, and not following your father into exile, or worse, is that you can be of use to me."

"I understand."

"You will need to be more forthcoming than you have in the past."

"I do not always understand what Mistress Hutchinson says."

"I doubt that. I believe you understand very well, indeed. But if you do not, then you must remember the words. It will be for me to decipher them."

There is a knock on the door. It opens and Eleanor comes in ahead of Master Wilson, Master Stanton, and a younger man I do not recognize. This man walks directly to the governor and greets him with an embrace. Master Wilson and Master Stanton, though, stand by the door and stare at me as though I am a loathsome insect in their path, and I must be removed before they can proceed. I take my leave, pressing myself against the book lined walls until I reach the door. When I do, Eleanor hauls me out of the room.

"Back to your plates, child," she says.

"Yes," I look toward the door, but Eleanor places her thick body, arms crossed in front of her chest, in front of it.

I start to head back to the kitchen, slowly, but then I hear Mistress Margaret call Eleanor from upstairs. I crouch in the space beneath the stairs where a trunk is kept. Eleanor's hurried steps rush toward me. I flatten myself on top of the trunk as she passes by, and then I listen to the steps creak beneath her weight. I make my way back to the door and press my ear to the keyhole.

"How is it with your wife, John?" the governor asks.

"The journey much fatigued her, but she is recovering and awaits her time and God's pleasure."

So the stranger is the governor's son, Master John Winthrop, Jr., who is returned to Boston from Connecticut, where he is governor, with his wife soon to take to childbed.

"And what news from the Pequots?" asks the senior Winthrop, and I can hear that he cares as much, or more, about the answer to this question as he does concerning the health of his daughter-in-law, soon to bring him a grandchild.

"They refuse to yield up the murderers of Captain Stone," the younger Winthrop says. "They do not agree neither to the quantity of wampum we have demanded."

"And the fort at Saybrook?"

"I fear it is under siege."

No-one speaks for a moment, and then Master Stanton's voice rises above the silence.

"These savages must be taught we are not to be trifled with."

"Is it not true that you are considering removing your family to the Connecticut, because you feel there is not land for your needs here?" Governor Winthrop's voice is honeyed but I detect the sharp edge beneath its surface. Master Stanton's laugh booms through the door where I stand and I jump back.

"Why, that has nothing to do with it, for me or any of us, am I not right?"

A chorus of laughs joins him, now, and then the solemn voice of Master Wilson.

✓ "The savages have no right to land that they do not improve. That is a point well-grounded and understood."

"We must get the General Court to act then," Master Stanton says. "We will raise a force and send it Saybrook."

"It would be meet to invite Master Dudley's counsel," the Governor adds.

"He will go along with us in this affair," Master Stanton replies. "His interest, as ours, lies that way."

"No doubt," the governor replies. "But he is but one and there are others who would oppose us."

"Ah, yes, and they have their one to lead them, do they not? I have seen her power with mine own eyes, and heard how she casts a spell."

"Then we must meet her power with mine." The governor's voice has steel in it now. There is silence and then the sound of a crisp piece of paper being unfolded and flattened on the desk. I can see the governor's hand, palm down, smoothing the paper. I have watched him do that a hundred times. He is a very careful man with his papers. I strain to listen, but their voices are now murmuring I cannot make out their words. I press my ear harder to the door. I must find out what they are saying, but then the steps creak again under Eleanor. I have no choice. I run past the stairs and back to the kitchen. When she walks in, I have a rag in my hand and my face is red from my haste.

"Good," Eleanor says. "Keep at it."

A moment later there is a knock at the door. I get up to answer it, but Eleanor bustles by me.

"You needn't bother," she says.

She opens the door and lets a young man in.

"The governor has sent for me," he says. I have not lifted my eyes from the plates, but I recognize the voice of Bridget's Tom.

"He is occupied, now," Eleanor says, "and bids you come again tomorrow."

"I will," he replies. I feel his eyes on me. "Is that you, then, Rachel?"

I look up.

"Yes."

"Could you tell Bridget..." he begins.

"You can tell her yourself," I reply.

"Yes," Eleanor says. "Rachel is far too busy here to be carrying messages back to that house."

Tom shrugs.

"It is of no matter. It is just that I wanted to tell her that I may be going away."

"Hush," Eleanor snaps, "have you no sense?"

I see Tom's lip stiffen as though he wants to say something he shouldn't, and then he just smiles.

"I can wait until I see her, can't I?"

"What happens in that house," Eleanor says, "is no concern of mine." She turns and stalks away. Tom looks at her back.

"So will you?" he asks me.

"No."

He takes a step toward me. I do not know his intent. He must see something in my eyes, and he stops.

"I will be going then," he says. "Tell Bridget I am going off to fight the savages."

After he is gone, I walk back toward the room where the governor had been meeting with his son and the others. The door is not completely shut. I edge closer to it and wait. I do not hear anything, and so I push the door open enough to look in. Nobody is there. His desk is neat except for one piece of paper that is all crumpled up into a ball. It is not like him to handle paper like that. I go in and pick up the paper, thinking I will throw it in the fire so his desk will be all neat again. But then I hear steps, and I thrust the paper up my sleeve and hurry out of the room just before the governor arrives.

Chapter Seven

After dinner, I go to bed and take the paper out of my sleeve where I have kept it hidden all day. The paper is covered in the governor's writing, and I am afraid that it is beyond my skill to read. I can make out a word here and there, but not enough to string them together.

Bridget comes up after a while. I have decided that I will not tell her about Tom asking after her.

"What is that you have there?" she asks.

"Something I need your help with."

She leans against me in the bed and peers over my shoulder.

"Who wrote that?"

"Can you read it?"

"Of course."

"Will you?"

"If you promise."

I consider for only a moment. My curiosity is great as my situation is perilous.

"Yes," I say.

She hugs me hard.

"Read," I say.

"It is a list."

"What kind of list?"

"Of heretical opinions."

"Whose?"

"Can you not guess?"

"Begin," I say, "slowly, very slowly." I want to hear every word alone before it is joined to the ones before and after it.

Bridget sighs. She is not used to patience or deliberation. She reads.

"A list of grievous heresies and errors in thought, spoken by Mistress Hutchinson."

Bridget puts down the paper.

"I am not sure we should read this without Mother seeing it," she says.

"Read," I insist.

Bridget shrugs and resumes. I look over her shoulder to see if I can match the words I hear to those on the paper. I cannot, and after a while I find the marks on the paper moving about and the words Bridget reads buzzing in my ear. I step back and only listen. I cannot make much sense out of what I hear. Bridget says a number, and then there is something I would expect Master Wilson or Master Cotton to say at meeting, and then a lot more about that something, and my head starts to ache. I know the words are in English but what they relate to in my poor life is more than I can see.

"Do you understand?" I ask.

"A little," Bridget replies.

"Keep reading, then," I say.

"My mother…" she begins.

"Later."

And she lowers her eyes to the paper and reads. I hear something about how we are passengers on a ship in a storm with mighty waves on a dangerous ocean. I watch her eyes move down the page. She pauses where the paper is creased and she cannot make out what is written. I look over her shoulder. The hand at the bottom of the page is different, the stroke bolder. Bridget's voice shakes as she finishes.

"Our course to salvation is twofold. One is war against the savages. Two is expulsion of the heretic. The first will enable us to do the second."

I take the paper from Bridget's hand and trace the letters of the words she has just read. I study them until I understand, and what I understand is how clever the governor and his friends are. They will turn our attention to the savages. Everybody fears them, even though some of them have accepted Our Lord. You can see it in people's eyes how they look at them, even the Christian ones, like they still expect an arrow in the back or a hatchet in the head. So, if we all fear them, we are together in that fear. The governor's ship will not sink.

But one must be thrown overboard. Even Bridget now understands that much.

"I will talk to your mother in the morning," I say to her. "I will show her this paper so she can read for herself."

"And will you, you know, the other?" she asks.

I am impressed by her stubborn self-interest.

"Yes," I say, "for I remember my promise to you."

After breakfast, before I leave for the governor's house, I seek an opportunity to talk with Mistress Anne. I have the paper carefully folded and tucked up into my sleeve as I come down the stairs. But she is by the front door, talking to Master Hutchinson about stopping by the cobbler to get the new shoes for young Samuel. Master Hutchinson has not paid much attention to me since I came to live in his house, and that is well. I have enough to do with Master Winthrop. So I step back up the stairs where he cannot see me, and wait for them to finish their conversation.

"You will remember, Will, won't you?" she asks.

Master Hutchinson is a tall, fair man, with a ruddy face, easy to smile, and slow to anger. I guess that comes from being so very prosperous and from having so many children, as well as a wife that knows her own mind more than most women I have seen. So, now, he just nods in his agreeable way, and then gives her a peck on the cheek.

It is remarkable that this woman, married to this man who is ordinary in every way except that he has a great deal of money, should be viewed by our governor as so dangerous that she must be sent away. She sees me waiting.

"Yes, Rachel," she says. "I have only a moment."

I feel the paper pressing against the flesh of my arm, and my head aches from the promise I have made to Bridget, for I know that in keeping my word I am exposing myself to Mistress Anne's disapproval, or worse. Still, I have never been one to worry too much about tomorrow when today is usually more than enough to deal with. I pull the paper out of my sleeve.

"If it please you," I say, "I think you should see this."

She takes it and reads the first few lines.

"How came you by this?" she asks.

"Bridget read it to me last night. I could not read many of the words."

"That is not what I asked you."

"I know, but you seem displeased, and I am afraid."

"Did you steal this?"

I begin to shake my head, and then I nod.

"It was crumpled on his desk. I was cleaning. I thought I would practice my reading."

"Is that all?"

"No. He is always asking me about you. I do not understand why. I thought maybe this paper would tell me."

"Did it?"

"Yes."

"Then let me read it."

I expect her to grow angry as she reads. I study her face, waiting for it to turn black. But it doesn't. As she reads, a smile forms slowly on her lip until she is grinning. When she reaches the bottom of the page, though, she frowns. Then she folds the paper neatly. "You must return this to where you found it."

"I cannot."

"But you must. Do not worry. You need not tell the governor you took it." She hands me the paper and I slide it again into my sleeve.

"Do you understand what the governor is worried about?" she asks.

"You," I say. "But I do not know why."

"Did Bridget read to you the part about the ship?"

"Yes, she did." I look down at my feet, and Mistress Anne smiles.

"You wonder how I can sink his ship?" she asks, and then takes my hand. Her touch, as always, is warm and reassuring. "He is saying that if the ship sinks, we all will drown, and if it sails smoothly, we will all reach our destination." She lifts her eyes upward, and I imagine she is looking toward heaven.

"And you do not thinks so?" That idea makes sense to me.

She shakes her head very slowly as if the very idea pressed down on her.

"No. For two reasons. I do not believe God punishes or saves one person because of what another does or does not do. And to use the Governor's figure, if we are indeed like a ship, I believe the Master of the Ship has not set the right course."

"And you do, know the right course."

"Yes," she says, and her eyes close. I want to ask her what that course is, but I do not dare. She snaps her eyes open, and I wonder if she has just been spoken to.

"He fears me," she says, "because he knows that I see what he is doing, how he is making a wall out of the Law of Moses, a wall that surrounds all of us, keeps us together like a flock of sheep, with him as the shepherd, but that same wall stands between us and our Lord. And I will strike down that wall, brick by brick with my bare hands, if need be, so I can leave Master Wilson's flock to walk with Jesus Christ."

"And other people. Are they to follow you?"

She shakes her head.

"I am not fit to lead anyone. I try only to help people see that they can find their own way." She looks at the paper again. "Do you see that the words on the bottom of the page were not written by the same hand as the rest of it?"

"Yes."

"Do you know…" she begins.

"There were several men there with the governor, talking I think about what is on this paper. There was the governor's son."

"It was not him," she replies. "The hand is too bold. Was Master Wilson there?"

"Yes."

"I see," she says. She takes her cloak off the peg near the door. "Now, I must be off, and you must to Governor Winthrop."

"There is one thing," I say.

"About the paper?"

"No," I reply. Without thinking, I place my two hands over my belly as though to screen it.

"You're not again," she says. "It is not possible. What makes you think so? Who is the man?"

Her questions run into each other and frighten me.

"No, I am not."

"Then who?"

I want to answer, but my tongue will not co-operate. She slowly shakes her head.

"It is Bridget, isn't it?" she says.

"Yes."

"And she asked you to speak for her."

"She is ashamed and afraid."

"Does she intend to marry, then?"

"I do not think the man is agreeable."

"I see," she says. "It is Tom, isn't it?"

"Yes."

"Do you know where to find him?"

"He will be at the governor's house tomorrow."

Her eyes sparkle in surprise and then anger.

"How is that?"

"He was there yesterday but the governor was busy. He is to come again today. He wanted me to take a message to Bridget, but I said I would not. He told it me, anyway."

"What was it?"

"That he might be going away."

"Find him tonight, if you can, and tell him Master Hutchinson has need of him tomorrow."

"Does he?"

"He will. As for Bridget. What does she want me to do, if she does not want to marry?"

"She thought you might be able to help her. In another way."

"So that is the way it is."

"I do not think she wants to stand on the platform like I did, or wear a letter like I do."

"No," she murmurs. "She is not strong like you."

I do not feel very strong. I feel as though I have been stepped on by the boots of the governor. And Master Wilson. And Master Stanton. And now I shall perhaps feel the weight of Master Hutchinson, as though I should have protected his daughter from herself.

I take my time walking across the way. The air is warm, and the snow is almost gone. The people I pass have small smiles on their faces as though to greet spring. Those smiles disappear, though, when they see the letter on my gown. Only one young woman, walking with babe in arms, nods at me, and keeps the smile on her lips. She does not dare greet me, though. I have become accustomed to this kind of thing, and so I just hasten my step and keep my eyes fastened on the ground as though afraid that I might trip over something, something like my neighbor's contempt for me, which I feel as much as the uneven ground beneath my feet.

As I walk, I hear the babe in the woman's arms cry. I cannot help myself, so I turn around. The woman has lifted the babe and is talking to it. The babe has quieted. My stomach tightens into an ache I had begun to think might have left me forever. Now I am reminded that I will ache until I die or until I have my own babe back in my arms. I am certain it lives and is growing up among the savages. I recall what I heard the governor and the others talking about, and an idea begins to form itself in my mind. But first I must try to do what Mistress Anne bade me do.

I intend to put the paper back on Master Winthrop's desk. But as soon as I walk into the house, I see Eleanor standing in the hall, waiting for me, with her arms crossed in front of her chest. I sometimes think that she stands this way so often because she is practicing how she will look when she is dead, only then she will be lying down instead of standing up.

"Maureen is sick," she says. She does not try to stop the smile that spreads up from her mouth to her ears.

"Again?" ask I.

"You know what to do," she says, and I think I hear a cackle, but her lips have not moved.

I nod and go up the stairs. Maureen is the new servant girl, just arrived from Ireland. Master Winthrop bought her from somebody who was going back to England and did not want to be burdened with her. She is healthy enough, it seems to me, but she is often sick in the morning when she is supposed to do her first chore of the day. Then, she recovers in time to do her other chores by the late morning. When she is sick, like she is today, I must do her job.

I make my way into their bedroom. The bed is unmade, of course, but my nose tells me where I must go first. It is in the corner. I pick up the pot. It is still a little warm. I hear the piss slopping around in it, and the stink attacks my nose. I hold it away from me and carry it down the stairs and out the back door into the field beyond. I find a small pile of snow in the shade of a tree where the sun has not reached to melt it. I empty the pot onto the snow, being careful to make sure it does not splash onto my feet, and I watch with a smile as the snow turns yellow. I am supposed to wash the pot out with water from the spring, but we have not done that all winter, and I do not intend to do it today.

Maureen is making the bed when I bring back the pot.

"You must be feeling better," I say.

"I was dizzy when I awoke." She smiles. "But I am fine now."

I place the pot back in the corner.

"I am sure you are," I say.

The governor is waiting for me when I come down the stairs.

"Rachel," he says. "I must ask you about something that has disappeared from my desk. I wonder if you know anything about it."

He does not wait for me to answer but walks through the parlor and into his study, beckoning with his arm for me to follow. I feel the paper in my sleeve. We pass the fireplace in the parlor, and I think about throwing the paper into it. But the fire is almost out, since Maureen has not yet tended to it, and just then the governor turns to make sure that I am following him. Instead of throwing the paper into the fireplace, I shove it further up my sleeve.

He enters his study and takes his seat behind his desk.

"Yesterday, I left a piece of paper on my desk. It was crumpled up because I thought I was not satisfied with the way it was written. Then, this morning I decided it would be wiser to see if I could improve upon my expression rather than throw away my efforts entirely. But, as you can see, there is no paper here."

"No sir, there is not."

"I remember that you were in this room yesterday."

"Yes sir. I left it when the other gentlemen came."

"So I remember. Yet, the paper was on my desk when those gentlemen were here. And this morning it is gone."

"Perhaps someone made the mistake of thinking you no longer wanted it, sir."

He smiles.

"Just my thought. Now was that somebody you?"

"No sir. That was not my meaning. I know nothing about your paper."

"I am sorry to hear you say that. I am to see Reverend Wilson later this day, and he had added a note to my own poor efforts, and this is what is troubling me. I wanted to meditate on what he had said before I question him further, but I do not recall how he worded his recommendation. Do you?"

"No sir."

"But you do remember seeing his words appended to mine. Surely, you saw the writing was from a different hand."

"I saw no writing, sir. Yours or his. Because I saw no paper on your desk, or anyplace else."

He rises, his face flushed. My hand starts to reach for the paper to push it further up my sleeve, but I make it stay down by my side. I do not think the governor would offer me the indignity of searching my clothing.

"Perhaps Maureen can help you, sir," I say.

"She is sick abed, I understand."

"She was, but she is better."

"Still, she is new to our family. I have not yet given her leave to clean this room."

"There are those who do not wait for leave," I say, remembering the stink of the chamber pot.

"Indeed," the governor says, "there are those who do not wait."

I turn to leave.

"A moment," he says.

Something in his tone is dangerous. I have heard it before. He uses it when he is about to ask a question to trap you instead of inquire.

"Do you know where Mistress Dyer lives?"

So that is it. This man has eyes and ears everywhere. He makes it very difficult to lie or to squirm around the edges of a fact.

"Yes," I say.

"Were you there a fortnight ago?"

"No, sir, why would I have been?"

"In the company of Mistress Hutchinson, perhaps?"

"No," I repeat. He looks at me and then smiles.

"That is all," he says.

Maureen is sitting on the bed she had been making.

"The governor is looking for a piece of paper he has misplaced. I told him I knew nothing about it but that maybe you did."

"A paper, you say, why would I be knowing about some paper. I cannot read. What would I be wanting his paper for?"

"I'm sure I do not know. Maybe you can explain that to him when he talks to you."

She wrinkles up her nose like a hog snorting, and closes her eyes in thought.

"Maybe I should go talk with him. To clear his mind of his misgivings about me," she says.

"He didn't ask me to fetch you."

"Still, I think I might."

"Well, then, do what you think is right," I say.

She gets up off the bed and heads toward the stairs. For a moment, I think I might place the paper in her bed. But I reject that idea. I do not think the governor would ever lower himself, or let his wife lower herself, by rooting around his servant's bed clothes. Instead I go down to the kitchen. Nobody is there and the fire is roaring in the fireplace. I pull the paper out of my sleeve, and throw it into the fire. I hear steps. I can still see the paper, so I poke it into the heart of the fire.

"That's right," Eleanor says. "It is a good thing to see you taking an interest and not waiting to be told what to do. Just make sure that bread is done before you take it out of the oven."

"Yes, I will," I say. I peer into the fire, until my eyes begin to water. As hard as I stare, I can see only flames and ashes.

"Did you drop something, then?"

I turn to face Tom. I have to admit he is a handsome one, tall, stout, with a sparkle in his brown eyes. But then I remember that Henry looked good until you got to know what a bastard he was.

"No," I say.

"Then what were you looking at?"

"Any fool can see that I was looking at the fire."

He smiles and shrugs.

"What did Bridget have to say to me?" he asks.

"Nothing. For I did not talk to her about you."

"I am disappointed," he says.

Eleanor bustles back into the kitchen.

"About your business, Tom," she says. "The governor waits for you."

"Tell her I will be at the Sign of the Jackal tonight," he says, and hurries off.

"What is that all about?" Eleanor asks.

"The silly boy thinks I am going to carry messages for him," I say.

For the first time, Eleanor smiles at me in a way that makes me think that she might have been a girl once herself.

"You know better than that, I trust," she says.

"Yes, I do."

I am alone in the kitchen tending the fire, waiting for the bread to bake when Maureen comes in, her face red. She grabs the poker from my hands and elbows me aside.

"What is the matter?" I ask.

"As if you do not know," she says.

"Surely, I do not."

"The governor was at me about that paper. Why would he think I took it?" Her blue eyes are set close together on her narrow face, and they now almost cross with her anger. I take a deep breath as though I could smell the pot.

"He is that careful about his papers," I say.

Her eyes switch from me to the fire. She pokes at a charred piece of the note and pushes it into the flame.

"I cannot read," she mutters. "That is what I told him."

"As did I," I say.

"He should look to those who can," she says.

"Yes," I reply.

"Seek him there, if you must," Mistress Anne says, "for I must talk to him."

"That is where I know he will be."

And indeed he is. He is at a table with two other young men. They have been drinking for some time, as I can tell not only by the empty tankards and the beer spilled on the table, but by the smell of their breaths as they talk. I know that smell very well in all its variations, depending on what my father had money or opportunity to buy or steal to drink. And they are breathing hard because they are talking about killing savages. There is another young man sitting alone at a table behind Tom and his friends. He glances over at them from time to time, but he does not join in their talk. His cheeks are covered by a scraggly beard. But he is not the one I came to find.

"Yes," Tom is saying as I approach them, "the governor himself told me this very afternoon that an order is to go out to raise a power and he promised me that I could be a sergeant if I was to bring a couple of stout lads, such as yourselves, with me." He lifts his tankard to his lips and swallows. He lowers his tongue out of his mouth to catch the beer that dribbles down his chin, and then he sees me.

"Why, Rachel, you are not Bridget."

"Why, Tom," I reply, "nobody can fool you, you are a clever one, I always say."

111

"Well, then, no matter," he says, "come sit down."

He motions to the tavern keeper's servant, and the wench comes over with another tankard, filled to the brim with beer. He pulls her down onto his lap, and she protests with a loud and unconvincing giggle. She does not spill the beer, which she slides across the table to me. Tom has his hand somewhere I cannot see, but a second later the wench jumps up, her face red and a smile on her lips.

"Now, I've told you, none of that," she says.

"Right, you have, then haven't you?" he says. "So," he says to me, "do you truly not have word for me from my Bridget."

"No," says I, "but I do from her father."

Tom's companions laugh, but his face is now serious.

"In truth?" says he.

"Aye," say I, "in truth. I am sent to fetch you to speak with Master Hutchinson."

"What about, then?"

"I cannot say."

"Cannot, or will not? Well, then, no matter. I guess I must content myself with what is at hand." He reaches his hand across the table to my breast. I suffer his fingers as they squeeze and roam for a moment, and then I start to pull back. He looks as though in puzzlement.

"Why, then, what signifies this?" and he traces the letter on my chest.

"Do you think then it is an invitation for all who might take a fancy?"

"Indeed, I do."

His fingers are still resting on my breast, and so I take hold of his hand, which is much larger than mine. I grab his fingers with one hand, and with the other I push his thumb back as hard as I can. His face reddens and he clutches at me with his other hand. I just push harder until his eyes begin to tear. Then I let his hand drop. He rises to his feet and leans across the table toward me, but I am much too fast, and he is not very steady.

"Why you," he sputters.

"Remember who sent me, and on what errand," I say.

"I will catch up with you some time," he says, and then he turns back to his friends. I am about to leave when the man at the next table motions to me. I shake my head because I do not want to wait for Tom to remember that I am still there. The stranger motions toward the door, and I understand that I am to wait for him outside. Tom calls to me.

"I will see Master Hutchinson before I leave. But not tonight, by your leave, for I do the governor's business this night, I do." And with that he and his friends laugh so loud that for a moment there is no other sound to be heard in the tavern.

The stranger is at my arm almost as soon as I am out the door.

"I went to war once," he says. He is holding a musket. The gun is almost as tall as I am. "Those boys in there do not know about war, but I do. I have come to try it again."

"I was thinking I would like to follow this war," I say.

"You can," he says. "You can go as a whore or a soldier. I can teach you how to do the one," he looks at my chest, "but maybe you know about doing the other." I feel my blood rush to my face, and he reaches for me. I step back, but he only wants my hands. His are warm and gentle.

"I see," he said. "I was unkind." He lets my hands drop. I study his face for the sneer or knowing smile I am used to seeing on the likes of Henry or Tom, the look that says my body is meat for their table whenever and however they want it, but that look is not there. His eyes are deep set and his face, young as it is, is lined with hard experience. I trace the letter on my chest.

"No," I say, "not you. This is unkind. Tell me if you still are of a mind about being a soldier."

He hands the musket to me. It is heavier than it looks. I try to raise it to my shoulder as I have seen men do when the parade. It digs into my bone. I let it slide butt down onto the ground.

"Can you show me, then?" I ask.

"Yes," he replies. "You can find me when you are ready to learn. I will be at the same table every night." He looks over his shoulder toward the tavern. "But if you do not see me, just ask for Martin Miller."

I put down the musket and take his hand. It is cool. I press his palm against mine. Maybe I can trust this Martin Miller.

Chapter Eight

Bridget is insistent. She cannot imagine I am serious.
"Are you really going to leave?" she asks.

"I have been thinking about doing so."

"You think your babe is still alive?"

"I do."

She closes her eyes for a moment and when she opens them they are wet with her tears.

"It is passing strange," she says.

"I know."

"That you would go where you might die to find the babe you lost, while I…"

"You do not need to say it."

"I cannot."

We hear the stairs creak, and we both turn to each other in the bed where we have been lying in the dark, knowing that before long Mistress Anne must seek us out. And now she has.

Usually, she walks with purpose, thrusting her short, plump body ahead as though fearful her destination will disappear before she reaches it. Now, however, she moves toward us like I remember seeing people as they walk behind the cart that carries the body of a loved one to the cemetery. Bridget seems to take note of her mother's serious intent, and she leans over to whisper in my ear.

"You did speak to her?"

Her breath is hot with fear on my cheek, but her hand which now reaches for mine is cold and damp.

"Of course," I say.

Mistress Anne is upon us but Bridget seems unable to pull herself away from me, as though she feels I can protect her.

"Bridget," Mistress Anne says, in a voice that is menacing on its edge but soft in its core, like the sharp teeth of an angry cat whose standing fur might melt in a moment's tenderness into a gentle purr. But Bridget sees only the points of the exposed teeth.

"Tom has spoken to your father," she says. "I am afraid that it was not much of a conversation, for his tongue was thickened by his drink, and his ears clogged as well. But your father did make him understand that he is to see you no more." She pauses and I think I see the claws as well as the teeth. "Tom now knows that when the time comes he will be held responsible."

Bridget's face reddens. She has not let go my hand, and she now squeezes it tight.

"Is that all?" she says. "What did Tom say?"

"That he is off to war. Your father said he wished him well, that he come back whole, and that he have coin in his purse when he does so that he can do what is right." Mistress Anne rushes these words as though they are distasteful, like some food not well cooked that she wishes to be rid of as fast as she can. She waits for Bridget to speak, but Bridget can only shake her head.

"Speak child. You had no agreement, did you?"

"No."

"Did he force you?"

Bridget looks at me. I shrug. I was not there.

"Did he?" Mistress Anne asks again.

Bridget draws her breath deeply enough so as to seem to fill her body with courage along with air.

"No, Mother, he did not."

"He is leaving you with your belly."

"I could not bear standing on the platform, like Rachel did," she says.

"That might be reason to have you do it," Mistress Anne says, but then her voice softens. "Your father is a practical man. He would not have you marry a scoundrel like Tom, and he would not have you bring shame on the family."

"Is it about business then?" Bridget says suddenly, and it is the first sign I have seen from her that she may not forever remain the spoiled child of the rich merchant.

"Do not try his patience," Mistress Anne replies. "Or mine." She reaches her hand to her daughter's belly. "Are you sure?" she asks.

"I think so," Bridget manages to reply.

"How many times?" Mistress Anne asks.

"Twice," Bridget says.

Mistress Anne takes a heavy breath.

Bridget looks at me and I shake my head. She wants me to ask about the special flower and I will not. She rises from the bed and whispers in her mother's ear. Mistress Anne does not respond right away. Then she steps back.

"That is not the way," she says.

"But I have heard about this flower," Bridget insists.

Mistress Anne shakes her head.

"There is such."

"Then why will you not give it me?"

"It is not the way." Her face looks weary, and there are lines reaching back from the corner of her eyes. She seems older than she was only a few weeks ago. She does not speak for a moment, but looks at her daughter through those tired eyes. "It is not the way," she repeats.

Bridget reddens.

"Would you have me on the platform?"

"No," her mother replies.

"What then? Am I to have the babe here?" She looks at me and I know what she is thinking. "I cannot do that."

Mistress Anne shakes her head slowly.

"You think only of yourself," she says. "But you were born lucky, for you will not have to suffer your shame here. We are to remove to Master Williams' new plantation at Providence."

"Because of me?" Bridget asks.

"No, child. Because of me," Mistress Anne answers. "I am to be banished and it is likely that I will be excommunicated as well."

"We should never have left England, then," Bridget says.

"Ah, but we did," Mistress Anne says.

We are in the woods, not far from the house. The moon is full and lights our way on a broad path between trees. We are looking for spikes of white flowers. Bridget says she heard her mother talking with a praying Indian who called the plant black snakeroot and that it could be found deep in the woods. She insisted I go with her and I agreed, for I could see no reason to refuse even though we do not really know what we are looking for, nor would we be sure if we found it.

Still, Bridget is desperate to find it, and I am restless. Since my conversation with the soldier last night, the idea has been growing that I should follow this war. I do not think I can endure much longer being squeezed by the governor every day as he seeks evidence to use against Mistress Anne. I have no idea what that might be, but every time he looks at me, even if he does not say a word, I know he is waiting for me to offer him something that will pay him back for his generosity in sparing me the fate of my father. Sooner or later I will say something that will place Mistress Anne into his clutches.

I cannot tolerate that thought. The war will give me a way out.

We are well into the woods now, and the moonlight does not penetrate the shadows of the trees. Bridget stumbles and I catch her.

"It is no use," I say. "We cannot see what we are looking for, even if is here, and I am not certain of the way back."

"You return home, then, if you must."

She throws her shoulders back and stares at me. She looks like a petulant child who is not getting what she wants. When I do not respond, for what can I say to her in this mood, she lets out a loud rush of air from between her teeth and turns her back to me. She stares at the ground, and then lifts her eyes to a path that leads between two trees and deeper into the woods. The light from the moon turns the trunk of one of the nearer trees white while the other remains black. Bridget pauses by the first and lowers her head to stare off into the darkness beyond, and then she moves off in that direction. I let her go until I can hardly see her in the shadows before I follow. If I am to die from a wolf, or an Indian, or some evil spirit, I do not want to die alone.

I hear her crashing through the underbrush ahead, but I can no longer see her.

"Bridget," I call, but she does not answer. I am afraid to yell more loudly because I do not want the wolves, the Indians, or the spirits to know our whereabouts. For all I know, the specter of that poor, deformed babe is in these woods. I listen for her steps and when I think I hear them I walk in that direction. I see a figure moving in the shadows. When I get to that spot, the figure is gone. I am sure that it is hiding behind the stump of a tree that has been broken in half by a storm. I turn to flee but I do not know which direction I have come from. It seems there are now two paths, and I don't know which one I was on. I plunge onto one of them only to be stopped within a few feet by a thick web of branches that slaps me across the face. Something stings my eye shut and the tears roll down my cheek. I stumble back to the broken tree but now I cannot see the second path. I crouch and try not to cry. I have not heard Bridget's steps in several minutes. I expect any moment to hear her scream as some creature's teeth rip through her flesh.

I sense something behind me but I am too afraid to turn to it or to try to flee from it. I sit with my eyes shut waiting for it to grab me. Maybe when it has hold of me I will be able to fight with it. Just before the large hand covers my face I smell something familiar and then I know I can relax even while I am being pulled against the rough wool texture of his coat. I reach my hand over my head to feel for his face. My fingers reach the coarse hairs of his beard, brush against his nose, and then move along his cheek. He is patient while I make this exploration. One hand has remained over my mouth and nose, but now the other takes my hand and guides it to the low stump of scarred skin that rises over the hole where his ear should be.

"Aye," he says, "it is me." He keeps his hand over his mouth. "Let us wait for your fine friend to get farther lost into the woods, and then we can talk."

His hand smells of rum, and although I cannot see it, I know it is covered with grime, as I do not remember ever seeing it otherwise. Yet, strangely I am not repelled. Indeed, I am comforted by the very familiarity of his crudity. I do not struggle, and he drops his hand after a few moments when he is sure that Bridget has strayed far enough way. He turns me toward him.

"Do you not want to spit in my face?" he asks.

"I could think so, but to what purpose?"

He widens his mouth in a half smile that gives passage to the rum fumes.

"My girl," he said, "ever the practical one, which you get from me and not from your poor mother whose head was ever in heaven where she now is, but whose feet scarce touched the ground, even when she was walking on it."

"Do you have a proposition for me, then?" I say, for I know he does nothing for nothing. "And what will it cost me, though I have naught to give thee?"

"Only this. A name."

"Of he who has my babe?"

"Aye."

"The price?"

I can just make out the shrug of his wide shoulders in the shadows where we stand.

"That you may remember me in your prayers, and make it right with my grandchild when you get her back."

I am stunned.

"When did you find Our Lord?" I ask.

He laughs now, a black laugh from the depths of his heart, hard as rock.

"I have not looked, so I cannot find. That is for you and the babe."

Suddenly I am in his arms in a suffocating embrace, and the next moment, with my eyes still closed, and my nostrils still wrapped about the scent of him, I am alone with only the whisper of a breeze in the trees, and a few moments later, I hear Bridget's plaintive cry.

She is lost, and I must lead her home. I look again at the two paths, and now the one we had taken before seems clear. I recognize the sapling where it begins so I call to her and she follows my voice to me. She is carrying the stalk of a plant. A sad, pale bloom dips from it.

"Do you think 'tis this?" she asks.

I have no idea what plant she holds, but she looks so desperate, and soon I hope to be free of her problem.

"Surely," I say, "it may well be."

She brightens and follows as I turn to home.

We are in bed. Bridget will not let go the of the plant, which in the candlelight now appears to be a common weed with no power to remove what Tom has placed in her belly. She lies there staring at the dried-out stalk. Then she drops it between her legs and closes her eyes. Her breathing quickens. She opens an eye to peek toward the stalk, and then she runs her hands over her belly. I cannot stand it.

"Time," I say. "It needs must take time."

She looks at me with renewed hope in her eyes.

"Do you think so?" she asks. "In truth?"

"Yes," I lie. I want to quiet her so I can concentrate on the one strange sounding word my father whispered in my ear before he disappeared into the wood, for that word must lead me to my babe. A name, he gave me, and a confirmation that the plan growing in my poor head might indeed bear fruit.

I am surprised to see the empty places at the table the next morning. The older girls who have already eaten are doing chores, cutting vegetables for stew or kneading dough. I do not see the bigger boys. They must be out cutting and gathering firewood. Little Samuel is playing with a toy wooden cart. He is wearing his new shoes, and he stops from time to time to tug at them. They are stiff and must hurt his feet. The children always finish their breakfast first, leaving the table to the adults and Bridget. And me. But today, I see only one trencher and it is at the edge of the table where I usually sit. I look first at Patience, but she turns her face from me so I am treated to a side view of her hawk nose, which I note is pointing at the ceiling. I think of the stories I have heard about turkeys caught out in the rain who drown when the water fills their upturned noses, and I start to smile. Patience, though, can hear me smile. I know that is not possible, and yet it is true, for she brings her face around and fixes me with those hard eyes of hers. She motions me to sit at the table. She ladles the warm samp onto my trencher, slowly until it is filled to the brim. And then she pours in a little more, just enough to cause the samp to overflow onto the table.

"Eat," she says. "You can clean up your mess after." She walks to the other side of the kitchen and busies herself peeling some potatoes.

But I do not pick up my spoon. Instead, I let my eyes roam the table. I open my lips to ask my question, but she hisses at me and turns her back. I dip my spoon into the trencher so it clunks against the wood, and then I slurp the samp into my mouth. I do this several times, and she leaves. I wait, and a few minutes later, as I expected, Mabel slides into the room. She walks at a brisk pace as though to pass by me, but then she stops. She glances over her shoulder and then leans down to whisper into my ear.

"They've taken Bridget to see Master Cotton." She glances toward Patience. "Will and Anne raised their voices as I have never heard them before, even though their door was closed and my room right next to them, so I could hear, but not make out the words. And when they came out, I stepped into the hall as well, and their faces were dark like somebody had died." Her words tumble on top of each other all in a breath or two, and then she straightens up and walks to Patience. She picks up a potato and another knife and scrapes at the skin, her face red.

And somebody might as well have died, I think. Oh, Bridget, what are they going to do with you? Master Cotton will pray over you, but I doubt his words can lift the babe out of your belly. Surely Mistress Anne knows that. But maybe not her husband, or mayhap he is not thinking of any cure, only that Master

Cotton convince God to forgive his foolish daughter. I cannot believe he wants anything else. He is not the type of man to be angry for very long, and although he does not seem to pay much attention to his large family, I do think he loves them all just the same.

That thought causes my stomach to tighten, for I now in my mind's eye see not Will Hutchinson's kind eyes but the fierce and defiant face of my father. His head turns and I am staring at the hole where his poor ear used to be. I feel myself softening toward him, and I recall how gentle his hardened hands could be like a little while ago in the woods when his palm covered my mouth and nose. He whispered then a name, his lips close to my cheek. I smelled his breath as always when he spoke. "Find Nanawag," he said, "and you will find your bastard babe. He is the one I sold her to. He is going to take her to his people down the Connecticut, where the governor's soldiers are going. You will know him by the long scar that runs from his ear to his jawbone on the left side of his face. I should know. I was there when the blade cut him."

I remember these words, and I almost forgive him. Almost.

The air is warming, and there is a mist blowing in off the harbor. It carries the smell of the ocean. The breeze clears my head of thoughts of my father. I should be walking straight across the common to the governor's house, but I turn instead to the path that leads to the harbor. I hear the gulls calling to each other in the mist. Maybe they have lost their way, or perhaps a young bird has strayed too far from its anxious mother. The closer I get to the water the thicker is the fog until I can no longer see the path. I let my feet find it, but they cannot see the body and I lose my balance as my foot comes down on something soft. I catch myself before I fall and regain my balance. I stare down until I am sure. I am standing with one foot on each side of a body that is now stirring. A snore rises from the place where its head must be. I am relieved that whoever it is still breathes. I begin to lift my right foot above the body so I can continue, but the snoring has stopped and I sense eyes looking toward me. I wait, and the snoring starts again. I lean down. I am standing over Tom. His eyes are closed. An empty bottle lies on the ground near his cheek. I start to step over him, but his hand grabs my leg.

"Bridget," he says.

I pull on my leg, but his hand tightens.

"A kiss," he says, and his hand moves up to my knee.

I lean down and touch my lips to his. I taste his spit mixed with his beer. I press my lips a little harder and he relaxes his hold on my leg. I free it and bring my foot up hard. I have learned this much about men that where they feel the most pleasure they also experience the most pain. He grunts and rolls over. I wait for him to roll back onto his back, and then I spit his spit out of my mouth onto his face and move on.

The harbor is on my left. The mist has lifted, and I can clearly see the sailors working on the ship at the town dock. One is way up in the rigging doing something with a furled sail. Others are mopping the deck. Some kind of cargo is being hauled up the gangplank. I am staring so hard at the ship I do not hear the steps behind me until it is too late. I feel his breath on my neck before his hands seize my shoulders. I brace myself but in a moment I am spun around and I am looking up into his face. His breath still reeks. He drops one hand and rubs himself where I kicked him.

"That was not very kind of you," he says. I find myself looking at the place he is rubbing, and I see the bulge. I cannot deny my curiosity, but he mistakes it for interest. He takes my hand and tries to force it there. I pull my leg back in an exaggerated motion, and he releases my hand and steps back.

"Oh, no love, once a day is enough. I only thought you were my Bridget and would offer me a little comfort before I left on that ship."

"And where do you think you are going?" I ask, although I know the answer.

"Why, to punish those savages what attacked our settlers in Wethersfield. I hear they took off two girls. You must know what they are going to do with them."

No worse than what you would like to do to me, I think. But I want to hear more.

"Were there none who survived."

He shrugs.

"That I cannot say."

"My master awaits," I say. I am anxious to be rid of him, for his words have given me an idea I want time alone to think about. I stretch on my toes and kiss his cheek. He is so surprised he steps back, and before he can say or do more, I turn on my heel and take my leave of him. I quicken my pace and do not turn around when as I expect he calls my name. My mind is awhirl with the story taking shape in it. I hear the cries of the savages as they attack us. I must hide. Father shoves me and my little baby brother beneath a pile of brush we use for kindling. I hear the footsteps and the hoots. I do not see my father get killed a moment later but I hear his body fall. My mother screams and screams and then she is muffled. I imagine they are dragging her away. I have my head tucked between my knees and so I do not at first see my brother crawl out from the brush. He wants to follow our mother. I reach for him but he is too fast. He is outside the pile. If I stick my arm out after him, I will be seen. I shut my eyes. I hear the thud of a tomahawk on his head.

It is a good story. It will do very well. I do not like how I do not save my brother. I think I would have if I had been at Wethersfield. But I wasn't and so I can say what I will and I will be believed. For a moment, I consider saving my brother and presenting myself as a heroine. That makes me smile, but I reject it. I want to be seen as a victim not a heroine, yes, a victim who only wants revenge. And that part is true enough.

I am so possessed by my story that I forget I am on the path to the governor's house. My feet continue walking without my guidance. And so I do not see Master Wilson in time. If I had, I would have found a way to avoid him. He is leaving the governor's house as I walk up the path. He seems deep in thought, and I think he is going to pass by me without lifting up his eyes. Every time I see him I remember how he pinned that letter on my breast and the blood begins to rush to my face. I take a deep breath and lower my head as we near each other. I have my eyes on the ground but I hear his steps. They stop. I want to keep walking as though I am unaware of his presence.

"Good morrow," he says, and I must stand still.

"Good morrow sir," I reply. I lift my eyes and see that he has a smile on his face. He looks up to the bright sun.

"Indeed, it is a good day. And how do you do? The governor tells me how pleased he is with your work." He lowers his gaze to the letter on my breast. I take his meaning and I run my fingers over the lines of the W.

"It does its office, sir," I answer.

"It and God must instruct you," he replies, his voice now the same one I have heard in the meeting house, only not so loud as he is standing only two feet away. I have never looked that close at his face before. His teeth are yellow and the lower ones crooked. It does not look as though he could safely bite into an apple.

"Yes, God and the letter," I answer, and I watch to see if he notices how I have changed the order. He only smiles more broadly.

"When God has finished correcting the way you walk, we will be able to remove that letter, for it too then will have done its service. But all comes from God, as you well know."

"Is that why you are so happy today?" I ask without pausing to wonder where the question came from. I guess I am unaccustomed to see his dour face broken so hard by smiles. He leans closer to me until I can smell his breath. It does not reek of rum or beer as my father's but it is nonetheless not very sweet.

"We," and he looks over his shoulder toward the governor's house, "only do the Lord's work," he says, and with a nod as though we share a secret he continues on past me.

Maureen is on her knees in the hallway moving a cloth over the floorboards. Her motions are so slow and with so little pressure it is hard to believe she is disturbing the dust or the occasional clump of dirt carried in on somebody's boot. I watch as she continues moving the cloth in the same circle without producing any effect, nor does she move on to another spot. She looks up at me, and I am startled by her expression. Her anger has tightened the flesh around her eyes so much that they seem ready to leap out, and it has hollowed her cheeks. She grinds her teeth without saying anything, and then she slowly rises to her feet. She thrusts the cloth toward me.

"You should have this, and the job it is supposed to do. I do not know why I should bother any longer."

"But surely, it is your task. Did not Mistress Winthrop herself tell you to do it?"

"That she did. But her husband is convinced that I am a thief, and he will not have me in this house a moment longer than is necessary. I am to be sent to whoever will buy my time."

"Thief?" I ask, but I know the answer. She guesses that I do and takes a step closer. She is taller than I am and probably stronger, but she will find that I am not easy. She leans toward me.

"That damned paper. You know very well which one."

I do, of course, but I shake my head.

"The one he has been looking for. He asked you about it."

I close my eye as if to remember, but what I am seeing in my mind is a pile of ashes in the fireplace that by magic turn back into a piece of paper.

"I told him I knew nothing of such a paper," I say.

I have always thought Maureen too lazy or too dull to pose a threat. But today there is fire in her eyes and she seems to be starting to get the glimmer of an idea. I take a step as though to pass by her and into the house. She places herself in my path.

"Just a moment now. I do remember on that day when he was going on about that paper I found you crouched by the fireplace stirring ashes that had no need of being stirred. What was you doing then?"

"Like you say, stirring ashes. You know how Eleanor is, how she must have her fire just so."

"There was no fire."

I nod encouragement.

"Of course not. That is why I was trying to get it going again."

Her face flushes in frustration, but I see she no longer cares. Her shoulders slump and her usual mask of sullen indifference forms on her face. She gets back down on her knees and runs her cloth over the same area yet again. I wait a second and then take a cautious step. She keeps her eyes on the floor, and I walk into the house. I stop by the fireplace in the kitchen and poke the ashes. I expect to see the white corner of the paper stick out from among the gray of the ashes and I hold my breath. There is nothing but ash, and I think I can breathe again. I wait still, staring at the charred pieces of wood amongst the ashes. Something moves in the far corner of the fireplace. It must be a hand come to reach out and pull me down into the fires of hell for my terrible lies. I jump back and feel something brush against my leg. The scream dies on my lips. I am too terrified to make a sound. I close my eyes. I hear a thump behind me. Something has my shoulder now. Slowly, I am turned. I squint one eye open. I am looking at Eleanor who has this huge smile on her face. She points to the floor where a dead mouse lies beneath her broom.

"Child," she says, "when did you become so timid that a mouse can frighten you so?"

I can only shrug. When I do not have an answer, and when I am talking to someone who suspects my wits anyway, as all us servant girls are thought to be dim, I play the part. Eleanor tsk tsks, and gives my cheek a pinch. Better to suffer such indignity, I think, than try to explain why the movement in the fireplace frightened me so. Eleanor slides the broom beneath the mouse and lifts it toward me. I know what she is doing, so I hold my hand to my mouth as though I would like to scream, and I roll my eyes in my best imitation of terror. I find it hard not to smile at my play acting as I have spent my life growing up in my father's house where I was the one who had to get rid of pests such as this fellow in front of my nose. My father was rarely sober enough to catch one, although I have seen him roast a fat rat over the fire when he was hungry and there was nothing else to eat, and when I was offered a bite I did take one myself. But now I act as though this little creature is about to devour me. Eleanor thrusts the broom a little closer.

"Here, now," she says. "It is dead, you know. And if it was not, why look at it. Do you think it could do you any harm?"

I nod.

"Silly girl," Eleanor replies. "Here take this." She turns the broom about so I can seize the handle. I hold it straight out so the mouse is as far from me as possible. "Now, see if you can carry it out the door," Eleanor says. I walk ever so slowly to the door and wait for her to open it. When she does not, I lower the broom to the floor with great care, being sure to keep the mouse on the broom head. I swing the door open, pick up the broom, and carry it and the mouse outside. I kick the door shut with my foot as I go through, and when I hear it shut, I let the mouse slide onto the ground. I pick it up by its tail. It is a skinny one. A drop of its blood drips out of its ears. Its eyes are still wide open. I wonder if it saw the broom coming down on its poor little head. And where is it now? Does it have a soul as we do, and if so is there a special place in hell or heaven for the souls of these creatures? I would like to ask Master Wilson that question someday. For now, I swing the mouse about and throw it as far as I can. I am just in time, for I hear the hinges creak as the door opens again. I turn to see that it is ajar a crack, but I am sure that Eleanor did not see.

"You see, it did not hurt you," Eleanor says, as she walks out. "Where did you put it?"

I shrug and point in the general direction where I threw it. She takes a few steps as though to find it, and then turns back to me. She holds out her hands and I give her the broom.

"The governor waits to talk with you," she says.

"Maureen…" I begin.

"None of your affair," Eleanor snaps, and there is no gentleness in her voice now. "Do not keep the governor waiting. Make haste."

I nod and trot into the house. I glance over my shoulder. Eleanor is still looking for the mouse. I do not know what she intends to do with. Perhaps she wants to bury it. I slow down my pace. He may be waiting, but I am in no hurry. His door is closed. I start to push it open, but think better of it and knock.

"Yes," he calls and his voice is cheerful. I remember the smile on Master Wilson's face and I can only guess that whatever made the one smile has added cheer to the other. I find him at his desk, as usual, and he is holding a glass over a large map. He motions me to him. He points to a name on the map. It is located where the land ends and the water begins. The printing is not very clear and I squint at the name he points to.

"Here," he says, and holds the glass over the name. Now the lines are bigger, but not much clearer.

"I believe it says 'Fort,'" I try, "but I cannot make out the next word."

"Excellent," he replies. "Fort, indeed, Fort Saybrook."

I do not respond and he seems disappointed.

"Have you not heard the name?" he asks.

I know what he seeks, and I offer him a crumb.

"I believe I heard some such name, you know," I look vaguely in the direction of the Hutchinson house.

"Indeed," he prods.

I do not add anything more, although I do remember how Mistress Anne's face reddened when she said that name, and how her husband only shook his head sadly, and then said another name, one I would not repeat to the governor. I remember he said 'Providence' slowly, with great emphasis. I thought he was talking about God, but then it became clear that he meant a place to which he might remove his family if things continued as they were so hostile to them in Boston. But I do not share any of this with the governor. He seems to expect my silence, and so he shrugs.

"I do not suppose you have heard anything more about this place."

"No."

"Or know where it is?"

"No."

"Child, can you find Boston on the map?" He hands me the glass. I hold it over the map and move it up and down and left to right. I see a large letter B at the start of a word, in the water next to a place where the land looks like somebody's arm poking out into the ocean. I point to it. The governor nods, and then he takes my finger and draws it from the B word down to the Fort place. In spite of myself, I am getting very interested for reasons the governor would never approve.

"We are sending our soldiers from here to there," he says.

I note that he has pulled my finger over the land.

"Are they going to walk, then?" I ask.

His eyes brighten.

"I have told Eleanor not to underestimate you," he says. "No." He takes my finger back to Boston on the map and guides it again down toward the fort, but this time he stays in the water. I nod.

"I have seen the new ship in the harbor," I say.

"That is the one."

"How long?" I ask. On the map, the distance is hardly more than the width of my hand. I have no idea what that means on the face of the Earth.

"No more than a few days," he answers. "Do you want to know why?"

In very fact, I do. Not so much the why, but the details. If I tell him I already know about Wethersfield, he might not give me the story I seek, the story that I will refashion to my own purposes. And so I frame my face as best I can to look like a child ready to be told a bedtime story and I nod my head. He smiles. Then he draws his finger up the map from Fort Saybrook along a blue line.

"That is the Connecticut River," he says, and continues to move his finger until it stops at a place where there is a long name that begins with the same letter I wear on my chest. "And that is Wethersfield," he declares. "Have you heard of it?"

I shake my head.

His face hardens and his eyes narrow.

"But surely Master Hutchinson and Mistress Hutchinson must have said something about this place."

"They only tell us servants what to do. Those are the only words we hear from them."

The lies come easily to my lips, and I am a little ashamed, but I remind myself that I am my father's daughter after all, am I not?

"But surely you have heard others talk about it."

"I attend to my chores," I say. "I do not heed gossip."

"Gossip, indeed."

He leans back as though he has nothing more to say. I cannot let him stop before he tells me more. I lower my face to the map and trace the blue line of the river as he had done until I reach Wethersfield, and then I run my finger over its first letter. I look up at him, and see that he is watching what I do.

"Yes, that is the place where the savages, howling devils that they are, attacked and murdered our brothers and sisters in Christ."

I remember overhearing his son and the others talking about how rich the land is in this river's valley. I guess he must mean that Christ is a farmer, too.

"All of them?" I ask.

He raises his eyebrows and stares hard at me. I wonder how I have offended him. Then his expression softens.

"No, by the grace of God, a goodly number survived."

"The others…" I begin, and I do not know why I want to ask the question, but that my head is filling with images of bodies covered in blood and arms and legs lying about here and there.

"Butchered," he says, as though to confirm my bloody thoughts. "Stripped naked and their bowels ripped out, their scalps lifted from their heads, the men, their…" His face is red, with some kind of excitement or anger. "I see you are troubled. You need know no more of this terrible slaughter."

In fact, I feel my blood rushing and my heart beating hard in my chest, but whether it is from fear or something else I do not know. I nod.

"I have heard they take prisoners and force them to become savages like themselves."

"So you have heard some tales," he says, with a smile as though he has caught me, like a cat with its paw on a mouse. But I will not squirm.

"When I was little, my father used to fill my head with such stories. I have tried to shake them out, but I am afraid some remain."

"Your father," he says, but does not complete the thought. "Those captives who are forced as you say, it would have been better that such of them as turned from our Lord and embraced their pagan gods had died."

"Yes," I reply, but I am not at all sure that he is right. Can it be our God prefers us dead? "Maybe some of them only pretend to worship their gods."

He reaches his hand to my chin. There is a tenderness in his eyes I have never seen before.

"They should die before permitting themselves to become apostate and blaspheme our Lord," he says in the very gentlest tone, and yet I it pierces me like the cold steel of a knife.

"Yes," I answer again.

He holds my chin a moment longer and then pulls his hand back to wave me away.

"About your chores, then," he says, all gentleness gone from his voice. He is again my master, and I leave with my head aching from the cold horror of his words.

Eleanor is waiting for me outside the door. My mind is still in Wethersfield and so I walk right into her. I look up startled into her face. She puts her hands on my shoulder and pushes me back with gentle force. She holds me at her arm's distance.

"Still thinking about that mouse, I warrant," she says.

I nod.

"We need some wood from the pile. Can you bring some in, for the pile is near where that mouse must be. Mayhap it will rise up and bite your nose." She finishes with a cackle that sounds something like a chicken laying an egg.

I put on my most serious face.

"I did not throw the mouse into the woodpile," I say.

"And you do not fear it will get up and find you?"

I pause a second to give the idea consideration.

"I think not," I reply.

I walk past dried stalks of last season's pole beans in the garden to the woodpile. I take my time choosing the logs I will bring in. I go behind the pile so I am hidden from the kitchen window where I know Eleanor is watching my progress. If I tarry too long out here, she will come after me in a temper. But still, I want very much to be alone. Perhaps it is the fact that I know that I will soon be leaving this place, very possibly for all time that makes every minute I still must spend here impossible to endure. I pick up the log on top, examine it, find that it is a little damp, and so I put it down on the ground. I select the next one. It seems to be dry. A spider is crawling on it, and I pick it off as gently as though the log was my babe's arm, for I am consumed with my desire to once again hold my babe in my arms. I close my eyes so I can remember the touch of her, and then I open my mouth.

"Nanawag," I say to the logs on the woodpile, "I will have my girl back."

I wait, half expecting the logs to respond.

I pick up two more logs and carry them into the kitchen where Eleanor is waiting. She eyes my load and then frowns.

"So little for so much time," she says.

"There were these things crawling all over the wood," I say. "I only picked the ones that did not have them on them."

I put the logs down and she inspects them one by one, turning them over.

"Right," she says, "we do not want to be eating no crawling things falling off the logs and getting into our food."

I do not know if she believes me. But I do not care.

When I return to my house, Patience greets me at the door, her face red with irritation. I look past her to see Mabel scurry by. She is carrying the heavy green velvet cloak I have seen Bridget wear. I remember remarking to myself how strong it contrasted to the snow on the ground, and how it made me think that before long it would be spring again. Patience follows my glance and nods.

"There is much work to do," she says. "Attend on Mabel. She will tell you what needs must be done." Mabel stops as she hears her name and turns back toward us. She beckons me toward her and I can tell by the look on her face she wants to tell me something. I nod and she continues walking but at a slower pace. I catch up to her as we reach the stairs.

"Master Hutchinson is taking Bridget to the new plantation in Providence," she whispers to me, although I have already figured out what all the fuss is about. Then she tells me something I do not know. "They go alone, for now. The rest stay here." We hear steps and know that Patience is coming after us. Mabel hands me the cloak, and says in a voice louder than she needs to. "Take this round back where there is a box waiting for it, and be quick about it. Then go up to her room and see what else you can find to pack up. We have not time for idleness now," she says just as Patience arrives.

The cloak is soft and thick, and I imagine it about my shoulders. I make my way to the rear of the house to a room that is used to store all sorts of things the family has no present use for, including several wooden chests. One of these is open, and I recognize Bridget's good gown, the one she told me once she hoped to wear when she wed Tom. I begin to drop the cloak on top of it, but first I must feel it about me. I put it on and hold it tight to my chest. I do not think I have ever been so warm or felt so protected. I begin to understand something about Bridget. A girl who is given a cloak such as this to wear enjoys a privilege and place in the world that one such as me can only wonder at.

"It looks very well on you."

I turn to face Mistress Anne and feel my cheeks redden. But I do not take off the cloak.

"You need not put it in the chest," she says. "Keep it for yourself. Bridget will hardly miss it."

I am about to thank her when I realize how impossible it will be for me to keep such a thing. I let it slide off my shoulders and place it in the chest. Mistress Anne watches but does not try to change my mind.

"Perhaps another time," she says.

"Yes, another time, or another cloak," I reply.

"You do know what is happening, do you not?" she asks.

I nod.

"Bridget is to go away to Providence with her father."

"And nothing more?"

"That you and the family are to stay here. For now."

"For now," she repeats. "And what do you hear at the governor's house?"

I am startled. She has never before asked me such a question. Before I can answer, she seems to recover. Her expression softens into something like apology, or even shame. She looks down at her feet and slowly shakes her head. I am very much embarrassed. It is not right that she should show such discomfort. She is my mistress and can ask me anything, as can the governor. The only difference is that I always want to answer her questions, and never his. I open my mouth to speak, but she presses her finger against my lip.

"No," she says. "I do not want to know, and even more, I do not want to put you in the same position as I know he does."

"But I would he pleased..." I begin, after she removes her finger.

"Don't," she says, her voice now regaining its usual command, and I stop. "It's just that I won't be able to protect you much longer," she continues, "and I am looking for a way."

"He means to force you away," I say. "He asks me things, about Wethersfield, and your meetings, of course, and just a little while ago, he mentioned Mistress Dyer..." I want to continue, but she shakes her head, and a sad smile is on her lips.

"So, you will tell me even though I ask you not to. But you do not tell me anything I do not know. It is only a little time before I am banished. Perhaps excommunicated." Here she pauses and there is great pain in her eyes. "Not that I am worthy of such a thought, but still it is hard to realize that one I trusted so will be the governor's instrument."

She does not have to say the name. I know she feels she is to be betrayed as our Lord was by one so very close to her, the same one I imagined baptizing my babe, who had us bury poor Mistress Dyer's deformed infant in the night. Until now, I would not have believed that Master Cotton's kindly eyes were those of a self-serving coward. I see his face again as I had in my dream of baptism. The skin slowly peels from it leaving only a horrid skull, with just the eyes still in their sockets. I shudder, and Mistress Anne takes me into an embrace. I feel her warmth for a few moments, and then stand back.

"He is only a man," she says, "looking out for his own interest, or perhaps he thinks he can better serve God by sacrificing me while retaining his influence with the governor. It is not for me to judge."

No, I think, but it is for me, and my anger rises so hot that I can only nod before I turn to go up the stairs to see if Bridget has any more clothes for me to drag down.

I have a cap I found among the things I was packing pulled down almost to my eyes, and my cloak wrapped around my body. Martin is sitting at a table by himself, a mug of beer in front of him. He nods at me. There is a loud thud coming from the table behind him. A fellow there has fallen asleep in the middle of saying something to his companions. They wait for him to rouse himself and finish his thought, and when he does not they laugh and continue their conversation. Their words are lost in the loud snores of the sleeper. One nudges him and the snores stop for the moment, and then continue. The table erupts in loud laughter. Martin waits for it to stop, and when it does, he takes a gulp, with his head tipped back and his eyes on the ceiling. He lowers his eyes as I approach, and then he wipes his lips with the back of his hand. This is a gesture I have seen many men make. He looks up and smiles. I believe he has been waiting for me. I sit down across from him, and he slides the mug toward me.

"I thought you would come," he says.

I raise the mug to my lips and throw back my head. I let the beer pour down my throat and make sure some dribbles down my chin. I bring my head down and draw the back of my hand across my lips. For good measure, I run my tongue over my skin to capture the beer that remains there.

"That is good. You will do well," Martin says.

I bring the mug to my mouth again, and drink. Martin reaches across the table and I shove the mug toward him. He tightens his face into a serious expression. His eyes search mine.

"There is a great deal more to being a man than drinking your beer a certain way."

"I do not intend to be a man," I reply, "only to be taken for one."

I realize I have spoken into one of the rare moments when the tavern was silent, and that I could have been heard by anybody who was listening. The snorer rouses himself and looks in my direction. I scowl at him. He shrugs and lets his head drop back onto the table. Martin puts his fingers to his lips to tell me what I already know. I frown to let him know that I am not that stupid.

"Yes," he says as though I have said my thoughts out loud, "but you must be more careful."

"Do you hear what is in my head, then?" I ask. I must wonder what powers he might have. Perhaps he is the devil or a wizard. But I care not if he will help me find my babe.

"Take another drink," he says and again pushes the mug across the table. It catches in a crack between the planks and starts to tip over. The beer spills and he licks it off his hand. I take the mug. If he is a wizard, he is a very clumsy one. I drain what is left in the mug.

"What am I thinking now?" I ask.

"That you would like another beer," he replies, and he takes the mug from me and holds it aloft until the serving wench comes by. She has a pitcher in her hand, but she does not pour into our mug. Martin reaches into his pouch and takes out a couple of coins. She takes them from him, and holds them in the light of the candle on the table so she can see what they are. Then she pours.

"And a mug for my mate, Richard," he says.

The wench looks at me until I turn away.

"He is a shy one, ain't he?" she chuckles and walks away. A moment later, and she is back with a mug. I reach for it and I feel her eyes on my hand. I snatch the mug and put my hand under the table. She looks as though she is about to say something, but then she shrugs as somebody else calls to her. Martin waits until she is out of earshot.

"I signed up today. It was easy enough. It seems the local militia is coming up short. This one is sick, and the other one has to run the farm for his widowed mother, and so they were happy to see somebody who wanted to go. They've got a clerk in the meeting house."

"All you do is write your name?"

He nods.

"Or your mark."

"I can sign my name good and proper," I reply.

"Good, Richard."

I smile.

"Yes. Richard it is."

"Do you not think the clerk might know you?"

I consider, and then shake my head.

"It is true enough the people in this town have had the opportunity to see me. But I do not think they were looking at my face at those times. And at others, why I am just another servant girl."

"Just the same, do what you can to mask your features." He crosses his arms in front of his chest. "Especially these."

I suddenly feel that my breasts are much larger than they are.

"Yes," I reply.

"Until the morrow," he says.

Bridget is lying in the bed. I have lit the candle, but she does not stir. I have a little piece of a mirror on the table and knife in my hand with which I am chopping off my hair. On the floor next to the bed is a small chest that contains the few personal items and the clothes she is going to wear tomorrow for her trip to Providence. It seems she must have been restless before she fell asleep, for she has kicked off our blanket, and her shift is up about her waist. I put down the knife and look at her bare legs. And at the dried weeds, crumbling to dust where she has placed them between her thighs.

Chapter Nine

Bridget is snoring and her hands hold what is left of the weed between her legs. The sun has just risen and the room is brightening. The other children, as well, are asleep. I slip out of bed and walk as quietly as I can toward the bed of the oldest boy. He is only a little bigger than I am, for he takes after his mother who is short and round rather than his father who is tall and thin. His shirt and breeches hang on a peg next to his bed. I reach for them. He stirs and I try to think of something to say when he opens his eyes, but he rolls over so he is no longer facing me. I snatch the clothes and without taking my eyes off him back away from his bed.

I go out of the room in the hallway, which is still dark as it has no window. I pull my shift over my head and start to step into the breeches. I do not know the front from the back. I find the lace that holds them up about the waist and see how it should tie. I step into them. They are coarse against my skin. I shiver although it is not cold. I wrap my bare chest as tight as I can with the piece of cloth I hid in my bed when I went to sleep. I do not have big breasts but they still can be flattened only so much. I fasten the cloth with a pin I also secured for this purpose. I start to smooth down my hair to pull the shirt on, and I am surprised for a moment when my fingers brush against the skin of my neck, but then I remember the pile of hair on the floor next to my bed. I lace the shirt up loosely. I need a mirror but there is none up here. I run my fingers down the front of the shirt. I think I can pass for having a boyish chest.

I am about to leave the room and I take one more look around. I gasp so loud I think I must be awakening everyone in the house. There on my bed is the gown, with its letter, that I have been wearing every day. I roll it up into a bundle, with the letter on the inside. It is an ordinary color brown, so that it now looks like I might be carrying my cloak or some such extra garment.

Outside, I try to walk as I imagine a robust lad would, but I feel foolish after a few steps and decide to move my legs as I usually do. My legs inside the breeches feel strange, and I sense the air on my legs where the breeches end just below my knees. I consider sneaking back into the house to find a pair of hose, but dismiss that notion. It is still very early and not many people are about, and for that I am grateful. As I approach the town common I see a shape coming toward me, and I prepare myself for my first test. It is an Indian carrying a pile of furs on his shoulders. He casts a glance at me, but I do not think he pays much attention. Still, I pull my shirt up to my chin and lower my eyes. After he passes, I find myself beginning to walk onto the path that leads to the governor's house. It is hard to keep my mind where it must be. I order my legs to carry me instead toward the meeting house, across the common.

I am relieved to see that there is a plank table set up beneath a tree in front of the meeting house, and that there is a man sitting behind it, as Martin said he would be, waiting for those who want to sign up to fight the savages. I slow down and peer at the man, who is moving his pen across a paper. He does look familiar. I remember his face, his pushed in nose and close set eyes, from someplace, but I am not sure where. He continues writing. I hear the scratch of the pen and begin to remember, but I am too nervous to be sure.

The day is unusually warm for spring and yet I am shivering. I approach the table and stop a few feet from it. The man waves me forward, but I hesitate.

"Come along, then," he says. "You look like you could use a good meal. We will feed you well enough before we send you off. You will need some flesh on you to stop those arrows." He lowers his gaze to my legs. "Forgot your hose, have you? Or have you none? Your legs are no more than sticks. Will they hold you up, do you think?"

He cackles like a hen, and continues waving me on. I am happy for his insults. I step to the table and try not to breathe too deeply. I do not want to call his attention to my chest.

"What is your name?" he asks.

"Richard."

He waits and I realize he wants my family name. I start to say 'Moore', but stop myself. I have forgotten what name I intended to use.

"I am just from Wethersfield," I reply.

He looks hard at me and I feel his eyes probing beneath my clothes to discover the truth of my body. I am finding it hard to breathe. I think my breasts are going to burst through the cloth that has them flattened against my chest.

He waits. There is a pen and ink on the table, and next to them a piece of paper with some words on the top and a few signatures below.

"Please, sir," I say, "can I sign the paper?"

He dips the pen into the ink and holds it toward me with one hand. With the other, he slides the paper to my edge of the table.

"Surely," he says. "But I will need you to write more than Richard. Wethersfield, you say? How long?"

"I was there," I reply.

His eyes soften just a little.

"Your family?"

I try to make my eyes water.

"Dead, sir. All dead." I remember my story. "My little brother. I could not save him."

He seems almost convinced.

"How old are you?"

I do not hesitate.

"Sixteen."

He reaches his hand toward my face. I start to pull back, but then suffer his touch. He runs his fingers over my smooth cheek and then above my lips and chin where there should be at least the beginning of a man's beard.

"I do not think so. You must have somebody to vouch for you. We are not papists here, sending off children on no crusade against the infidels."

"I will vouch for her."

The voice from behind me could as well come from heaven, it is so timely, and so unexpected.

"Mistress Hutchinson, is it?" the man asks. "Do you indeed know this lad."

"He has been staying in my house," she says.

"From Wethersfield, is he?"

"Yes. No doubt he cannot remember all that happened there. It was too terrible."

I turn to her and nod. I think I see just the slightest smile flicker across her face as she returns my glance, but then when she looks again at the man she wears the expression I know so well of one who is not to be questioned. It is a wonder how she can change herself in a moment. The man feels the effect.

"As you say, Mistress. Take the pen, Richard of Wethersfield," he says. I feel bold now, with Mistress Anne at my side.

"West," I say.

"Are you sure?"

I nod.

"Then take the pen Richard West. Write your name. Or your mark."

I start to scratch 'Richard West' at the bottom of the list on his paper. I realize I am not at all sure of the order of the letters for my given name, after the first one, so I write the *R* with bold strokes and then let the pen run across the paper. I recall seeing *West* on the Governor's map and write that one with some confidence. The man behind the desk watches my pen, and then he takes the paper from me and studies it. He motions to Mistress Anne. "If you please," he says. "The governor is quite particular in these matters." I watch as she writes her name in her bold hand beneath mine.

"I surely do not want to give the governor any cause for concern," she says. The man's face breaks into an expression that is half sneer and half smile.

"That you have done afore times, Mistress Hutchinson. I do think you know that, if you will pardon me saying so."

She stares at him hard for a moment, and then takes my arm and turns me away.

"Come, then, Richard. I must talk to you before you leave."

"Have him at the harbor for the morning tide," the man calls out.

"Is he not to be trained before he goes?" she asks.

He shrugs and I notice for the first time that one shoulder is higher than the other. Now I know him, the clerk writing down the lies that put that letter on my chest.

"We have had some trouble filling our quota," he says to Mistress Anne, "as there are some who have been complaining about this expedition with some effect in taking the wind out of the sail of those who might otherwise be only too happy to bring the Lord's sword down on those savages. But I expect you are aware of what I mean, Mistress."

I am close enough to her to see the muscles tighten in her jaw, but she says nothing.

"On the morrow, the morning tide, Mistress," he says. "The lad will learn what he can on board the ship that sails on the morrow." He looks down at his paper, and then raises his eyes as though he has just remembered something. He stares at me, with a little, cruel smile playing at the corners of his mouth. "Do you have a musket?" he asks.

I shake my head, and he turns to Mistress Hutchinson. She reaches into her pocket and takes out some coins. He shakes his head with a frown.

"Does this look like a gun shop, Mistress? I am not a smithy."

She hands him the coins.

"See that he gets what he needs," she says.

He takes the money from her and then passes it from one hand to the other until the coins clink against each other. Then he lets them drop one by one onto the table. "I cannot secure him a musket."

"Keep half the coins, then," Mistress Anne says, "and give the other half to his officer."

"On the morrow," he says once again, and this time he lowers his head over his paper until his nose almost touches it. He has nothing more to say to us.

After we walk out of his hearing, I stop and look at her.

"Why did you let him say those things about you without giving him an answer? I should have spoken up on your behalf."

"It is foolish to answer such as him, for he was only tempting me to say something he could then report to the governor for the case they are building against me. I do not want to give them anything more." She pauses and her eyes seem to be looking far away, or perhaps into the past. "I don't know why he bothers. He already has what he needs."

"And what is that?" I ask.

She does not answer right away.

"It does not matter. Bridget has seen to that." She looks down at the ground, moves her lips, but no words come out. She snaps her head upright. "It, nothing, matters to these men but that I be gone."

I have never heard her talk so, and I am frightened. We are standing between the governor's house and hers. I look toward her house, the very house I sneaked out of this morning like a thief, and I am ashamed. She embraces me, and my face brushes against the stiff linen of her gown.

"I know," she says. "You are a woman now, after what is yours, even though you must dress like a boy to pursue it." She kisses first one cheek and then the other. I feel something wet on my skin, and when she steps back I see the tears in her eye. I do not believe she is crying for me. It must be for Bridget, or for herself, as she thinks about being driven away when all she ever tried to do was speak the Lord's truth. I step back into her embrace and press my face against hers, and this time my tears join with hers.

"Go on, then," she says when we separate. "Go on, Richard, and find your poor, lost babe. I have dreamed of it. And I know she waits for you and will bide until you find her."

I try to bring my arms about her, but I am still holding my rolled up gown. I hand it to her. She opens it up a turn, and then nods and smiles.

"Yes, Richard," she says loud enough for any passer-bye to hear, "I do not think you will be needing this any longer."

She tucks my gown under her arm and walks away.

Martin is waiting for me at his table in the tavern. I have spent the day sitting on a fallen log in the woods behind Mistress Anne's house. I strained my ears to hear anything besides the usual forest noises of birds chirping and insects buzzing, or the soft splash of an acorn tossed down from a high tree limb by an industrious squirrel. It is amazing how many noises there are to hear when you really listen. But this was not a day for such idle thought. What I waited to hear was footsteps heading toward the house. When I could not stand sitting anymore, I got up and stood behind a fat old tree. I knew Mistress Winthrop would note my absence. She is a kind woman, but manages her household very well and does not take kindly to servants who do not show up.

And, indeed, just as I had sat down on that old log for maybe the twentieth time, I heard twigs snapping beneath thoughtless feet, and when I again took up my position behind the tree and peered around its thick trunk, I saw Eleanor come marching around to the back of the house, her heavy step throwing up dust and dead leaves behind her until she reached the garden and made her way through the rows of brown corn stalks. I was too far away to see her face, but I knew it must be red with her walk and her distemper, coming to fetch me or find out why she could not. The door opened and somebody spoke to her. I could not see who, but I did observe Eleanor throw back her shoulders and shake her head in disagreement. She spun around and walked away as fast as she came for a bit, and then slowed her pace as though thinking that she might as well enjoy the freedom from her chores for a little while before she had to tell Mistress Winthrop, and maybe the governor himself, that I would not be coming today. For I am sure that whoever spoke to her gave her that message, and that message must have come straight from Mistress Anne herself.

I sat back down on that log and dared not move. Of course, I was being cautious for little reason. Nobody was going to come looking for me here, for Mistress Anne knew I was biding my time before I left and everybody else in her household had concerns that had nothing to do with me, and as for Master Winthrop, he must have thought I had finally tired of his inquisitions and had fled. He had more important things to worry him than such as me, even with the letter on my gown.

I startled myself with that thought. I brought my fingers up to my chest ever so slowly. I knew that I was no longer wearing the gown, but I still expected to feel the frayed edges of that letter. When my fingers found nothing but the silly shirt I was wearing, I expanded my chest and breathed. I breathed as freely as I had in a long time, since that moment when that accursed letter was first pinned on me. The very air I took in tasted as sweet as an apple, ripe and fresh picked. I stood up and I wanted to scream my joy to the heavens, to God Himself, for I was sure that He would approve. I had learned that much from Mistress Anne's teaching over all these weeks, that the letter those men pinned to my breast signified nothing to God who could read the innocence of my heart. I did not understand why God had me suffer so, unless it was to teach me humility. At that notion, the sweet taste in my mouth soured somewhat. I did not think I could be pleased with a God such as that who would think it necessary so to humiliate me in order to convince me to love Him. No, I cannot be comfortable with such a God.

I am after all my father's daughter.

And I will think of God my own way and believe He wants me to recover my babe and live free of shame.

I look across the table at Martin, and I do not think he can understand any of this.

"Dick," he says, "can I call you that?"

"As long as you can remember my surname, which is West."

He nods.

"I see," he says. "I think I can remember that well enough."

He shoves his half full mug of beer across the table, and I drink. It is more bitter than I like, and I remember how my father used to say the drink in this tavern never did suit his fancy. Still, I have not eaten and I am glad enough to have something in my belly. After a few minutes, though, my head feels like it is going to float up from my shoulders. I place my hands on my ears as though to hold my head in place.

There is the clump of heavy boots on the wood floor, the sound of several male voices running into each other, and the scraping of chairs being pulled back. I look past Martin and see four young men sit at a table behind us. All but one has his back to me. I know the face of the one that I can see, but Tom is too busy with his companions to take any notice of me. I slide my chair to the left to have Martin block Tom's view of me. Tom looks up as he hears my chair move and looks directly at me, and I stop. There is nothing to do but play it out. I lift my mug and wave it at him. He waves his hand at me. There are not many candles on the tables and the room is gloomy. Maybe that is why he does not seem to recognize me. Or maybe he just cannot imagine that this young man he is looking at with shorn hair, sitting with another soldier, is the Rachel he knew. I settle back in my chair and down my beer. Martin looks back over his shoulder at Tom's table.

"Do you know them?" he asks.

For some reason, I do not want to tell him about Tom.

"No," I reply. "One of them waved at me. I suppose he sees us here as soldiers like himself."

"Are you hungry?" Martin asks.

"Yes."

He motions to the serving girl who is busy at Tom's table where he has his hands on her breast. She pulls herself away and approaches our table with her eyes on both of us. She does not get too close. I have the mad impulse to paw her breast, if only to feel what it is like to be on the other end of that kind of thing. I lift my hand from the table and she backs off a half step. I lean toward her and find her breast with my hand. She stands patient like a cow when you are grabbing its teat. She does not even look down at me. I close my hand just enough to feel the contours. I study her face for a reaction, but she offers none. I squeeze a little harder, and she places her hand over mine, and her expression softens. I feel her nipple harden, and I pull my hand back as though I had touched a hot iron. I wonder what she felt that made her change from indifference to something else that I have never experienced, except maybe when my own babe was at my breast, but I think that must be different. When Henry was all over me, I remember only fear, pain, and anger.

"I am hungry," I say, straining to take my voice down.

She now turns her eyes toward me. I expect to see anger or shame like I felt with Henry, but instead there is a twinkle.

"Aren't you the lively one?" she says. "And hardly weaned from your own mother, I warrant."

"Bring my mate here some of your stew," Martin says. "We are off to the Indian war, you know, and will not be sitting at a table being served so fine by such as you for a time, maybe never again."

She glances over to Tom's table where they are deep into their beer. One has his head down on the table, and the others are finding it difficult to form their words.

"God protect you then from those savages," she says as she walks away, "and bring you back alive."

When she returns with a trencher filled with steaming stew, she leans her hip against me as she sets it down on the table before me. I almost think she is inviting me to touch her again, but I am through with that. She leaves after a moment or two and I wait for the pressure of her body to leave with her. Then I begin to eat. The stew is hot and overly spiced, and the few pieces of sad meat in it are more fat and bone than anything else, and yet it fills my stomach and I eat without pausing for conversation. Martin does not seem to mind. He watches and sips his beer until I am finished.

"I have never asked you why…" he begins.

"Do you need to know?"

He shakes his head.

"You must have your reason," he says. "And I do not think that your head is filled with the idea of killing savages."

"Not kill them, but find one."

He studies me, and I feel unclothed beneath his glance. But still he cannot guess. For some reason, maybe the beer, I am enjoying his confusion. My mind cannot settle itself.

"It cannot be a man among them who abandoned you."

"No," I reply.

His eyes brighten as though remembering something.

"Or a woman?"

"You mean like that one over there," I say, looking toward the servant girl who is bringing mugs of beer to the table of recruits. At the next table is one sitting by himself. He is snoring loudly. He turns his head in his sleep, and I see his mole. She pushes against his shoulder and he tumbles to the floor. She stands over him and pours a little beer on his face. As he rouses, she swings her hips so that the bottom of her gown floats over him. He looks up. I expect to see him smile, but his face is red with anger or shame. He pushes her to the side and gets to his feet.

"Whore," he mumbles. "Leave me be."

For answer, she lifts her gown and the shift beneath it to reveal a glimpse of her bare thighs.

"Do you not want some, Oswald?" she asks, and now she has her gown even higher so that the hair between her legs can be seen. She steps toward him, still holding up her gown.

He motions her away, but his eyes do not move from her legs until she lowers her gown. He shakes his head, and again mouths, "Whore."

I hear the word and remember how it was hurled at me. I feel my own face flush, and he turns his eyes toward me. He cannot focus well, but he stares for a few moments, and then he makes his way to an empty table. He sits down with his head resting on his arms atop the table, his eyes on me until I turn away. The girl shrugs and then dips her fingers into the mug and licks them. Tom beckons her toward his table and she leans over his shoulder to set the mugs down. He does not take his eyes from her.

I turn to Martin who has been watching me watch the girl and Tom and his companions. Martin empties his mug and starts to get up.

"I have paid for a room for us," he says. "No doubt we will be sharing it with those over there if they manage to climb the stairs."

I feel panic for a moment, but there is no other good choice. I must sleep somewhere, as we leave on the morning tide.

"You will be safe with me," Martin says. He leaves a few coins on the table.

I get up, and take his arm.

"It is my babe," I say.

"Your babe?"

"My babe that my father sold to one of those savages who we now go to fight."

"Are you sure?" he says.

"My father told me as much, and the bastard that he is, I trow he was not lying when he told me."

145

"I see," Martin answers.

Concern replaces confusion in his eyes, and I feel overwhelmed and dizzy. I hold onto his arm as we walk toward the stairs. We pass Oswald's table. He looks up at me, and his lips move in silent words. I hear loud laughter coming from behind us. I turn to look. The servant girl is still at the table with the recruits. She is drinking beer. One of them has his hand on her breast. Tom has reached up between her legs. She is laughing.

"You will be safe with me upstairs," he says again.

I nod. But I am not sure how safe I want to be. As I follow Martin up the stairs, I hear Oswald mutter that word again. I pull in my chest and tell myself he must be looking at the servant girl.

There are two beds in our room. Each one is just wide enough for one person. The beds take up almost the entire room, with just space to walk between them. The one on the right is shoved under a window. There is a chamber pot in the corner that has not been emptied in some time. I am trying not to breathe too deep. Our landlord has told Martin that he has rented the room to the six of us, Martin me, and the four down stairs.

Martin looks from one bed to the other and then at me. He shrugs and sits down on the bed near the window. He tries to open the window, but it is stuck. I kneel on the bed next to him and help him push. We both take a deep breath of night air. With the window open, we can hear the voices from the inn downstairs. I think I can make out the servant girl's laughter, which is now more of a squeal. The male voices are a chorus of merriment beneath hers.

There is a thin wool blanket on the bed. We stand up and Martin peels the blanket down, showing the straw mattress beneath it. He lies down and kicks the blanket further off him with his feet. He looks toward the other bed. I shake my head and crawl in beside him. I start to smile. It is ridiculous. I am going to discover what it feels like to be a woman while I am dressed like a man. Martin seems to see the jest, but then his arms are around me in a way that has nothing to do with what I remember Henry doing to me. Then his hand is at my waist looking for something.

"This is the first time I have tried to take off a man's breeches," he says.

I want to giggle but then his hand finds what it is looking for and I feel first the night air on my flesh and then his warmth.

When we finally go to sleep, the other bed is still empty and laughter floats up to us on the night air. Martin places his mouth near my ear.

146

"In the morning, Rachel, you must be Richard again. Aye, Richard it must be, until we are back from these wars."

"It may be so," I reply. "But it is not morning yet."

We are awakened by the sound of confusion coming up to us through the cracks in the floorboards and the open window. I look across to the other bed. It is empty. Martin is on his feet and going toward the door. I follow.

From the head of the stairs, we see Constables Middleton and Grover walking toward the table we were sitting at last night. They are followed by Oswald and James Burlington, the owner of the tavern. He is a small man, with a head like a bird with a long, narrow nose and a bald head. He is wearing his apron and his face is flushed with excitement. He points to our table. I am sure that he is showing where we ate, and that in a moment he will turn around and lead the constables up the stairs toward our room. I pull on Martin's arm, but he does not respond. Burlington takes the constables past our table. We go down a few steps more so we can see. Burlington stops, his head moving back and forth on his thin neck like a startled sparrow. Tom is standing on legs that seem ready to bend in different directions. The servant girl's gown is torn and her hair is flying out behind her head. She has her hands on her hips. Tom's companions are still sitting at the table trying to rouse themselves. One does and says something that makes the girl stomp her foot in anger. Constable Middleton steps among them, and they are quieted by his great size.

He turns back to Oswald. Oswald beckons him to come closer. He whispers something in the constable's ear. Middleton listens, and then he nods. He looks at the others. He motions them toward the front door, and the men stumble toward it. The girl does not move at first. She is trying to fasten her gown with a piece of lace. Constable Grover pulls her hands down so that the material separates and the breast I had fondled the night before can now be seen. The constable gazes at her for a moment, and then he pushes her by the shoulders toward the others who are now going through the door.

Oswald watches them leave. His face wears a look of excited triumph. I do not know what he thinks he has just conquered.

I know I should feel for the girl. Perhaps she brought her ruin upon herself. They will say she offered her body to them. That is true, but she did only what she had to do to keep her place. Mayhap she already has a babe at home. I think I have heard such a story. I imagine she might have been forced, just like me. She must have thought she could stop her game after she collected a few coins,

147

but Tom and his friends did not agree. Nobody has to tell me this. I see the night's activities in the anger in her eyes, and the smirking smiles on the faces of the men. She will say she was raped, and nobody will believe her. But I am not thinking about her. I had not let myself worry about Tom going off to war with us and sooner or later figuring out who I was. He is a scoundrel, but he is not a stupid one, at least not when he is sober, which is not much of the time, but would be more so as we got ready to fight the savages.

I do not think that he will be coming with us. Master Winthrop and the other magistrates will at least want to hear his story. He will tell them that the girl is a whore who tempted them. They will believe him and sentence her to be whipped. Tom might be fined, or he might feel the lash as well. I do not care.

We sail on the morning tide.

Chapter Ten

I have been sick for a week now. We have been sailing through one storm and another, and our little ship rolls this way and then that. Many of the other soldiers are also sick. Some have fouled themselves where they lie and the stench makes me want to take in air through my mouth while I shut my nostrils. Martin says I should try to spend more time up on deck, but just looking at the waves causes my stomach to churn and my bile to rise. I prefer to lie on the half of a hammock that we share, and I cannot tell Martin why.

The first day we were on board the ship our young lieutenant was teaching those such as myself who are new to war how to use our weapons. He had us in pairs, practicing the thrust with the sword. My partner was Oswald. He had his helmet pulled down almost over his eyes, but I could not mistake that mole with its red hairs. I do not think he recognized me, for he was sweating mightily and wiping his hands across his eyes to clear his sight. He was having a deal of trouble with his sword, and I was getting the better of our combat until I stopped trying so hard. I did not want him to pay more attention to me than was necessary. He got frustrated and bade the two next to us to change so as to get a variety, he said, of opponents, and I was very glad. Since then I have stayed below decks as much as possible to avoid meeting him again.

I have not told Martin about Oswald. I suppose I should, but somehow I am ashamed because Oswald knew me as the woman on the platform with the letter on her gown. And Oswald looked at me that night at the tavern as though he saw right through my male clothes to that woman I was. I don't know what Martin would do if he knew about Oswald. I am afraid he would abandon me. That makes no sense, and yet that is what I feel.

"The sea air is what you need," Martin says. "You can close your ears to what Master Wilson has to say."

Master Wilson has come with us to be minister to the troops and we have been told that he is going to speak to us above, on the deck. I imagine he will tell us how we are on a mission from God to punish the arrogant savages who have killed so many English at Wethersfield and other places. I do not doubt that he is right in this. But I hope that God also intends for me to find my babe and take her back home with me.

"I do not feel well enough," I say to Martin.

"The air will be good for you," he repeats as though he thinks I did not hear him the first time, and he looks at me in puzzlement. "It is foul down here."

I cannot argue with that, for every breath is proof of what he says, and so I roll myself out of the hammock. Others are starting to move toward the narrow ladder that leads up. Those of us who are not sick make their way up without hesitation. The rest of us struggle to stand, and then to walk, as the ship continues to roll. Once the sick ones start to climb up I see a tall, skinny soldier cling to the ladder as his body shakes, and then he ducks his head and empties his stomach. My turn comes, and with Martin behind me, I start up the narrow ladder leading to the deck. My foot slips on a rung and I have to squeeze the ones my hands are wrapped about to stop from falling. I feel Martin's hands on my hips, and I remember how his body felt against mine. But then the ship pitches and my stomach with it. There is a muttering of impatience coming from behind him, and so he pushes and I force my feet to find the next rung, and then the next until my head comes through the hatch and I blink in the sun that is forcing its way through the cloud cover. There is a breeze and I feel a little better as I make my way to an open space near the railing. I look about and do not see Oswald.

We are gathered in a kind of half circle looking at Master Wilson, who stands on a barrel. I guess he needs to be looking down at us to talk to us, or maybe he thinks he needs to be a step closer to God. I look at the faces in the crowd for the one with the mole. I think I see it across from me. Its owner has his hands across his eyes to block the sun that he is facing, and he seems to be squinting in the direction of the minister. Master Wilson starts to talk but his voice is lost in the wind that snaps the sails. He speaks louder and the wind stops for a moment. He smiles as though he thinks God has quieted the wind so that he can be heard. But then the breeze stirs again, the sails fill, and his cap flies over the rail. He looks at it as though it is flying to heaven, but then it drops into the water. He starts his sermon again, but we can hear only an occasional word. He looks toward the master of the ship who is standing near the helmsman. The master says something to the helmsman, who turns his

150

wheel. The ship turns until the wind no longer fills our sails, and Master Wilson can be heard.

He talks at length about God and the savages and how they have affronted both us and Him, and how He will use us as His instrument to punish their insolence. His voice rises and falls, more lulling than uplifting. But then he changes subjects, and his tone is charged with energy. He tells us the story of Sodom. He says we are the firebrand plucked out of the burning that was Sodom and Gomorrah and yet some of us still deny God and return to their abominations. He pauses and his eyes roam over us and I am sure they stop at me and Martin. He raises his pitch almost to a scream. Before we sailed, he says, the Lord God plucked four firebrands burning with their lust from the tavern where they and the Jezebel who incited them were found by the constables fairly lolling in their sin. It is good they were found, he says, and denied the chance of polluting our holy mission. Let us pray, he says, that we all heed God's providence in so instructing us against the temptations of our weak flesh. And he bows his head. I stare at his bald head until Martin's hand pushes the back of my head down.

But I am not praying. I am remembering the story of Sodom so I can understand why Master Wilson has chosen to talk to us about it. I recall that Sodom was a sinful place, where all sorts of unnatural acts were performed by the people there, and then I see what he is worried about. He thinks some of these young men might take pleasure in each other, for surely there are no women excepting myself for them. At the thought, I press against Martin and hide my smile behind my hand.

Master Wilson is still preaching, directing his words heavenward, but they hum in my ear like the buzzing of a fly. I close my eyes and wait for the buzzing to stop. When it does, I look up to see that everyone is looking over the rail. I turn in that direction, but another soldier has forced his body between me and the rail. I wait for him to have his look and give me a turn, but he does not. There is an excited murmur. I feel a crowd pushing against my back, and I smell the stink of unwashed bodies and the fetid breath of those who have a short time ago been vomiting. I look for Martin, but I do not see him.

"Give us a look," I say into the ear of the fellow in front of me. He does not respond. I dig my elbow into his ribs. He is a head taller than I am, so when he turns to see who has nudged him, he is looking over my head. His face is marked with the craters that the pox leaves, and one nostril has been slit for some offense. I guess the governor does not mind sending such as him to fight the savages.

"Down here," I say, and push my thumb into his belly hard enough to get his attention.

He looks down.

"I said I would like a look," I repeat.

He thinks a moment, and then nods as though he now understands what I want.

"Land," he says, "I was looking at the land."

I lean into him, and he steps back enough to give me room to reach the rail. From there, I see something rise up above the water on the horizon.

Martin is now behind me. He places his hands on the tall fellow's shoulders and moves him further away from me, so he can stand by my side.

"That must be Saybrook," he says.

We row ashore in shallops. Our lieutenant, a young man not much older than me, tells us where to sit. I take my place and look over the side at the waves, which are black and rippling like huge snakes. The lieutenant thrusts an oar into my hands. I look at his fingers around the oar. They belong to a man who has never given them hard usage. Martin sits across from me on the bench that runs from one side of the small boat to the other, and he has his oar in the water. The wind has picked up and the waves are high. We lean our backs into our oars and make slow progress climbing up a wave and then sliding down the other side. Sometimes we seem to perch on the ridge of a wave like a nervous chicken sitting on its egg, and at other times we rock in the valley between waves until the next one crashes down on us and leaves pools of water at our feet. We fight our way through the white surf and then clamber over the side of the shallop. Our clothes and faces are coated with salt and our hands and backs ache. We start to make our way toward the shore. I cannot see well. I try to rub the salt from my eyes and still I am looking through it and the rays of the sun. What I think I see strikes fear into my heart. There are shapes moving about, and they do not look like our soldiers.

The surf batters us, and one after another we are knocked down by the swirling waters. We are wearing steel corselets and helmets. Some of the helmets are steel, but mine is leather, and it is too big for my head. It would fit me if I still had my hair. Martin has the same long barreled musket he had when we first met. A few others also have muskets of various sizes and types.

Some have pikes. I have only a sword at my side as the lieutenant thought I was too small and weak for any other weapon. I take it out and use it as a cane to maintain my balance. Martin is trying to keep his musket out of the water. A wave knocks him to his knees, but he holds his musket above his head. With my sword planted in the sand beneath the water, I am able to lean on it while with my other arm I help Martin back to his feet.

Just as he stands, I find myself under the water still holding on to my sword with one hand so I swirl about it. The weight of my armor pulls me down as I struggle to regain the surface. I do not know how to swim but I kick my feet and pull at the water with my free hand. I feel myself moving through the water, but then I bump my head against something hard, and I open my mouth with the shock. It fills with sand. I am on the bottom. The helmet is now over my eyes. I try to shove it back, but it remains pressed against the top of my nose. I gather my feet under me and spring up and find the surface just as I think I can hold my breath no longer. I stand and push again at the helmet. This time I manage to slide it back so that I can see. I am facing away from the land and another wave is about to knock me down. I put my hand over my face and duck under the wave as it crashes on top of me. I wait until I think it must have passed and I start to rise. I hear splashing near the surface, and I am sure that the savages on shore have shot their arrows at us. I want to stay under the water, but I cannot. A hand grabs my free arm and I struggle against it. I try to swing the sword upward toward the savage who has hold of me, but I cannot bring it through the water. The hand raises me until my head is again in the air. I am about to try my sword again when I see that on the other end of the hand holding my arm is Martin. He pulls me all the way up. I see that my comrades are still standing about, with their eyes on the shore.

I swipe the water from my eyes but I am looking into the sun. The figures on the beach look like they are glowing. Some seem to have halos or horns on their head. They are jumping up and down making gestures at us. We have all stopped with the same thought in our heads. We have landed at the wrong place. This is not Fort Saybrook. This is the Indian fort up the coast that we are supposed to be attacking.

"Keep moving," the young lieutenant shouts. His voice sounds like a reed above the wind. We do not move.

"Move, damn you," the lieutenant screams. "Go to the shore. There is nothing to fear. Those savages are under Uncas and they will fight with us."

I do not know whether I believe this. The lieutenant is too young to know what he is talking about, and those savages on the beach look too strong for us. But first one, and then another of us, starts to walk toward shore. I look at Martin. He shrugs and takes a step forward.

We wade closer and now it is clear that there are thirty or forty savages waiting for us, their faces painted in bright colors. Some are carrying bows and arrows and others have brutal looking wooden clubs. They stare at us as we approach. They seem to be mocking us. Some point at us and laugh while others turn to their companions and run their hands across their necks or over their chests. I look back toward the shallop that is beached on the sand. I cannot row it back out myself.

The savages have formed a line, and we straggle past them. Our lieutenant places himself between us and them, and I am feeling a little better about him. One of the savages comes forward and says something to the lieutenant. He listens and then nods. He motions for us to continue walking into the fort. We are almost past the savages when one shouts out at us.

"English, are you fish or are you warriors?"

I know he is talking to me, but I do not look at him. His comrades join in with similar comments that sting my ears. Martin takes my arm.

"You can sheathe your sword, now," he says.

I realize that I have been swinging it about in front of me as though to clear a path. I slide it back into its sheath. We walk through the open gate of the fort and then it closes behind us, and I am happy that the savages are on the other side of the wall. They may be fighting with us, but I do not trust them.

Inside, we are greeted warmly by the soldiers of the fort. Our lieutenant trots ahead to a man wearing a steel helmet, bright in the sun. It has a crest front and back, and feathers sticking up out of the steel as decoration, although I do not think it would do him any more good than my poor thing if one of those savages chose to knock him on the head with one of their sharp tomahawks or wooden war clubs. Either one, I think, would do the job very well. He is talking to two girls, one about my age, and the other a little younger. They look very frightened, and their clothes are torn and stained with mud. The lieutenant approaches the man in the crested helmet as a servant walks toward a master. It is interesting to see how the same person who lorded it over us now has to dip his head in front of somebody even more powerful than he is. The other man motions him to come forward and points to the two girls. He

154

says something and the lieutenant nods and then bows toward the girls as if they were ladies even though they do not look any more special than I am, or as I am when I am dressed as my own proper sex.

"I will find us a place to sleep," Martin says. "No doubt we will share a tent with others."

I take his meaning and show my regret in my expression rather than words, for there are many other soldiers milling about and it would not do for them to hear what I would really like to say to Martin, how much I want to feel him pressed to me again as he was that night in the room above the tavern. But we have decided that we must wait, that if we are fortunate enough to survive, we will go someplace where we can be together without fear.

I look toward the two girls.

"I would be careful about going over there, Richard," he says. "I have heard that those two girls were captured at Wethersfield. Mayhap our lieutenant will ask you if you know them."

I consider for a moment, and then shake my head.

"I do not think so," I reply. "I have not told him my story. And if I did, he is not likely to pay it much mind. I am only another soldier to him."

"Prepare an answer, in case you are mistaken," Martin says and then walks off toward a row of tents against the eastern wall of the fort.

There are now a number of soldiers listening to the captain, for that is who I think the man with the feathers in his helmet must be, as he talks to the two girls. He seems to be doing most of the talking. I get close enough to hear what he says, but I position myself behind a fat soldier, wide enough to hide me and at least one other of my size. As I listen, I begin to shiver, and at first I think it is because I am still wet from wading through the surf to shore. But the sun is out and it is warm enough. No, the chill comes from what these girls say once the captain gives them a chance to speak. He is asking them questions that they are afraid to answer. His voice is strong and clear. I can make out his words with no trouble. Their answers, though, tremble and fade. I step a little closer, but the bloated body of the soldier in front of me stops the words from reaching me. I start to edge to his side, leaning my ear into an open space between the one in front of me, and another a few feet away. But then I stop. The girls are talking about how their village of Wethersfield was attacked and in spite of my brave words to Martin I know that I should keep myself hidden. I sneak a look from behind the soldier shielding me, and I think I see our lieutenant casting

155

his eyes about as though he is looking for me. I should make my way to where Martin is, for I see him standing in front of a tent, and waving me toward him. But I cannot. I must hear what these girls have to say. It is as though I have known them my whole life, that I was in fact in Wethersfield, hiding with my little brother who was killed, while these two girls were taken, perhaps after seeing their parents killed as mine were.

"Did the savages offer you any impropriety?" the crested helmet demands.

The girls do not answer.

"Captain Mason," our lieutenant says, "I do not think they well understand your question."

The captain wheels about to face the lieutenant and looks at him as though he is only now remembering that he is there.

"Is it not a simple question?" he demands. "I want to know if the savages raped these two girls. How else did they survive? Why were they not killed, or made slaves, or adopted into the tribe? These are the ways captives such as these girls are most usually treated."

"The Dutch…" our lieutenant begins.

"Damn it all," the captain replies. "I know all about the Dutch trading for these girls. I want to know what happened before." He turns again to the older girl and tries to soften his tone, for she looks like she is about to cry.

"Did they hurt you?" he asks.

She shakes her head.

"In any way?"

"No." Her voice is a thin whisper.

"Did they offer you any uncleanness?"

I hear that word so familiar, and I want to throw off my man's soldier clothes and run to her side. Unclean, I want to shout, it is the woman, you think, who is unclean, and even as you say the word you are covered in your own filth. I take a half step toward the girl, with my hands on the laces of my shirt beneath my armor, but I stop as I see the girl about to respond. Perhaps she can speak for herself. She seems now to understand what she is being asked. Her eyes brighten, and her voice is stronger.

"Yes," she replies, "but I was so sore afraid of offending God I could not."

"Did they force you then? Did they lay hands on you?"

"Only to point us in the direction we must go. And to tie us together, a rope about each of our waists."

"They were afeard we would run away," the younger one says. She seems bolder than her sister. "As though we would know which way to run if we did get loose. And then they fed us, although the one who did said he did not know why they were wasting food on us as we would be dead by the morrow."

Her bravery melts as she recalls these words, and she sits down on the ground and weeps. The captain starts to lean toward her as though he would comfort her, but then he stops. He does not know what to do. He straightens up and adjusts the helmet on his head. He is ready to battle but not to calm a frightened girl. He marches away, but he is alone, and not at the head of his troops. The lieutenant steps forward and kneels next to the girl. He says something into her hear, and brings a shy smile to her face.

"Yes," she says, "our bondage was because of God's displeasure at our wayward ways, but our redemption, too, is from Him."

The lieutenant stands up and leads the two girls away. I want so much to talk with them. I know I can give them ease. I can see in their eyes that they have said what they know these gruff men want to hear, but in their hearts there is a pain they cannot reveal, except to me, and yet I must hold my tongue and still my feet that want to carry me to them, and continue to pretend to be one of these men.

Martin is squatting outside the tent he has chosen for us. He motions over his shoulder toward the interior of the tent.

"They are talking about the savages. Those that are to fight with us. They do not trust them. They think they must have a guard outside the tent at all times. I said I would take the first watch, as I was waiting for you."

"What do you think?" I ask, and I remember the savages we passed on the way into the fort, how they menaced us with their weapons and scorned us with their words.

He shrugs.

"I do not know. But as I was sitting here, I heard a couple of the officers talking. He said this Uncas would prove that the English could depend on his warriors. Wait until tomorrow, this Uncas said, and you will have no reason to doubt his word."

I sit down next to Martin. My head aches. I am still cold even though the air is warm. My mind is back on that snowy day. I am again being dragged by the savages to the hut where I will give birth. I see their grins and smell their animal skin clothing. "We will cut you open later," one of them says and laughs. I shake my head to clear that memory, and it is replaced by another, my father, his breath heavy with rum, snarling at Mistress Anne and then the rough hands that pull my babe from me.

I know that our ministers cannot agree whether they have souls like us Christians or are as soulless as the dogs they keep. And I am sure they think my father's soul is as black as hell. And mine too for that matter. So, is it better to have no soul like the savages for then our death would be the end of all life and not the beginning of the eternal torment that awaits such as my father and me. I do not know why such thoughts have come to trouble my poor head now. The soldiers have come to fight against some savages, and with others. I have come only to find my babe. My father, with his black heart, has told me who has her, and she is hereabouts somewhere. I can almost feel her breath against my breast.

Martin reaches for my hand, but I pull it away. I stand and go into the tent and find a corner for myself. There are three other soldiers lying or squatting on the dirt floor. They look at me as though they expect me to say something, but I turn my head away and close my eyes. When Martin comes in, he lies down near me, but not next to me. I hope he understands. I do not think I can explain myself to him, for I am not sure why I am feeling this way.

I make my breathing regular as though I am sleeping, and I lie still while the buzz of conversation in the tent dies, and I am alone with my silence.

We are roused in the morning by the war hoops of the savages. I jump up and reach for my sword in the shadows in the corner of the tent. I find it and struggle to pull it out of its sheath. When it is half way out, it catches on something and I cannot make it move any further. Across from me, I hear muttered curses as the other soldiers bump into each other. I find Martin, with his musket loaded and at the ready, peering out between the flap of the tent. I want to tell him to pull his head back inside before it is split open, but before I can he lowers his weapon and turns back into the tent.

"What is it?" I demand.

"Uncas and his men have brought the proof they promised."

I slide the sword back into the sheath, and then try to pull it out again. This time it comes out without a problem. I test the sharpness of its blade and return it to its sheath. I walk across to Martin. He puts up his hand.

"It is not a pretty sight," he says.

I pull his hand down. I do not want to be protected by him, not now, perhaps not ever.

"Do you think I am so delicate?" I ask.

He shakes his head and shrugs.

"I forget," he replies. "Come, then, and see for yourself."

I hesitate. Now that I have insisted on my right to see whatever horrible spectacle awaits outside our tent, I am not so eager. But I part the tent flaps and poke my head out.

I find myself staring at a head, no more than ten feet away. It is one of four heads, each atop a wooden spear in the hands of a savage whose body is painted in the colors and manner that I remember seeing yesterday when we arrived at the fort. They are standing in a line before our officers. The one they call Uncas is talking to them. He draws his hand across his throat and then turns to point at the heads. The captain in the feathered helmet nods toward Uncas. Our lieutenant is standing off to the side. He does not seem to be listening to what Uncas has to say. He is looking at the heads, one after another, and then he turns away. He bends down and clutches at his stomach for a second or two, and then he straightens up. When he looks again in my direction, he has set his face in a hard mask.

Three of the heads are turned toward Uncas, the captain, and the lieutenant. I see only their black hair hanging down over the top of the spears. The last one is directly in front of me, and he faces me. His eyes are open, and his jaw has dropped so it looks as though he is in the middle of saying something. There is a huge, purple bruise on his forehead where he must have been clubbed. I wonder if that blow killed him, or if his body had received a mortal hurt from an arrow or musket bullet. Somehow it seems wrong to present only the head without the body.

I step out and look a little more closely. The savage holding the spear had been facing away from me, but he hears my step and turns around. He grins at me and thrusts the spear toward me. I cannot stop myself from cringing at the thought that the head might come flying at me. The savage laughs.

"He is dead, do you not see?" he demands.

I take a step toward him to show that I am not afraid. I note the long, straight black hair, dark eyes, and painted cheeks of the savage's head. I look at the others atop their spears on either side of me. They are all Indian heads being displayed by other Indians. I concentrate again on the one before me. I see the dark red of his blood on the shaft of the spear. His teeth, clearly visible in his gaping mouth, are very white. He looks as though he has something important to say. Perhaps he does. Perhaps he can tell me what it is like to be dead and separated from his body. Is it like the ministers say, that the soul flies off somewhere to wait upon the Last Judgment when it will be reunited with the body to spend eternity in bliss or pain? And if it is what happens with such as this poor fellow in front of me, whose body is in one place, and his head in quite another. Mayhap these heads will find it hard to find their bodies. And can these eyes looking back at me, see me? Is that why we close the eyes of the dead?

I feel a tug on my arm.

"It will be time to eat, soon enough," Martin says.

I gesture toward the heads. Martin shrugs.

"I imagine those are Pequots, and that Uncas is showing our captains that he can be counted on to fight and kill those Indians who are our enemies."

"And how are we to know these are Pequots?" I ask.

"We could ask them, but I do not think they will answer."

Uncas shouts something in his language to his savages, and they say something back to him. Then they trot through the open doors of the fort. The heads float above them as they run as though they are being carried on the breeze. I wait for the doors to be closed behind them, but they are not.

"I thought the show was over," Martin says.

Before I can answer, there is again the sound of the savages' devilish screams and then a shape comes rolling through the open door. It comes to a stop in a cloud of dust opposite our tent. This one has his head on his body. But there is a rope around his neck. His face is red, and at first I think it is more of their paint, and I wonder what this fellow is going to do. But when he gains his feet again, he is standing not ten feet from me and I see that the red is blood, and that his eyes are filled with either fear or rage or both. Uncas has hold of the rope. He walks past the captive and continues until the man must follow along or be choked. Uncas drags him to where the captain is standing.

"Here is one we have saved for you," he says. "He calls himself Kiswas, and says he has lived among the English, and can speak your tongue, and know your thoughts. In your thoughts, he says he sees only fear of Pequots like himself."

The captain pulls himself up so he is at his full height, his bright helmet now catching the sun and sending it into the captive's eyes.

"Kiswas it is. You were not so bold when you ate with us."

Kiswas spits on the ground in front of the captain's feet.

"You are very brave now," he says, "with your Mohegan friends. But we Pequots care not for them or for you. Alone, you English would not dare to harm me."

The captain's face reddens for a moment, and then he takes a step back.

"What do you think we should do with him, Uncas? Do you have another spear to put his head on?"

"He is not ready to die so fast," Uncas says. "Leave him to us, this proud Pequot, and he shall see if we Mohegans are worthy foes."

"Take him," the captain says, and he walks away.

Uncas motions two of his men to come forward. One holds Kiswas while the other takes the rope from about his neck. I think Kiswas is going to fight for his life, but he stands there, his arms crossed before his chest, his chin high, and his eyes staring straight ahead as to the place he thinks he will soon be when the Mohegans are through with him. They tie one end of the rope to one of his legs. Then they pull on the rope until his leg is lifted off the ground and he is standing on one foot. He looks ridiculous, as though he is trying to do one of their strange dances. Then they tie another rope to the leg that is still on the ground and then they motion to their friends. Fifteen or twenty of them grab one rope, and the same number the other. They whoop and howl, but do not do anything as yet. They look at Kiswas. Then one group give a little yank, and then the other does the same, and Kiswas' feet come flying up and his head bounces on the ground. They start to pull on the ropes in earnest.

I retreat into the tent. I do not need to see what they are doing. I wait to hear him scream, but he does not. He is showing how brave he is, I suppose. After a while, I do hear Kiswas moan and his tormentors shout their glee. Then there is silence. And finally a shot from a gun breaks the quiet of the morning.

The next morning as we prepare to march, a fifth head sits atop a spear, which like the four others has been driven into the ground. We walk past them and listen to the buzzing of flies circling the dead flesh.

Chapter Eleven

The sun beats down on us as we march. I wonder if this heat is a sign of God's displeasure with us. Mayhap He is giving us a little taste of hell before we get there. I do not think Master Wilson would explain this weather in that fashion, but he has stayed at the fort where he can sit in the shade and drink something cool.

Every step I take hurts. My leather helmet slides down onto the bridge of my nose and digs into my flesh. My corselet rides up and into my neck, where it feels like a hot iron. The scabbard rubs against my leg as I walk, and my feet are swollen in my boots. I dare not look up into the sun for fear of dizziness. Sweat coats my flesh.

My comrades are muttering curses. I would join them, but my tongue feels swollen. I do not believe I can make it form the sounds of a word. I have come to depend on Martin at times like this. Up until now, I have never seen him in an ill humor, or sad, or fearful, or angry. His mood is as constant as the sun in the summer on a cloudless day and at night I have been able to crawl into his warmth when the dark hides us from the others' eyes. We do not do anything more than lie close to each other as everybody else must do either because we are in the tent where there is little room, or as now when we are sleeping outdoors on the ground and huddle close together for protection against the savages, hoping that the arrow or war club will hit our neighbor before ourselves, although none would have the courage to say so to his fellow, none that is except Martin when he is in his usual good humor. But even he seems to be feeling the strain. He has not smiled in a couple of days. He swipes at the insect that buzzes about his ear. He misses the bug and the palm of his hand comes down hard across his ear and cheek. His skin reddens, and he shakes his head in disgust.

"Damned mosquitos," he says.

I have never heard him curse before, or even say anything in such anger.

"Damned what?" I ask, for I do not know the word.

"Mosquitos, I said. That's what the little bastards are."

I put my hand to his cheek and feel the bump begin to form. I have half a dozen of my own, wherever my skin is exposed. They take turns itching. When one stops another starts. I imagine it feels something like what it must have been like for those papists who put on their hair shirts to show how they could suffer to serve their God.

"Mosquitos?"

He removes my hand and draws his nail hard across the bump until it bleeds.

"Yes," he says. "The Spaniards call them that."

I am surprised.

"They look like English gnats to me, only with a bigger appetite. Where did you hear such a name for them?"

He looks at me like he has forgotten who I am, and then he shifts his glance as though to a distant place.

"I did have a life before I met you," he says, and then he speeds up his pace so I have to trot to keep up with him. Our company has been walking in twos in a straggly line with much space between each pair. Our officers have tried to keep us closer together, for our safety they say, but it is too hot, and we simply do not care. I think we might even welcome an attack from the savages to take our minds off how uncomfortable we are. But now Martin is walking so fast that he has to slow down before he runs into the two soldiers ahead of us. I catch up to him, but do not try to talk. It would do no good, and I have nothing much to say anyway.

Behind us are the savages who are supposed to be fighting with us. I cannot look at their painted faces without feeling fear. I have seen savages dressed like English in the meeting house, and some of them can speak better than me and, for that matter, dress as well or better. But these are not like those. These are more akin to those who traded with my father. Or those who whooped insults at us when we landed at Fort Saybrook. And they were the very ones who reduced other savages to a head on a spear to feed the flies and then rot in the sun. Those very ones now walk behind us but so quietly you cannot hear them. To know they are there, you must turn about and look for them, and then sometimes, as though to taunt us, they will seem to disappear as soon as we shift our eyes in their direction. I have heard that they are servants of the devil

163

himself and can fly through the air like witches who have signed the devil's book. I don't know about that. But I am not comfortable with my back always to them, and so from time to time, I turn and walk backward with my eyes on them.

Of course, some of the savages are in front guiding us, and I suppose that is a good thing for else I do not think we could find our way through this wilderness of tall trees and deep shadows that turn the day into night. I think that our savage guides are leading us into the darkness where their comrades wait to ambush us. I fight my fear. I have never used my sword but I am not afraid to test its blade if I must. Martin has his musket and his broad shoulders. And if all else fails, I have my feet.

Master Wilson led us in prayer the last night we were in the fort. He said that he was sure God wanted us to punish these arrogant devils who slaughtered our innocents at Wethersfield. He seemed to be looking at me when he said that. I wondered, while he spoke, if God will punish me for my lies. I was shocked to realize that I did not feel such a punishment would be more than I deserve, and that my first worry was that God in His justified anger at me would strike down those close to me, my Martin, and my babe. I almost walked up to Master Wilson to confess my lie, and then I recalled how coldly he fastened that letter to my chest, and I took a deep breath before mouthing my silent prayer to God to forgive me and if not at least to spare my loved ones.

Now I hope that He has concerns elsewhere in the world and will leave us to our own ways. Master Wilson had spent most of the voyage sick in his cabin. He said such sickness was an affliction from God to remind us that our help is only in Him. Master Wilson is a learned man, who has read many books and has studied the words of the Holy Scripture. I am sure somewhere in those words he has found instructions from God, telling him to stay safe behind the stockade at Fort Saybrook whilst we walk between savages front and back toward other savages who await us with their bright weapons at the ready. I look toward the heavens, hoping to hear the Lord speak to me as he does to Master Wilson. I hear a bird high in a tree and then a mosquito in my ear. I almost smile at my foolishness. For the first time, I think of Mistress Anne. I believe she would have smiled too if she was here by my side right now reading my thoughts as she could do.

We march all day, and as the sun sets we are told to find a place on the ground to sleep. Tomorrow, our officers say, will be a most busy day. We are very close to the savages' village, which is well fortified and within are warriors with their bows, and war clubs, and some perhaps even with muskets sold to them by English traders who care more about their purses than the safety of their fellows. We must remember to say our prayers and ask God's help in the forthcoming battle. I have tried to talk to God this afternoon. I do not think He is listening to me. Martin bows his head. I do not know what he is thinking. I am never sure of his thoughts, and he does not give them voice. Perhaps he is praying. Mayhap he is studying his right boot, which is wearing through at the big toe and will soon have a hole there.

Without saying a word to each other, we understand this might be our last night together. We find a place beneath a pine tree a little removed from the huddled bodies of our comrades, but still within the protection of our sentries. The ground beneath the tree is thick with needles. Martin smooths a place for us and we lie down together. The clouds have been drifting in all day, and now they hang low and dark over us. Every once in a while, I can see the moon. It is only a sliver of yellow in the black sky. I imagine it is God's eye and he is closing it because he does not want to see what is going to happen tomorrow. The air is warm and so thick it is hard to breathe. We can hardly see each other as we lie down on the needles. We must be invisible to the others. After a while, we hear snores rising from those closest to us. They act as our cue. We have not talked about what we are going to do tonight, but we both seem to have the same thought. I feel Martin's hands on my hips drawing me to him.

Later, Martin says he has to go piss, and I hear him stumbling through the trees into the darkness. Then, he curses and I know he must have walked into something. It is quiet, and I stretch my body in the warm air. I do not want the night to end. Steps are approaching, and I open my arms for Martin. A hand comes down across my mouth.

"I know who you are," a voice says.

I reach up toward it, and my hand finds a face. I try to draw my nails across the flesh, but his other hand traps mine. My finger is resting on a bump on the man's face. I do not need the light to know that red hairs are growing out of that ugly lump. I dig my teeth into the hand over my mouth. I taste his blood, and then he is gone. In a little while, Martin comes back and lies down next to me. I do not tell him anything.

Martin falls asleep with his arms about me. I close my eyes, but I cannot rest. After a while, I roll away from Martin. He grouses in his sleep and reaches for me, but then relaxes back into his slumber. I sit up and stare at the black sky. The sliver of the moon emerges from behind a cloud. I want to bathe in its light, and so I stand up with my eyes shut. I think I can feel its warmth, but then another cloud hides it, and I am chilled. I lie down again next to Martin so that his warm breath can reach my neck.

It seems I have just fallen asleep, when we are roused by our lieutenant who is walking among us to wake us. The sun is not yet up. The men complain and the lieutenant curses. For those who will not rise, he finds their ribs with his boot for encouragement. When he reaches us, he stares down at us for a moment, and I realize that I do not have my corselet on and I am very much aware of how my breasts must be pushing out my shirt. I have stopped binding them as soon as I started wearing armor. I have been dreaming of my babe all night, and when I awoke, my breasts felt full as though I was going to offer her suck. I wait for the lieutenant to say something, and I think I should roll onto my side or stomach, but that would only mean he would nudge me with his foot. Martin stands up. He must understand my problem. The lieutenant is still looking down at me. I can just see his eyes in the dark, and I hope that he cannot see me any better than I can him.

"Good morning, lieutenant," Martin says. "My mate was not feeling well last night, but he will be fit and ready in a moment."

"See that he is," the lieutenant replies. "I do not want to have to come back to rouse him."

I sense more than I see the lieutenant shake his head in disapproval, but then he walks away. The moon is visible now, as the clouds have drifted off, and the air feels cooler. I grope about for my corselet, my helmet, and my sword. Martin's hand finds mine as he is looking for his powder pouch. I hold his hand when he tries to withdraw it. I want to feel the warmth of his flesh. He squeezes my fingers and then pulls his hand away. I roll up our blanket. Beneath it is my sword on one side, and Martin's musket on the other. I adjust the scabbard against my right thigh and lift the sword half way out. I run my thumb over the blade, as I have seen the others do. It is certainly sharp enough to cut off a savage's head.

I am brought back to those heads on the ends of spears, and I feel a little sick. I see again the one that stared at me as though it had something very important to tell me, if only if could find a way to move its lips and form words. I think it wanted to say that it was only the first of many, that this day's battle would see many bodies abused by various weapons, and there would be more dead on the ground than can be held up for display on spears. I slide the sword back into the scabbard. I realize that at some point, I don't know when, I had stopped hating those who hurt me, not because I no longer felt the resentment but because my anger made me unhappy. Perhaps it is my feelings for Martin that have caused this change. I do not know. I do think that I must survive this day. If I have to kill somebody to do that, I will.

We are formed into our columns. Uncas is at the head walking with our captain. Some of his savages are at his side, and the others are at the rear, as before. It seems to me that there are fewer of them than there were yesterday, and the rumor going up and down our line is that now as we approach the fort, our savages have lost their heart and have chosen to fade back into the forest. It is still dark, but our eyes have adjusted to the pale light cast by the narrow moon, and the glow of torches carried by a number of our soldiers. Martin nods toward those carrying the lighted brands.

"What do you think of them?" he asks.

"Why, to light our way."

"No," he replies. "I have never before seen such a strategy but for one purpose. We should not want to show the enemy where we are unless we had another use for that fire."

I understand and shudder. An order is passed down the line from the head of the column to cease all talking and for the torch carriers to fall back and let everybody else pass them. We continue walking a little further when we are motioned to stop. Martin nudges me.

"We are very near, now. You do not have to go in," he whispers in my ear.

I feel both insulted and relieved. I respond to the insult.

"And why not?" I ask, and I can feel my jaw jutting out as it used to do when I would try to make my father do the right thing, like chop some firewood instead of heating his own insides from a bottle while I shivered in a corner. I realize I have raised my voice to an almost normal level and somebody from the front of our column says "Hush" in a harsh whisper. I put my face next to Martin's and as we talk our breaths mingle.

"You came for your babe," Martin says.

"She is inside," I reply and as I say the words I am sure she is.

He does not say anything right away, and I want to see his face.

"It would be better if she is not."

I understand. I look back at the torches.

"Then I must go in."

"If you do..." he begins, but does not finish the thought, for what instruction can he offer?

If I could, I would crawl into his skin, I think, and come out only when it was all over.

"Yes," I say.

His hands are busy with his musket. He has shown me before how he must pour powder down its barrel, and ram the ball after, pour a little of the other powder onto the firing pan, and at last light the match cord. His hands move with great speed now, not as they did when he was teaching me.

"Do you have a match?" he asks.

"No," I reply.

"I will be back."

And off he is toward the back of our line where the torch carriers are. He returns a few moments later carrying a small twig smoldering at its end. He holds the twig to the cord until it too begins to burn.

"It is a good thing it is not raining," he says. "Else this would be good only as a club, and a very clumsy one."

I realize he is talking to me this way to keep my mind occupied.

Those in front of us begin to walk again. There must have been a command from the front of our column but we did not hear it. We start to walk. We have been moving between the trees on a narrow path. It must be one that the savages use. It had been so narrow that we had difficulty walking side by side but now it is widening, and we soon see why as we break out from between the trees and we are within twenty feet of the stockade. It looks like a row of closely planted trees covered in shadows that hide the spaces between them. I stare a little harder, and see that I am not looking at live trees, but trunks lashed together and driven into the ground. It looks very solid and I wonder how our leaders expect us to crash our way through it. It is also high enough to make scaling it very nearly impossible. Perhaps we are going to set the walls on fire, but even I understand that it is not easy to light a log on fire with a torch and in the meantime we would be alerting the savages within. There must be another plan, and there it is. A rough door in the line of logs that forms the stockade, and we are heading straight for it.

There is a howl from atop the stockade and it is followed by more, one after another. Those at the front of our column are now running toward the door. And overhead come the arrows from the top of the stockade. One flies by me and lands in a tree at the side of the path. I watch as it quivers back and forth. Martin pulls it out and throws it to the ground. He lifts his musket to his shoulder and sights at a savage on the stockade who is pulling an arrow back on his bow. He pulls the trigger and there is a loud explosion in my ear and a puff of white smoke. Martin steps back against the force of the musket on his shoulder. We cannot see through the smoke. Another arrow whizzes over our head.

"Missed," Martin says, and his hands are again busy loading his weapon.

Our soldiers are thumping against the door to the stockade with a log. Others of our soldiers also fire their muskets and the smoke thickens and burns my eyes. The arrows are raining down on us, but I do not think anybody has been hit. We hear a scream and then a shout from our soldiers near the stockade.

"One less savage," somebody shouts.

The thumping continues and then stops. The door swings open, and we are rushing toward the village. I take out my sword and hold it bravely in front of me. I am trying to convince myself that I can use it to pierce a savage's chest and find his heart. But I do not feel the necessary anger. Martin grabs my arm and pushes me to the side as our fellows continue by us.

"You wait here," he says.

"I am not afraid," I lie.

"Of course, you are." He pushes me again, and this time I stagger back into the trees at the side of the path. I lose my balance and drop to my knees. I steady myself with my sword and rise. But there is more smoke and I cannot see Martin. The soldiers with lighted brands are now going by. One stops and turns toward me. He lowers his torch. It is Oswald. He takes a step toward me, waving his torch. His eyes are bright. I do not know if he even sees me. It is as though he is looking through me.

"Whore," he says. He steps closer and now I can feel the heat of his torch. I hold my sword out in front of me. A hand grabs Oswald's shoulder and spins him around. It is Martin. Oswald looks at him and mutters something I cannot hear. Then, he trots after the other torchbearers.

"Who is that?" Martin demands.

"I do not know him," I say.

"He seems to know you, and not in a friendly way." He points as though to indicate I should retreat back into the shadows. I nod and wait for him to go. He catches up to the last of the torchbearers and moves past them into the fort. I wait a moment or two, and then follow. From inside, I hear shouts and screams of the wounded. Then as I reach the door the sky is lit. For a moment, I think the sun has awakened, or perhaps God has cast down his thunderbolt. But as I step through the door, I see what has happened. At my feet, next to the door is a savage who has fallen from the top of the stockade. A musket ball has taken out half of his face. He seems to be breathing still. I thrust my sword toward him, but stop before my blade reaches his chest. His one good eyes watches my blade and when it stops he smiles, and then the smile becomes a sneer. Another of our soldiers, it is the officer with the shiny helmet, is at my side. He takes the sword from my hand and plunges it into the savage's chest. He twists it and then pulls it out.

"He would have done the same for you, lad," the officer says. "Do not give one of them the chance."

And then he turns and walks into the fort as though he was marching in a parade. I follow and find that I am in hell. I expect to see hundreds of savage warriors. I cannot make out much for all the smoke, but the first person I see is a woman whose long black hair is smoldering. One of our soldiers grabs her hair and run his sword through her neck. Her blood gushes out, up into the air like red water thrown up from a bucket. She sinks to her knees and her blood comes down on her head. She remains kneeling, her eyes wide open and staring at the soldier. He kicks her on the jaw and her head snaps back. She falls to her back and he stands over her for a moment, shaking his hand which seems to have been burned when he seized her hair. When she does not move, he looks about for somebody else to attack. But all he sees are women and children. He spits in disgust and motions him to follow. I nod, but do not.

The wigwams of the savages are on fire. There are red flames everywhere. The savages are running about. Some of them are burning and they roll on the ground. Our soldiers are skewering them with their swords, shooting them with their muskets, and then clubbing them rather than reloading. I see the one who sliced the woman's throat kneeling next to a charred body. Here and there are grown men among savages trying to fight back. But there bow strings burn and snap. Some of them hurl themselves at our soldiers and embrace their enemies as they receive a death blow from a sword or lead ball fired into their chests at such close range that their skin smokes around the hole.

Children are running wild about looking for their mothers. Some are screaming, others are mute. Terror and confusion mix in their eyes. Mothers hold out their arms for children, any body's child. One woman scoops up a child and runs toward the rear of the stockade. Maybe there is another exit. I watch her run and see a soldier sight his musket at her. There is a flash from his matchlock and the now familiar explosion of sound. She keeps running. He takes a step or two after her, and then shrugs. He turns just in time to see a warrior savage running at him swinging his war club. He has no time to reload, so he holds up his musket to ward off the blow of the club. The club bounces off his musket and glances against his helmet. He drops his musket staggers back. The savage raises his club to deliver a death blow. I can only watch. My arms and legs refuse to obey my command to move. I do not know what I would do if I could move. I am supposed to help my comrade, but would I?

I do not have to answer the question. Another soldier's sword runs through the savage's back and comes out his chest. His eyes register his surprise that instead of killing his helpless foe, he has been killed. The soldier who had dropped his musket picks it up and swings it hard against the savage's head. Even from where I am some distance away, and even amid all the noises of pain and anger, I can hear the thud as the musket stock crashes against the savage's skull. The one with the sword pulls it out by pushing against the savage's lower back with his foot. The savage falls to the ground, and the soldier with the musket nods his thanks to the one with the sword.

Nobody is paying any attention to me. Not even the savages. It is as though they cannot see me. I pinch my flesh to make sure that I have not been killed without my knowing it. My nails bite into the skin on my arm and I feel the pain. And then for further proof a savage comes running at me. He is aflame from his knees to his belly, but his eyes are free of the fire, and they are focused straight at me. He is screaming an awful howl, and he is swinging what looks like a huge war club over his head. He is only a few steps from me, now, and I can smell his burning flesh. He starts to bring his club down toward my head. I thrust my sword at him and he runs onto it. I feel his weight against the hilt of my sword, and I dig my boots into the ground to keep from being driven backward. His club falls to the ground and I am looking into his eyes, no more than a foot from my face. His mouth is still moving, but there is no sound. The fire that is roasting his middle now licks my blade and travels up my sword, which becomes so hot I can hardly hold it. I remember what I saw the other soldier do. I raise my boot, press it through the flames into his stomach, and push. He falls off my blade. I lean down to look at him. The fire continues to eat at him. I do not think that he feels it anymore, unless he is already in hell. But then I stare at the smooth skin of his face, a face that has never known the troubles of a man, for this body at my feet is that of a child no more than ten or twelve years old.

I look up to the sky. I see that the moon has disappeared, and the sun has not yet risen. There is nothing but blackness above. I wonder if God has turned His back on this desperate scene. Or if He intends to open up the earth and swallow us all. I am sure Master Wilson would disagree. He would see some special providence, as he likes to say, in this darkness, that it is aiding our soldiers. And he is a most learned man. He must be right. I can almost smile thinking that.

But the boy on the ground in front of me brings me back to why I am here. He is somebody's son. And I must find my babe. I do not doubt she is here and that she is in danger. I fear that she is, or soon will be, dead. I look wildly about. I am in a small circle of calm because the fighting has moved toward the rear of the stockade where a number of the savages are trying to break through or climb over the walls and so escape. Smoke rises everywhere, from burning bodies and the reeds and bent saplings of the wigwams, all now aflame. Some on the ground are moaning, crawling away from one fire toward another. I walk toward the first wigwam on my left, looking at each body on the ground as I pass. Here is an old woman, who escaped the fire so her wrinkled flesh is not charred, but it is stained with the blood running from the wound sliced into her chest. Approaching her is a little child, crawling on its knees. My heart leaps until I see what is between the child's legs, and I step aside so that the little boy can reach the old woman, mayhap his grandmother. He does and a smile broadens his chubby face. He pokes her arm and waits for her to move. I can watch no longer, but out of the corner of my eye I see a young woman gazing out from behind the wigwam I am approaching. I turn away to give her an opportunity. I do not hear her, but I can imagine how she darts to her babe and swoops it up in her arms. I pray she finds a safe haven somewhere.

When I turn back, the babe is gone. I make my way to the wigwam. It is smoldering, smoke rising above it and settling in the spaces between the bent sapling frame. Its reeds are charred and black. I stoop to enter. I can see nothing inside, so I crawl on my hands and knees and feel the ground. I think I hear breathing from the far corner, but when I get there I find nothing.

Back outside, I almost stumble right into Martin.

"It is a good thing I am not a savage," he says. Blood is dripping down from his forehead to his chin. One cheek is blackened.

"I was thinking..." I begin, but my hands find his face, trace his wound, and pause on the darkened skin. It feels warm.

"The powder," he says. "Goes off too soon sometimes, or too late others."

I see that his right hand has a burn mark too. I wonder if it is from the powder as well, or the fires raging all about, perhaps on some savage. I choose not to ask.

"I know you are looking," he says, with his hand on mine against his face. "But I believe I have found what you seek."

"Where? Why did you not bring her here?" The questions tumble out of my mouth, and I squeeze his hand to my lips. I do not care who sees us. He points to a wigwam across the way.

"It was not safe," he says.

"Is it now? I cannot wait."

He motions for me to follow. I want to run ahead, but he holds my arm.

"Stay with me," he insists, and I do, following him toward the wigwam until we are almost upon it, and then I run toward it. I expect to feel him try to hold me back, but he does not. Like most of the others, it is still smoldering, like the dying embers in a fireplace, only these are not the kind you would want to stir back into life. I drop to my knees before the place where the door flap should be, but it has been burned off. What remains is the structure of saplings bent into a frame on which the flap hung. The entrance is narrow and bent from the fire. I have to squeeze through it. As I do, I my arms brush against the frame, and I feel my flesh singe from the heat, and for a moment, I fear that I am trapped in the doorway and will burn to death. But I will myself to push myself past the entrance and into the wigwam. I glance up and see that in some places the saplings are still glowing red, and toward the rear a part of the structure has started to collapse where the fire has eaten entirely through an upright.

The sun has risen, and I can see more clearly in this wigwam. There is a woman lying on the ground next to the circle of stones the savages use for a fireplace. There is a dark red stain of dried blood on her back where a musket ball entered her body. Her hands clutch her deerskin skirt. Her long black hair is spread on the ground next to her. She has an ugly wound on her forehead where a clump of her hair has been pulled out by the roots. Somebody tried to scalp her but stopped for lack of skill, time, or opportunity.

I am disappointed. I do not want to see yet another dead and abused body. Martin is at my side. I did not notice when he came in.

"Look, more closely," he says, and points to her skirt. At first, I see nothing, but then there is a movement, and after that a little hand emerges. I reach for the hand while Martin rolls the woman off the tiny body. I am looking at a babe. I place my hand next to its face and examine its pale flesh next to mine. They seem to be the same hue. And her eyes, they are blue, just like mine.

"Are you sure?" he asks.

I want to say yes, my heart says yes, but I cannot be certain. I start to shake my head, when a face appears staring into the wigwam from its side. The face has a long, jagged scar running down it from ear to neck. The face stares for a moment at me and then at the babe.

"Nanawag," I say.

The face nods, and then the butt of a musket comes crashing down. Martin has heard me utter the name and looks as though he is about to ask what I have said when we hear the thud of wood against bone, and the face disappears. He runs over to the place where the savage had been standing, stares down at him and then seeks the owner of the musket. My attention, though, is on the woman. She is now on her back. I stare at her bare breasts. I wonder if she has given my babe suck. I pick up the babe and clutch it to my chest. It holds my eyes, but then turns to the woman she thinks is its mother. I stand up and walk away. She squirms about in my arms and her mouth seeks my breast, but she is stopped by the steel of my corselet. I feel helpless and ridiculous.

"He is gone," Martin says, and he is talking about the soldier who crushed the skull of Nanawag. Then he notices how I am holding the babe against my chest to no purpose. "We will have to find a wet nurse for her," Martin says.

I am about to offer an angry reply that I can and will take care of my own daughter, even though I know he is probably right, when through an opening burned in the front of the wigwam a figure holding a musket appears. Somehow I know who it must be before I see his face. Martin follows my eyes and takes a step forward. He thinks he is welcoming a comrade in arms who has just protected us from an enemy. I know better. The only question is what he intends to do.

Oswald stoops through the opening in the front of the wigwam. The match cord on his musket is lit. I can see it sizzle and smell it burn. He cradles the musket in his left arm so that it is aimed to the side. His eyes glance at my babe and then rise to my face. He does not see, or perhaps take notice of Martin.

"You want to be careful with your musket," Martin says. "There is nobody here you would want to shoot."

For answer, Oswald lifts his weapon to his shoulder and sweeps it toward Martin.

"I be careful," he says. "All the time."

Martin makes a motion as though to push the barrel of the musket away from him. Oswald steps back and out of reach. He sights down the barrel. Martin looks toward me for an explanation.

"What is it you want?" I demand.

"Whore, show yourself," Oswald says in a voice strained with anger.

"What would you have with me?" I ask.

I have known that this moment must come from the time we stared at each other when I was standing on the platform. I do not know why he hates me so, but I somehow understand that his hatred is mixed with his lust for my body. It occurs to me that he cannot decide whether he want to kill me because he cannot have me, or rape me so that he can. Whichever it is I am determined to disappoint him.

He thrusts the barrel of his musket at me. Its match cord still burns, and his hand is on the lever of the trigger. He pokes the barrel next to my babe and against my corselet so that the sound of metal on metal clangs. Martin moves as though he might grab the barrel. Oswald's eyes shift to him, and Martin understands their message. He will pull that trigger unless Martin backs off. Martin does, and Oswald holds the barrel against my chest.

"Put your bastard down, and take your armor off so I can see the whore that is hiding beneath it."

I lower my babe to the ground and urge her away. She looks at me.

"Go," I say and push her toward the corner of the wigwam.

She does not move. I point to the dead woman, and give my child another shove. She smiles and starts to crawl toward the woman. I stand up and undo the laces at the bottom of the sides of the corselet. When they are undone, Oswald pulls back his musket. The mole on his nose seems even bigger and uglier, and I realize that his breathing has become labored. He motions me to take off my corselet. I lift it off. I think of striking him with it, but his eyes have shifted to my babe who has begun to cry. She is sitting next to the woman with her mouth on her breasts. Her cheeks sink as she tries to draw milk and when nothing comes she starts to howl. Oswald points the musket at her for a moment, and I drop the corselet to the floor. As it thuds to the ground he turns back to me.

"Where is your letter, harlot?" he demands.

"I have traded it for this," I reply, pointing with my left hand to the armor at my feet, while my right reaches for the hilt of my sword.

"A rare bargain," he replies. "But not a good one, not a just one in the eyes of the Lord."

"You are right, my friend," Martin says, and I stare at him.

"Take her before the Captain, to show how she has made a mockery of him," Martin continues.

Oswald seems to consider.

"No," he replies, "I think not. This harlot is mine. See how she stares at me, but I will not be tempted. The Captain be damned."

Martin takes a quick step and places himself between me and Oswald.

"Then you must decide. You have one ball in your musket. And there is me, and there is her."

I see that he has a long bladed knife in his hand, and I do not know where it came from.

"And there is also the bastard," Oswald says, and swings his musket around again toward my child. I throw myself on the ground next to her, my back to Oswald. I clutch her to me, and I now understand how the dead woman received the wound on her back that killed her. I wait to hear the explosion and to feel the ball rip through my skin, and I try to focus my thoughts on our Lord who must be looking down with gentle mercy in His eyes, but all I see in my mind's eye is my babe's face scrunched together, her lips moving as she howls in her hunger.

I hear the explosion, but feel nothing. There is the sound of a body falling behind me. I smell the powder. Martin is lying on his back. The ball has penetrated his armor and found his breast. Blood seeps out. Oswald has started to reload his weapon. He is ramming a ball home in the barrel. I pull the knife out of Martin's hand and rush at Oswald. He starts to swing his musket at me but my knife finds his arm. He drops his weapon and looks at me, startled. His expression has undergone a marvelous change. Tears leak from the corners of his eyes, and his face has collapsed into the soft flesh of a boy who knows he has been caught doing something wrong and has been punished. He clutches his arm, bends down to his knees, and crawls out of the wigwam.

I kneel next to Martin and drop my face next to his lips. I yearn to feel his breath, but there is nothing. I kiss his lips, and pick up my babe. She has stopped crying and is working her thumb in and out of her mouth. I take her on my lap and rock her until her eyes close and she sleeps. I grasp Martin's hand. It is still warm. I hear the tramp of soldier's boots approaching the wigwam. I squeeze the hand. I think I feel it return the pressure. I study his eyes. In them, I see his encouragement to take my leave of him. The boots have almost arrived. I can see the dust they are kicking up. I crawl toward the opening at the front of the wigwam, clutching my sleeping babe to my chest. I duck my head to peer out. I am looking at a pair of boots encrusted with dirt and blood. A sword blade shines next to them. It, too, is stained with blood. Its owner has been busy this day. A face replaces the boots. It is the lieutenant. I back up, and he looks about him. He points to Martin.

"Is he alive?" he asks.

His question stirs hope.

"I do not know," I answer.

"Come out then. With your babe. We will attend to him."

I do not move for a moment, and when I do it is back to Martin.

"I must stay with him until I know," I say.

The lieutenant shakes his head, and then I see another face, next to his. It is Oswald.

"You must come out," the lieutenant repeats.

I shake my head. The lieutenant motions to soldiers behind him. They enter the wigwam and take Martin's legs. I think he stirs, but I cannot be sure. They start to pull him out. I raise his head off the ground and hold it while he is taken out. They lift him and carry him away. I start to follow, but the lieutenant's sword is in my path. I blink in the sun after the darkness of the wigwam.

The lieutenant studies my body. I realize I still have my sword on, but my head is bare and my corselet is on the ground in the wigwam. I do not care. I am no longer in disguise. He looks puzzled.

"Are you not Robert West from Wethersfield?" he asks, although his voice indicates that he is beginning to understand.

"Yesterday, I was. Today, I am Rachel Moore of Boston, who has come to find her babe, stolen from her arms and traded to these savages."

"That child is yours?"

"Yes."

"How know you that for a surety?"

I turn my daughter toward him and hold her up so that her face is next to mine. She blinks in the sun, but he can see her eyes next to mine.

I point to the wigwam. "Over there, inside is a savage woman who was taking care of my babe. Outside, dead or badly wounded, is another savage. He is the one who bought my babe from my father. If you look at his face, you will see an old scar that runs from his ear down to his neck."

Oswald has been standing back out of respect to the lieutenant, but now he steps forward. Arrogance and hate have returned to his face. His arm is bound.

"She is who she says she is." He points at my babe with his good arm. "And that is her bastard. When I tried to bring her before you, she did this to me," and he holds up his wounded arm.

"Only after you attempted to shoot me and my babe."

"Enough," the lieutenant says. His voice has deepened, it seems to me, after this day of war. He seemed a boy playing at soldiering yesterday, but now he is grown into a man. "We have had a great victory today. I will not have you spoil it. You," he says to Oswald, "join your company. And you," he takes my arm, "come with me and we will see what the captain wants to do with you and your babe."

"But…" Oswald begins.

"You can tell your tale to the captain later, if you choose," the lieutenant says. "But think you whether you want to have to explain how that man we have just taken out of this wigwam came to be shot."

"In time," Oswald mutters, "if not here, at home, I will indeed bear witness to what I know." He trudges off.

178

I look about the village. The wigwams are still smoldering, and I hear moans from wounded savages lying here and there. Our soldiers seem to have received few hurts. They are forming themselves into lines as though to march. Across from them is a group of savages, women, some old and stooped, others carrying babes in their arms, and children clutching at their mothers' legs. The women's eyes are dark with a fury they aim at the English soldiers who stand so close to them. The children look about them, stunned and confused. Some wander toward the bodies of the dead or stare at those still alive. There are many more savages on the ground than standing. And of those on the ground, dead or barely alive, almost all are women and children. I see only a few men among them. A half dozen of our soldiers have their muskets pointed at the women and children. Yesterday, they lived in this village. Today, they are captives.

The lieutenant leads me toward our soldiers. I hear muttering about revenge for Wethersfield. Others are smiling at the cowardice of their Indian allies who never entered the village. Uncas is talking to our captain. Some of his warriors are nearby. He seems to be explaining something. He slaps his chest several times, and the captain nods, as though in agreement.

"Stay here," the lieutenant says to me.

He approaches the captain, and waits for Uncas to finish. When he does, and walks away with his warriors, the lieutenant points to me and says something to the captain. They talk for a few moments. I see their lips move, but I cannot hear them. I feel very tired. I do not care what they are saying. I want only to know about Martin, and to feel the warmth of my babe's body pressed against mine. The captain approaches. He bends down to look at my babe.

"Turn her about," he says, "and hold her up to your face."

I do, and he studies us for a moment.

"Let me see your sword," he demands.

I shift my babe to my left hip, and pull my sword out. He takes it from me and examines the blood on it.

"Have you used this on the savages as well as the one you say tried to kill you?"

"Yes," I answer.

"I have heard that she did indeed kill at least one," the lieutenant says.

The captain strokes his cheek. His eyes are bloodshot and his cheeks streaked with sweat.

"I do not know what to do with you Rachel Moore, if that is who you are. You can leave the child with one of these savage women and put your armor back on, for if you want to act the man, you can. Or you can join those women and children. Choose." And he turns on his heel and walks away.

"My Martin?" I call out after him, but he does not stop. The lieutenant comes to me.

"I am no surgeon, but his wound is very bad. He may be dead."

The words chill my heart. I look at our soldiers, who are now staring at me as though they had never seen me before. Some of them are whispering to each other. I can well imagine what they must be saying. I take a step toward them, and then stop. I stand between them and the captives. I gaze back and forth between the two groups. Then, I turn my back on the soldiers and walk toward the savage women and children. Before I can go two steps, the lieutenant is in front of me. He points to my sword. I remove it from my belt and hand it to him. By the look in his eyes, I think he is going to wish me well, but he just takes the sword, pulls it out of its sheath to test its blade, and then turns away from me.

I feel the eyes of the savage women and children on me. Perhaps I should fear them, for they have seen me run my sword through a man who was someone's husband, or brother, or father. I shift my babe in my arms and walk toward them. There are a half dozen of our soldiers busy tying ropes about their necks. The children have been separated from the women, and there are no men. One of the soldiers steps in my path. He is holding a rope. I see his intention, but he is too quick, and my arms are not free. In a second, the rope is looped about my neck as well.

"Is that the way of it, then?" I ask, but out of the corner of my eye I see that Oswald is in charge of this detail. He offers me a sneer and then turns to tell one of the other soldiers what to do. He is puffed with his importance, and I dearly wish that I had slashed his throat instead of his arm. I take my place in the line with the other women. For answer to my question, the soldier tightens the rope about my neck. I am suddenly pulled forward, and I see that another soldier has tied the other end of the rope around the neck of a young woman. Her noose has caught a hair and her head has been pulled back so that it seems as though she is looking up at the sky. She is trying to free her hair, but seems unable to grasp the rope. I am yanked forward.

"I have the idea," I yell at the soldier holding my rope. He grins and makes to pull on the rope again. I trot toward him as he pulls, and he winds up on his back. His comrades laugh, and I stop so that I am standing above him. He mutters a curse and snatches at my legs. I stagger but do not fall. He stands and spits at me.

"Indian whore," he says. "Whose babe is that you carry?"

He hauls on the rope so that I am drawn toward him. He is short and broad, so I am looking into his face. It is an ugly face, long like a horse with big ears, and large, yellow teeth. He gropes between my legs, and I cannot move away, nor strike at him without letting go of my babe.

"Let us see whether you are man or a woman," he says, "or maybe a witch or wizard." I feel the pressure of his fingers. "I saw you act the man well enough with a sword in your hand, but here you are holding a babe like you was a woman. I believe you must be a woman," he says and he moves his hand back and forth between my legs. I clamp my thighs tight so he cannot remove his hand even if he wanted to.

"Are you satisfied, then?" I demand.

He offers a smile that he believes is an invitation.

Oswald has come up behind and grabs him by the shoulder. I release the pressure on his hand, and Oswald shoves him away.

"Enough of that, George," Oswald says.

"Right," George replies. "Who would want to drink from that well." He looks at me as though I have things crawling on my skin.

"Depends how thirsty you are," says another.

"Leave it be," Oswald says.

"Right, you are," George replies. He relaxes his hold on the rope, and I take my place in the line. I wonder whether I should offer my thanks to Oswald when I see that look in his eyes that tells me it was not any warm feelings toward me that caused him to get between me and this George. It had to be something else, like he was planning to get me alone for himself when the time came, or he truly thought he should protect George from defiling himself with me. I do not know which I find more offensive, and decide not to think about it more, but keep my eyes open for anything Oswald might have in mind. He walks away with his arm around George's shoulder.

The woman in front of me is still struggling to free her hair. But now she has stooped forward so that she could see George's abuse of me. I look at her hands. They are badly burned, and yet she has her fingers squeezed between the rope and her hair. Her eyes glisten with tears. I reach my free hand toward her. She stiffens, for a moment, but when I smile at her, she removes her fingers, and permits me to use mine in their stead. The rope does not want to loosen. She holds out her arms and I hesitate only for a second before placing my babe in them. She curves her wrists and forearms to form a cradle, and my babe settles without a whimper. I use both my hands to loosen the rope just enough to free her hair, and she trembles in her relief. She had been in great pain.

We stand and wait. The officers are talking to each other. Fragments of conversation from our soldiers drift toward us. I hear that a number of savages have escaped, and they are to be pursued and hunted down wherever they might hide. I see that the women are straining to hear the same words, but they do not seem able to understand them as well as I do. The woman in front of me looks at me with a question in her eyes.

"They are going to chase after those of you who have escaped."

"Thank you," she replies.

Oswald comes back, but does not look at me. He motions us to start marching, and we follow him toward the place where the gate to the fort used to be. We are flanked by soldiers. I recognize a number of them, but they do not look at me. It is as if they cannot see me. Or I have become one of these women who are not worth their time to look at, for we are to be disposed of by some people in authority. As soldiers, they do what they are told. But they do not look unhappy, and I understand why. They have the easy job of taking us wherever we are supposed to go. Their comrades have the much more difficult and dangerous task of hunting down those who have escaped and who are now hiding somewhere like wounded animals.

Some of the women on the line have babes strapped to their backs on boards. The fatigue in my own eyes teaches me the advantages of that method of carrying a child. But a bigger problem is that my babe is beginning to stir, and I know she will want to suck. She has opened her eyes and seemed to study my face. I smile at her, but she scrunches up her cheeks, and her face reddens. She claws at my breast, and in despair I open my shirt. She lunges for my nipple and I feel her hard gums seize it. She puffs her cheeks and sucks, but gets only air. My poor breast aches and my heart feels as though it must break. She tries one more time, and then pulls back her head and howls. The soldiers walking by our sides now glance at me. The woman in front of me turns and holds out her arms. She has undone her shirt, and I can see that her breasts are full.

I hand my babe to her, and she attaches herself to the woman's breast. She sucks again, and drinks. I do not have to ask the question. She has no babe strapped to her back, for hers is back in the village somewhere, lying in the hot sun with nobody there even to give it a proper farewell. The woman has tears in her eyes, but she forces a smile. I am glad my babe will not starve but it is so hard to see her at this other woman's breast instead of mine.

I lace up my shirt and watch as my babe feeds.

If anything, it is even hotter as we walk toward Saybrook than it was when we were marching toward the savage's village. Nobody is saying much. The women are sullen and when they do talk to each other I cannot understand their words, although I am beginning to learn a few of them. I walk with my babe until she gets restless and hungry and then I hand her to Malawaha, for that is what she calls herself as best as I can say it, and then I watch as my babe sucks on another woman's teat.

Malawaha knows this upsets me. We communicate with our eyes, and gestures. I think we understand each other as well or better as those who use words. I have my own feelings about words, as I have said before, and I am content to talk to Malawaha in this manner. She has let me know that her own babe was smaller than mine and it is dead, and that her heart is as full of sorrow as her breasts are full of milk. Feeding my babe, she lets me know, is a comfort and a relief in both ways. But seeing how I yearn to feed her myself, she has promised to show me how to do that.

We have stopped for a rest, not because we are tired, but because the soldiers, still wearing their armor, want to refresh themselves in the shade and to drink from a small brook that we are about to cross. They take off their helmets and dip them into the water, and then drink or pour the water on their heads. My thirst increases with each drop of water I see splashing to the ground.

"Oswald," I say when I see his face with its ugly mole, "do you think we can have a drink?"

"You can," he says, "but not the others."

"Why me only?"

"For you were Christian once, and when we get to Boston I have hopes to see you correct your ways."

"I will take the water, then," I reply, "and think about another baptism."

He dips his helmet into the brook.

"Beware of blasphemy," he says, as he hands me the helmet.

"I always do," I answer, "it is this heat that addles my poor brain." I take a long sip of the water, and then hand it to Malawaha. Oswald is looking back toward the brook, where two soldiers are splashing each other like children, and when he turns to me and see what I have done his face reddens. He starts to seize the helmet from Malawaha, and when she tries to pull it back from him, her poor, charred fingers cannot hold it and it drops to the ground. I go to pick it up, but Oswald stomps his foot on my hand as it is about to seize the helmet. I can only watch as the water, every last drop of it, drips out of the helmet and into the dust of the ground. He picks up the helmet and positions it back on his head.

"I should know better than to trust you with a kindness," he says, and stomps away. I watch as he approaches the two soldiers in the brook and yells something at them. They bow their heads like children and splash out of the water. A moment or two later, and we are again walking. My tongue aches more for the little water that refreshed it, and it feels like it is stuck to the roof of my mouth. I see the apology in Malawaha's eyes, and I shake my head as hard as I can. I want her to know that I do not fault her, and that Oswald is the one to blame. I thinks she still finds it hard to understand how I, an English woman, can be on her side against the English soldiers. As we walk through the trees, she suddenly drops to one knee, and I think she is failing because of weariness and the heat, but she picks up something from the ground and then continues to walk.

It is dark when we approach the fort at Saybrook. As the doors open, a cheer rises from the soldiers inside. Oswald, who is walking at the head of our column, squares his shoulders and answers the cheer with a loud hurrah. His comrades follow. We walk in and feel the eyes of the soldiers, some curious, some angry, on us. I feel a breath on my neck, and I know before I turn who it belongs to.

"You know," George says, "I can come and get you later so you don't have to sleep with these savages."

I look at him until he turns away with a shrug. We are led to an open area in the fort where there is a log planted in the ground. A soldier approaches me, and I prepare to defend myself. He reaches for the rope about my neck, and I pull back.

"You need not worry," he says, and seizes the rope. With a few quick movements, he brings it over my head. I begin to relax and rub the soreness from my neck when he ties the rope to my foot and the other end to the log. I see that we are all tethered to the log like animals set out to graze in an open pasture. Maybe we are supposed to visit each other, as we are now no longer tied together. The children seek out their mothers, and those who cannot find their own and are left standing alone are gathered in by the women. No child comes toward us.

Two soldiers start a fire and hang a pot over it. We are told that we can eat from it, but we are given no bowls. After the pot has heated for a while, we take our turns, starting with the children, approaching the pot and scooping up what's inside it with our hands. What we are eating is a watery gruel that seeps through our fingers as we bring it to our mouths. It has no taste, but it feels good going down into our bellies. Malawaha's hands are too sensitive from her burns, so I bring the gruel to her mouth, and I feel her lips as she licks my hands clean.

"For your babe," she says, "I eat for your babe."

I sit with Malawaha while she gives my babe suck. When she is done, she hands her back to me. Then, she reaches into a little pouch she has concealed at the waist of her skirt and shows me what she had picked up earlier in the day.

"Take these nuts," she says. "You can crush their meat and boil it, and feed it to your babe, if we are separated and you cannot find another woman for her." She hands me the pouch and I tuck it into the waist of my breeches. Malawaha's eyes follow my hands and then travel down my legs, and a little smile on her face becomes a giggle she cannot stop. I find myself grinning like a fool in return, and my face feels odd, it has been that long since I felt happy enough about anything to smile.

"You are a funny looking man," she manages to say.

"I know." I hug my babe to my chest and do not feel at all like a man.

"What is her name?" Malawaha asks.

I have never given my child a name. I thought of doing so right after she was born, but when she was wrenched away from me, I did not have the heart, and all the long months I dreamed of holding her again, I promised myself I would name her when I held her again. To think of a name when I did not have her would mean she was dead. At least that is what I told myself. So, now, I can name her, and I would like to give her my mother's name, but my father never uttered it, and I never heard it from anyone else. He would say 'your mother', but never her name.

"I do not know," I answer.

"It will come to you," Malawaha replies, "when it should."

And it does that night, as I lie on the hard ground beneath a starless and moonless sky. She will be Hope, for that she has been and will be for me.

Chapter Twelve

The voyage home has been quick and very unpleasant. We have been kept below decks the whole time, and fed just a spoon of gruel and a thimble full of water each day. Many are sick and the stench in the still air down here makes you want to keep your nostrils shut against it. Malawaha is the only nursing mother among us, and I fear her milk might fail if she does not eat enough. When the spoon comes to me, I hold it in front of Malawaha's mouth. She shakes her head, but I press the spoon to her lips.

"For Hope," I say.

She nods and swallows.

A little later, I hand Hope to her and watch as she feeds, and then smiles. The hunger in my belly eases. Then Malawaha hands her back to me, and she falls asleep in my arms. It is as though I have eaten as well.

We hear the ladder creak under boots, and a moment or two later, Oswald appears. He is carrying a cocked pistol as though he needs to protect himself from a dozen or so starving women and children. Mayhap he does.

He walks to me, and extends the hand on his wounded arm. I see that some blood has seeped through the bandage. His wound has not yet healed. Perhaps it never will. I can hardly bear the sight of him, for his face brings back that moment when I lost my Martin. Oswald seems to know that I do not want to have anything to do with him, and yet he delights in coming by to see how I am. And each time he does he makes sure that I see his wound. If he is waiting for an apology, he will be disappointed. Today is no different, as he looks first at the dark brownish red stain on his bandage and then at me.

"The air is fresh and soon we will be able to see the harbor," he says.

I do not answer.

"You do not belong down here," he says.

I look around me at the women and children lying on the rough planking of the hold, their eyes dull, too weak or too deep in despair to look at us or to talk to each other. I wonder if I appear as desperate as they do. Part of me feels that I belong with them, but another part would love a breath of fresh air, even in the company of Oswald, who for his own reasons is attempting to be kind to me. I point to Malawaha.

"She must come with me."

He shakes his head.

"I am not interested in her."

Which means, I think, that he is interested in me, and I am about to turn away when a little puff of air seems to slide down from topside.

"You and I have business together, some new and some old."

"You know I need her."

Something of the old sneer forms on his lips.

"To feed your..." he pauses "babe." His lips settle into an unconvincing smile, and I know that he was about to say a different word beginning with the same letter. "Well, then," he continues, "come up with her, or without her, I care not. I was only offering you a chance to think about renouncing your newly acquired savage ways before we come into the harbor."

"That is a lot to ask from a little fresh air," I reply, but he has already started up the ladder and does not respond. Malawaha has been watching and listening to this conversation. I beckon her to come up with me. She hesitates. She does not trust Oswald, or any English man or woman. Nor do I, or savage either for that matter.

"Come on," I call to her.

We climb up the ladder. As we do, some of the other women lift their eyes toward us, but it is with a weariness that barely defeats their melancholy. Oswald is waiting for us with two other soldiers, muskets at the ready, as if they half expected a rush for freedom from the women below. They relax when they see it is only me with my babe and Malawaha. She stays so close to me I can feel her breath on my neck.

"There," Oswald says and points. I can just make out something long and low on the horizon. I squint and stare and think I see the three humps rising a little higher than the surrounding land. I feel my heart begin to quicken and I wonder why, for Boston surely has not been very kind to me. And then I understand. I am hoping that Mistress Anne will be there waiting for me.

"What will they do with us?" Malawaha's voice is a whisper in my ear and yet Oswald, standing nearby, must have heard.

"Sell you," he says. "Some wants to kill you, but others want to put you to use and to make a few coins." He leans toward Malawaha and lets his eyes roam over her from head to toe. "I imagine such as you might fetch a pretty price. My comrades are now hunting down your warriors and will kill them. Maybe one of them is you husband."

"And which do you prefer?" I ask. "The money or the killing?"

"That depends," he replies.

"On what?"

But he walks away without answering, and I know what he will not say.

Malawaha takes my arm. I look into her eyes and see her fear and confusion. She has been so strong until now, but she stares at the harbor the same way I gazed on the platform that I thought was going to be a gallows. At least I knew what they thought I had done wrong. She only knows that one night she and her babe were sleeping in their wigwam when hell arrived and she woke to fire and blood. She turns around toward the stern of the ship.

"I should not be here," she says.

"What good would it do you to be back in your village? If you were there, you would be dead."

"Is that so much worse?"

I start to answer that life is always a better choice, but I remember there are times when I do not believe that any more than she now does. Without words I do what I can, and that is to throw my arms about her. I step back, take one more breath of the fresh air and one more look at the approaching harbor, and then I lead her back down into the hold.

It seems as though the whole town has come out to see us walk down the rough gangplank onto the town pier. We again have ropes about our necks, but tied this time only in pairs. I suppose they were afraid that if we were attached to each other as before, one might fall and take the rest of us with her. And then where would be the profit or the spectacle of death that Oswald says we are to provide? I have refused his offer for special consideration, which means he would have escorted me without a rope. And where was I supposed to run? I ask him and say I have come this far with the others and will remain with them. He sighs and picks at his mole and loops the rope around my throat, giving it just a bit of tug to show his disappointment at my ingratitude. As we start down the gangplank, I strain my eyes for a glimpse of Mistress Anne. I see Master Winthrop and Dudley and Oswald's father Stanton, and other

189

townspeople whose faces I can recall, but nobody from the Hutchinson household, and certainly not herself.

"You will not find her," Oswald says, and I am beginning to wonder if he is forever going to be my personal demon, poking me with his pitchfork to puncture every bubble of comfort I begin to feel. Still, I cannot resist the temptation to ask.

"How know you that?"

"My father told me, before we left, that she was to be banished and excommunicated."

"Maybe she was not…" I begin, but he shakes his head.

"My father has the confidence of the governor."

"Aye," I reply, "I know the governor's mind about Mistress Hutchinson, better than you or your father." It is a foolish boast to make, but I am satisfied to see Oswald raise his eyebrows in surprise and look at me as though seeing me for the first time. He wants me to explain, but of course I will not.

The governor is standing at the bottom of the gangplank as my foot finds the pier. Master Cotton is at his side. The captain is a few feet away, and he points in my direction. He must have told them how I was found. I cannot imagine that they have anything good in mind for me. Master Cotton steps forward and takes my shoulders in his hands and gives them a little squeeze. I believe he is trying to show kindness.

"So you have returned to us," he says. "Like the prodigal son of the scripture. Tell me child are you ready to embrace our Lord once again and ask Him for His mercy, for surely he will extend it to one such as you."

"One such as me who has sinned? Is that what you mean, Sir?" I am being impertinent, but the rope about my neck gives me courage, for the only thing worse that can now befall me is that I will be led straight to the gallows and hanged for the unrepentant sinner that I am. At the thought, I remember Martin and almost smile, but then I feel Hope at my breast and know that I must manage to continue living, at least until she is old enough to take care of herself.

Master Cotton does not reply. His face is creased in sorrow. But there is something else in his eyes, something I cannot put a name to until he turns to Governor Winthrop with a shrug of his shoulders that seems to say that he can do no more with me. He fears the governor. I would not have guessed that this confident man of God could walk in fear of any mere man, and yet I know I am not mistaken. I am even more sure, now, when I see the governor nod to indicate that he understands, for he, too, has failed in his governance of me.

It is a marvel that I have so flustered two such powerful men.

"Your answer, child," Governor Winthrop says as he steps forward. "What say you to Master Cotton?"

The well-remembered voice of authority melts my courage. I am again the servant girl suffered to empty the piss from the chamber pot in the governor's house. I fight my own fear. I take a breath and straighten my shoulders. I feel Hope's warmth, and the way her hands seek me. I am not, then, the same girl as when I left dressed as a soldier.

"Child," the governor says, his hand at his beard in the familiar gesture, "we have come here to redeem you, for I was as your father when you ran off to war."

"Pardon, sir," I reply. "I did not so much as go off to war as to find my babe." I hold Hope up, as though he had been unable to see her until now, and feel very foolish doing so.

He nods with that smile on his face that I know I cannot trust.

"Of course," he almost coos like a dove, "seeing your babe in your arms softens our offense at your leaving us so suddenly."

I want to know what he is after. I look at Master Cotton for help, but he is gazing at the women and children now gathered on the pier under the watchful eyes of the soldiers and the curious glances of the townspeople. The governor follows my glance.

"Master Cotton can tell you that you have nothing to fear from me, that I am a forgiving man, when those who have aggrieved me find it in their hearts to mend their ways."

The words are out before I can consider their danger.

"Mistress Hutchinson..." I begin, but stop when I see the sudden flash of dark anger roll down the governor's face from forehead to chin, like a black cloud blocking the sun. He waits a moment.

"But she did not mend," he says, "even though Master Cotton and the other godly men bent every effort in instructing her."

I am beginning to understand, but I will need space and quiet to make sure I am right. For now, I must discover how I can turn the governor's offer of forgiveness to my advantage for the sake of my Hope. I see the governor's glance look past me to Malawaha, who is standing behind me with her head down, perhaps hoping she will not be noticed. I feel that if she could free herself from the rope about her neck she would slip into the water and permit herself to sink, and the only thing stopping her from doing that now is the other end of her rope is around my throat. He strokes his beard.

"I have made arrangements," he says, "to take you back into my household and to see that Master Cotton himself attends to your spiritual estate."

"Do you mean me to live with your family?" I ask.

He pauses, as I hoped he would, and I want to give him an alternative.

"I would prefer to live with my babe in my father's house, if it still stand, or make another like it if it does not."

"I cannot have you live alone."

"I am waiting for my husband, who is with the army chasing those who survived the attack."

"Your husband, indeed?"

"Yes."

"Were you married, child?" Master Cotton asks. His eyes drop to my chest for a moment, as though he expects to see my letter of dishonor there. Then he puts his soft hand on Hope's cheek and there is a tenderness in his eyes I well remember, and I even recall my old dream of having him baptize my babe. This is not the time, I think, but mayhap before too long I can ask him.

"I believe we are in the eyes of God," I reply.

"Indeed," Governor Winthrop intones, and the word works its way into and chills my bones as once it did. Out of the corner of my eye, I see Oswald approaching with his father. Master Cotton has turned to greet them Winthrop looks like he, too, would like to welcome Oswald back and congratulate the father on the son's safe return. I cannot permit him to do that.

"How is Eleanor?" I ask.

The governor turns back to me.

"Eleanor? She tries but she needs help, and my Margaret has not been well." He smiles. "We need you back. You know our house."

"I can work for you again, if it please you," I say. "I do not think my husband will object."

"Your husband," the governor mutters. "It would be right for you to prepare a home for him. See if your father's house can be made comfortable. If not, speak to me. Come to work tomorrow morning. At the usual time."

With a will of its own, my free hand goes to my chest. He understands.

"There is no need to talk about that, as you now have a husband." And he is off, arms outstretched to embrace Oswald. Governor Winthrop says something to Oswald, who nods, and walks to me. He places his fingers between my neck and the rope and lifts it free. I realize my hand is still resting on my chest, and I let it drop. His eyes follow the motion. They glint with some thought he still will not express.

"So you wait for Martin?" he asks instead.

"Yes."

"Do not fear. I will not tell."

"There is nothing you can tell," I reply.

He shrugs.

"Perhaps. You are free to go."

I take two or three steps, and Malawaha is right behind me. I continue, and I hear her gasp. The rope has been pulled tight about her neck. Oswald has the end of it in his hand.

"The governor said nothing about your savage wet nurse."

"My babe…" I begin.

"Can suckle a white woman's milk," he replies. "We can find one for you."

I remember the nuts in my pocket.

"I will manage myself."

"Do as you must." He yanks on the rope so that Malawaha is pulled away.

"I will help you," I call after her. "Do not fear." But she continues to walk away with her head down, and I do not know if she has heard me.

I am alone on the pier. The clouds have blackened and the wind has picked up. I can feel and smell the onset of a summer rain storm. I tell myself to head for my father's hut, but my heart directs my feet to the town common. Up ahead, I see the governor making his way ever so slowly to his own house, but that is not my destination. He looks up at the threatening sky and then quickens his pace. I wait until he is at his front door, and then I turn my back to his house and walk toward hers.

I do not know what I expect, certainly not to see her waiting for me. The house looks much as I remember it, but it has that feel to it that vacant houses do. I walk around it to the garden in the back and see that is has been overtaken by the weeds. I try the back door, and to my surprise it opens. I enter and my steps echo in the emptiness. I place my hand into the ashes of the fireplace, and

193

they are stone cold. I need to explore no further. Sadness blankets me, and I go back out and direct my steps to my own house.

Its front door is swinging back and forth in the wind. The sky is very black now, and the rain beats down on the thatched roof. It look as solid as ever. I find a large stone and prop the door open to let in a little light as I enter. I reach into my pocket and feel the two matches that are there. I recall how Martin gave them to me with a smile and said I should make the fire, just as though we were sitting in front of our own fireplace instead of out in a field with a thousand savages waiting to do us harm.

I cannot risk striking a match yet. There is a strong draft coming through the open door. I could close the door, but then I would be in complete darkness, and what if the match fails? And I do not dare put Hope down, for fear she will crawl away in the dark and I will never see her again. Or she will be snatched up by one of those women I have heard about who have horses hooves for feet and who suck the blood of babes.

I sink to my knees with Hope on my hip and crawl to the fireplace. I used to hang our last candle on a hook just inside the opening to the hearth where he would not find it and yet far enough from the fire so it would not melt. I reach my hand in and find nothing. Hope is starting to make those little cries that announce she is about to wake up in a full throated roar demanding to be fed. I grope about for another minute until I remember that the candle would be on the other side of the fireplace. It is there, just as I last left it. I take out my match and strike it. It sputters, but Hope shifts her weight in my arm and I drop the match. It goes out.

I must put her down. I lay her on the floor with my foot against her and try again. This time the match flame holds and I can light the candle. I can just see the pile of straw I used to lie on. I swear I can still smell my own piss rising from it. No matter. I wait for the candle to drip and then place it on the floor. I lay Hope on the straw and close the door before the wind can blow out the candle. She sits up and looks about. For the moment, she has forgotten that she is hungry. I almost think she is smiling.

I pick up the candle and in its light I find the stump of another on the table. It is on its side, and I can imagine my father knocking it over with a drunken swipe of his hand. I stand it up and light it. Hope's eyes are following the dancing flames on both candles.

I find some dry kindling in the fireplace and one charred log. Within a few minutes, I have a small fire going, and Hope is now staring at it. She seems fascinated by the fire. She scrunches up her nose and narrows her eyes. I imagine she remembers the last time she saw flames in the Indian village. She begins to cry, not a howl of hunger, but a sound that seems burdened with her terror. I want to pick her up, but I know she will soon remember she has not eaten.

There is a pot hanging in the fireplace. It has the crusty remains of something on the bottom. I scrape it clean as best I can with my fingernail, and then open the door. It is raining hard now. I put the pot on the ground to collect some rainwater.

Back inside, I take the candle from the table and look under it. He was always dropping things, and sure enough, I see the glint of a blade. I pick up his knife, the one he used to cut the thatch. I run my finger over the blade, and it is still sharp. As careless as he was about most things, he always kept his blade keen.

I sit at the table and take out the hickory nuts. I decide to try one, and save the others. The knife slices through the shell, and the meat drops onto the table. I take off my boot and with the heel I crush the nut meat into a pulp. I retrieve the pot. It has a little water in it, perhaps just enough. I scoop the pulp into my palm and scrape it off into the pot. I place the pot back over the fire and watch the mixture bubble. Malawaha did not tell me how long it should cook, so I wait a few minutes until Hope starts to scream in earnest.

I remove the pot and wait for it to cool. I place it on the floor next to the stool and pick up Hope. I dip my finger into the paste and offer it to her mouth. She sucks my finger as though it was my breast. I love the feeling of her tongue against my skin. I offer her more, and more, until it is gone.

I lie down on the straw next to her. The rain beats on the thatch roof. Hope goes to sleep. I put my cheek near hers so I can feel her breath.

Eleanor's face fights a battle between joy and disapproval when I show up at the governor's door. I understand the disapproval, for in her eyes I must be a most ungrateful girl, to have turned my back on her master's generosity in receiving me fresh from my shame on the platform and with my letter on my gown, and giving me an opportunity to redeem my reputation in his service. All of this I can see in her expression, but I do not know how to read the happiness I also see there fighting for a place on her plain and wrinkled face. Perhaps she rejoices at my safe return. Or just as likely, she sees in me a relief from her burdens.

I shift Hope from one arm to another. I am unwell this morning. I do not know why, although a suspicion is beginning to grow in my mind. All through the night I heard my father's labored breathing, his snorts in his dreams, and his slurps as he roused to drink once again. After a while, I put my hands over my ears and lay there with my eyes open. If I concentrated on the sound of the rain, I did not hear his snores, and when the rain stopped, I heard nothing but the sweet breaths of Hope. I lay there until the sunlight crept in beneath the door.

To my surprise, I found an old shift and gown. I took off my breeches and man's shirt and dressed again as a woman. I wondered if Hope would notice, and she did seek my breast as soon as she awoke. I felt better in my old clothes, but I do not want to resume my old life. I managed to start the fire again and prepared another nut for Hope. I had enough left over to put in a little jar I found on the mantle. There was no food for me, yet I was not hungry and I am not now. Yet, Eleanor asks.

"There is still some samp in the pot in the fireplace," she says. "I expect you have not eaten."

"But I have," I reply, for I do not think I could look kindly upon even the most royally prepared breakfast.

"What about your babe?" she asks. "Surely, you have no milk."

"No, I don't, but I have this." I show her the jar I have brought with food for Hope.

She takes the jar from me and examines it contents.

"It is made from hickory nuts," I say.

She nods, but her expression tells me she does not understand.

"Is that something you have learned from the savages?"

"Yes." I wait for her to question more. I want her to be satisfied. She must be my friend, and if not that, at least not my enemy. "Is there still a cradle in the nursery?"

"Yes."

"Can I use it?"

She frowns. She is not used to making decisions.

"Ask Mistress Margaret, then," I say.

"She is sick and not to be disturbed."

"I cannot do much work with my babe in my arms."

She holds out her hands.

"I will take her," she says. "But you must find the time to mind her, and not let her interfere with your chores."

"Where do you want me to begin?" I ask.

"With the chamber pots," she says. "You know where to find them."

And I do. My nose leads me to the corner of the large bedroom upstairs, with its windows on two sides, and its large, soft bed. Mistress Margaret is in that bed, and she lifts her head off the pillow as I enter. An expression of confusion crosses her face.

"It's me, Rachel," I say.

"Rachel," she repeats, and lets her head fall back onto the pillow. I come closer and see that her face is flushed and there is sweat on her forehead. There is a rag in a basin of water on a stand next to the bed. I dip the rag in the water and lay it on her forehead. She smiles, but does not open her eyes. I locate the chamber pot in the corner of the room where it always is and carry it down the stairs. I pause at the foot of the stairs where I see a new rug, probably just arrived from London, on the floor. It is a marvelous affair of blue with golden threads running through it, and I have to fight the very strong temptation I feel to empty the chamber pot onto it.

It does not take me long to remember the house, every corner where the dust collects, or chair that is always in the way. I pass by Master Winthrop's study. Its door is shut, and I am just as glad not to enter it. I spend the day polishing pewter, scrubbing floors, and cutting up vegetables to help Eleanor prepare the stew for dinner. When the governor, who has been out all day, returns for the meal, I make sure I am in another part of the house. I do hear him question Eleanor. I do not know what she is saying about me, and I hold my breath waiting to be summoned, but no summons comes.

I continue with my chores, keeping myself busy even when there is nothing to do. I stop by the nursery every hour. When Hope is awake, I feed her. I find a nappy for her and change her, and then sit in a rocking chair with her in my arms pretending that I am in my own house. Then, I put her back into the cradle and rock her until she is again asleep.

Later, in the afternoon I hear the front door open and see that Master Cotton has arrived. I have been running a rag over the banister as though to polish it although it already shines.

"How are you, my child?" he asks.

Before I can answer, the governor emerges from his study and beckons Master Cotton in. He looks at me, and then walks in with the minister, but does not close the door behind him as he usually does. He takes his seat behind his desk, and motions Master Cotton toward the one other chair in the room. Again, his eyes catch mine, but he says nothing.

"Do you need something?" I ask.

"No," he replies.

I start to go up the stairs. But the open door beckons. Eleanor is asleep in the kitchen. I make my way back toward the study. I stop some feet from the door, but I can hear their voices clearly.

"You do remember Mary Dyer, do you not?" the governor asks. He almost sounds as though he is talking to a child who cannot remember his lesson. I am shocked to hear such a tone delivered to Master Cotton who is revered as the most godly man in the colony.

"I do," Master Cotton replies. His voice is firm, perhaps a little angry.

"You had an opportunity then to put an end to the spread of her pernicious poison, and you did not."

"I deemed it a private matter."

"Private! When the commonwealth lay sick from her blasphemy, and you had the physic in your hand!"

"I did not see it so," Master Cotton replies, and this time his voice is less certain.

"God has granted us another opportunity," the governor says. "You have heard of her monstrous birth."

"I have."

"Is it not God's providence?"

There is a long pause. I dearly want to look in to see how Master Cotton is sitting in that chair. I can well imagine the glint in the governor's eye. I have seen it before.

"It is," the minister says.

"A most fitting subject for a sermon?"

Another pause.

"Yes."

I have heard enough, more than enough. But I am to hear even more, for when I seek Eleanor in the kitchen to inquire if she has anything more for me to do, she is fully roused and a smile plays on her lips, a very unpleasant smile such as one wears when about to say something intended to remind you of your foolishness.

"Do you know about your former Mistress?" she asks.

I know she refers to Mistress Anne, but I seek safety in my shell of pretended ignorance.

"I see that she has a fever," I reply.

Eleanor frowns.

"No, you slow witted girl. It is no wonder you are always in trouble. I speak not of Mistress Margaret, your present mistress, but of Mistress Anne. Surely, you remember how she took you in."

"I do."

"And how she violated God's commandment prohibiting preaching by women."

It is futile to defend Mistress Anne in this household, and so I say nothing.

"Well, after you went off to war," Eleanor continues, the smile now growing wider until it extends to her ears, forming a new line that cuts through the wrinkles of her cheeks, "her impertinence could no longer be suffered, and so the governor, who had been so very patient, was forced to seek her removal. She was banished as a threat to the well-being of the commonwealth. And the ministers tried to correct her errors of religion, and when they could not, she was excommunicated. Master Cotton himself, with great and unseemly sadness I must say, offered the judgment of the ministers that she must be expelled from the church."

I remain dumb, although Eleanor pauses so I can respond. When I do not, she points to the pot in the fireplace.

"Before you go home, if that's what you call that place, and why you will not stay here with your babe in comfort, I know not, but before you leave, build up the fire beneath the pot. You are welcome to stay for supper, if you please."

I kneel before the fireplace and begin to poke the embers into a fuller flame. I know she has more to tell me.

"They say she was delivered of a monster while she was at Aquidneck. It is no wonder."

She waits again, but I do not turn around. I continue to fuss with the fire until I hear her chair scrape, and I know she is leaving the kitchen. After she does, I go upstairs to the nursery, and pick up Hope. I would run home if I were not afraid to stumble and fall and hurt my babe.

Chapter Thirteen

It is lecture day, and I am late when I arrive at the meeting house. I have no doubt what Master Cotton is going to talk about. The governor seemed to want me to know in advance, and that is why he left the door open so I could overhear his conversation with the minister. The subject is going to be unpleasant, and I thought about not attending, but I have no money for a fine and I cannot bear another whipping. I do not believe the magistrates would be in a mood to show me much mercy. I see Malawaha is on the end of the last bench. I find a seat next to her. She holds out her arms for Hope, and I give her to her. I look about me and see that I am sitting among the Indian women and children. There are only about eight or ten of them.

"They have been taken away on a ship," she says.

"What about you?" I whisper, for I see that Master Cotton is about to speak. She shrugs.

"I am in the house of the soldier with the…" she hesitates and points to her nose.

I look toward the front row where I see Master Stanton and Oswald. Malawaha nods. Oswald turns around and catches my eye. He makes a gesture with his hands but I do not understand what he intends, nor do I care. He does it again, his face flushed, but then his father sees who his son is staring at and says something to him. Oswald points to the door as though telling me to meet him outside, and then faces the minister.

Master Cotton looks uncomfortable behind his pulpit. His eyes travel to the front rows of benches where the governor and the other important people sit. He is about to say something and I know it will have to do with Mistress Anne.

Yet, he hesitates and the air of expectancy among the congregation increases. Some shift their feet and others stare about as though expecting somebody to say something or do something to help the minister begin talking.

He looks down at his open Bible, then up toward the ceiling. He takes a deep breath and begins.

"God's providence has again been wonderfully manifested unto us, and so I am moved to begin today's service by telling you what I have heard from our friends in Aquidneck in Narragansett Bay, whither Mistress Hutchinson and some of her followers have gone."

At the mention of that name, the congregation seems to hold its breath. I do, too. Malawaha is nursing Hope. Her eyes are directed toward the pulpit, but they are closed, and I can only imagine what she is feeling as I see a smile form on her lips.

"You remember, of course, with sadness as I do, how we not very long ago, after long and prayerful consideration, excommunicated and banished Mistress Anne Hutchinson for the many errors in her opinions, which she spread among us like a plague. Some of us, then, had fallen under this woman's spell, for she is an enchantress, a woman of ready wit and special parts, make no doubt about it. Even I felt myself becoming bewitched at her apparent piety and godliness, until God chose to alert me to my folly."

It is more like the governor than God, I think, and I wonder how this cowardly man could have fallen so far. He, who Mistress Anne followed here from England, and who was her teacher, is saving himself at her expense, and she not here to defend herself. The governor has a club held over his head, and that club, I now assure myself, as I had thought, is the kindness he showed Mary Dyer and her family.

"She has given birth to a monster," he continues. "A thing that scarcely can be called a child, a thing of twenty seven lumps, that seem to have been produced entirely from the man's seed with nothing from the woman herself, whereby God teaches us the error of her proclaiming that righteousness is not to be found in our nature, but only brought to us by the presence of Christ in His Saints. This is a blasphemy that denies the possibility of a commonwealth such as ours to be based on law as administered by our magistrates."

This description of Mistress Anne's teaching does not resemble what I recall hearing her say, the warmth of her heart and the generosity of her spirit. It is these men with their words that they parse into nonsense that makes no sense to me. And to many others, no doubt, too fearful to raise their voices in protest. I let my head sink to my chest. Those about me might think I am praying, but what I am doing is shutting out this horrible noise, these words like pitch being smeared on Mistress Anne's character. She is gone, but they still fear her, and I take a small comfort in that. When Hope is through nursing, I take her back from Malawaha and hold her to me and shut my ears to all but her breathing. Malawaha looks to me for an explanation, but I can offer none she would understand.

After the service, we are confronted by Master Stanton as we are about to leave. He has waited at the front of the meeting house and steps into our path.

"Mary," he says, and Malawaha does not respond. He places his hand on her shoulder.

"You know I cannot pronounce your savage name, which is forbidden now as are all words of your language. So Mary you are."

Malawaha looks at him.

"Come with me, now," he says. They leave and I do not try to follow. I join the last few out the door. As I step into the sunlight, I find myself in front of Oswald.

"I want to speak to you," he says, his voice louder than is necessary to cover the short distance between us. "I like you better as a woman."

I try to make my way around him, but he steps in front of me. I look into his eyes. They are bright with some excitement. He takes my arm. I pull it hard, but he is stronger than I thought he would be. There are still a few people standing about and talking. Out of the corner of my eyes, I see Master Cotton and a white haired man with their heads almost touching. They turn together and stare at us.

"What would a gentleman like you want to do with one such as myself," I say, and try again to walk by.

He does not answer. He keeps his grip on my arm and leads me away. We walk in silence until we can see my hut. He stops and puts his hand on Hope's cheek. She stirs with her eyes closed, but her mouth opens. I almost think she is going to smile at him, and I hug her to me.

"Your babe," he says.

"What about her?" I hold her tighter. She opens her eyes and wrinkles up her nose as she focuses on Oswald. She starts to cry.

"I could feed and clothe her if..." he pauses.

I understand.

"You cannot be thinking that," I say. I pull away from him and continue toward my hut. He catches up to me with long strides, and again places himself in my path. The tension has left his face. I realize that he did not know how to say it to me, and I have helped him out.

"What would your father think of such an idea?"

He reddens, and then sets his jaw.

"I do not care. I can provide. When I am twenty-one in two years, I come into my inheritance."

"He can take it away."

He smiles.

"I am his only son. He has promised me land in the Connecticut valley that the late war has made safe for us. He does not want to move there. He has said it is an opportunity for a young man. He will be angry at me, but not so angry that he would sell the land to someone else. He loves land," he stops and a look of sadness crosses his face, and for a moment I can almost feel sorry for him. "He loves land more than he loves me," he continues. "And I will explain how I am doing God's work in redeeming a sinner. He may not understand. Perhaps Master Cotton can advise him."

"Have you thought that I might not want the man who shot the man I love?"

He nods his head up and down with violence. I start to walk again and he comes with me.

"Of course. I am not stupid. But I felt God was speaking to me."

Something was speaking to you, I think, but the voice was not coming from inside your head. I look down to where his legs join to see if it is talking to him now.

"I wait for Martin."

"I have heard that he died."

I do not, cannot, believe him.

"We can have your Indian woman as a servant and wet nurse," he says.

I point to my belly.

"There is something you should know, then."

He follows my hand with his wide and starting eyes.

"You lie," he says, "to put me off."

"Wait but a fortnight or two, and then I will show you. Your own eyes will not lie to you."

"I care not," he replies.

We are in front of my hut, now. He looks at it as though he has never seen it before. It is possible he has not even though he may well have walked by it

204

a hundred or a thousand times. People who live in large houses such as he does do not see the little ones like mine.

"Would you live here with me and my babes?"

He looks genuinely shocked.

"Of course not."

I step toward my door. He starts to get in the way, but then he backs off.

"I could, you know," he says.

I swing the door open and then close it behind me.

I have not seen Oswald for a couple of days, and my life is settling into its old routine at the governor's house. Eleanor is doing less and less so that I needs must do more and more. I do not mind. I like keeping busy. I try to tire myself so that I will sleep, for I still hear my father's breathing at night. It is growing a little fainter, but until it stops I lie staring at the underside of the thatched roof. And every day I walk by the harbor seeking news of a ship coming up from Saybrook. I am sure that one will arrive carrying Martin back to me. Until then, his absence is burrowing a hole in my heart that will not close nor heal.

I hear a knock on my door. I have just finished feeding Hope, and have even managed to eat a little stew that I have taken home from the governor's kitchen. I am expecting no visitors, and so I think it must be Oswald. But it is not.

"What is this my son tells me?" Master Stanton demands. It has been very hot, and the sweat has dripped down his fat neck and stained his stiff white ruff.

"What has he told you?"

"Not what he should have, no doubt, how you have lured him into your bed."

I have to bite down on my lip hard enough to feel the pain so as not to laugh.

"He has never been there."

Master Stanton reaches a gloved hand toward my belly, and I suffer his touch so he can be sure.

"He says it is his."

"It is my husband's."

"The one they call Martin Miller, if that be his name?"

"Yes."

"My son says he was shot and mortally wounded."

"He would know, wouldn't he?"

"Would you not?"

"We were both there."

"Is he not dead?"

"I think not."

"Do you not want to marry my son?"

I wonder if there is some guile in this question. If I say no, will he think I am insulting him and his wealth? Mayhap he will think I am only feigning my lack of interest. If I say yes, he will not believe me, or if he does, he will offer me something to change my mind. That is an attractive thought, but I choose another course.

"I am already married."

"That is not what I asked you."

"But that is what my answer is, and it is the answer of an honest woman."

He reaches into his pouch and takes out a fistful of coins. He extends his hand to me, and I let the coins fall into my palm. I curl my fingers so they will not fall, but I do not close my hand on them.

"There is something I want more than money, and it is something you can give me."

His eyes brighten. I see what Oswald meant about what his father loves. Land and money. He wants me to make the offer. He did not get rich by accident.

"The one you now call Mary. Give her to me. For my service in the war. And..."

"Yes?"

"For my promise that never will I agree to marry your son, no matter what he promised me."

"Even when he offers you a chance to live on a thousand acres of rich soil, with servants of your own."

"To empty chamber pots, as I do now."

He pulls his nose back as though he could smell the piss.

"Yes."

"Even then," I reply. Better a thousand chamber pots than one night in bed with Oswald.

He holds out his hand, and I pour the coins back into them. He squeezes the palm of his other hand over them, and then drops them into his purse.

"I will have papers drawn up. And you shall have Mary."

"And you shall have your son, to do with as you think best."

He does not know how to respond to this last, but decides to accept it without anger. He even gives me a little bow, and then leaves.

I go to sleep that night more easily. I do not hear my father's breathing for more than a few minutes, and I dream of sharing my little hut with Malawaha.

The next morning I see a ship tied up to the dock. I hurry toward it. A crowd has begun to gather, as it does every time a ship arrives. I prepare to push my way through, but people step aside to let me pass, as though I was a lady, but the truth is that they do not want to stand too close to me. I have heard the whispers in the meeting house, and on the common on my way back and forth to the governor's house. Some say that the governor has been too kind. Others say I should have been sold into slavery like the other savage women. They all fear being infected with whatever I have that has made me as I am, a woman who lost herself several times, but most when she lived among the savages and came back with a rope about her neck just as if she was one of them. I am just as glad, now, to let them step back so I can get close enough to see who is coming off the ship.

My heart leaps when I see that several wounded men are making their way down the gangplank, walking with hesitant step. One has his arm in a sling. Another uses a crutch. The third has his arms about the shoulders of two of his healthy comrades. I study them, their faces, their bodies. None of them is Martin.

I place myself in their path. The one with his arm in the sling looks familiar, but I cannot recall his name. He looks at me with a puzzled expression. I cannot tell him that we served together.

"Are you back from the war?" I ask.

He nods.

"There were a few of us hurt too bad to come home right away. We stayed at Saybrook until we mended."

"I am waiting for my husband. He has not returned yet."

"There was one still there."

"Was his name Martin? Martin Miller? A tall man with a musket?" I am prepared to give him more details, to force him to remember seeing my Martin recovering from his wound, but he starts to shake his head.

"I cannot be sure. But he was hurt very bad. The surgeon did not think he would live."

"But..." I begin.

"He was still alive when we left. Pray for him."

"I have been."

Malawaha is squatting in front of my hut when I return that evening. She gets up and walks toward me.

"He said I am to be your servant."

"No," I reply. "You are my friend."

"But he said you bought me."

"No. I traded for you. I got you and he got Oswald."

She puts her hand in front of her mouth and laughs into it.

"I do not understand," she says.

"It is not important."

Later we have found more straw to enlarge my bed.

"Do you not want to sleep there?" Malawaha asks, pointing toward my father's bed on the far side of the hut.

"Only when Martin comes," I say.

We lie down on the straw with Hope between us. Malawaha offers her breast. Hope fastens her mouth to it and drinks.

I lie awake in the silence after they both fall asleep. In the morning, we will think about how we will manage. It does not matter what we do as long as we do it together.

I close my eyes with my hands over my belly. Inside, Martin's babe is growing. Every morning and every night I will go to the harbor and look for the sail that will bring Martin back to me.

Until then, I have my Hope.

Chapter Fourteen

Oswald did not wait very long for me to change my mind. Like his father he could not abandon his dream of land. Within a couple of months, he left for his acres with his new bride, fresh from London on his arm. And now word has come back that he has been elected a magistrate in Hartford, and that he has a son. I wonder if the boy has a mole on his nose like his father.

Bridget came back from Aquidneck with her babe and a husband. I do not know who he is or where he came from. I met them walking on the common, and she looked through me as though I was not there. They have moved into her old house, but people say they are selling the furnishings and will soon leave.

Hope is big enough to walk now, and sometimes she tries to pick up her brother Martin. She has begun to speak. She says "mama." I point things out to her in our hut, and she says them with a great big grin on her face. But when I put my hand on Martin and say his name, she will not look at him for more than a second, and she will not attempt his name, for it seems he is not important enough for her attention.

Malawaha stayed with us until this past spring when we bought her a passage on a boat going to Long Island where she thinks some of her people moved after the slaughter at Mystic. She said she loved us, but she yearned for her own people. She did not know if she would find them, and if she could not she would seek shelter among the Montauks or other peoples on Long Island. But of one thing she is sure. She does not want to be English any longer.

She pleaded with me to come with her, and I thought I might. But I had to refuse. I am still waiting for Martin. I refuse to believe he is dead. And if he is not, I have to ask myself why he has not returned to me. The thought came in a still moment of winter night last year, carried it seemed by the rattle of a wet snow against my door, that he was never mine as I was his. I must remember how our paths crossed by chance that evening in the tavern, how he never did tell me where he had come from, or what he expected to do after the war. And, yet, I do believe he loved me.

Perhaps he found another war to fight in and does not know that we are here waiting for him.

And there are other wars. We have heard about the one in New Amsterdam between the Dutch and the Indians. That is the one in which Mistress Anne and her younger children were killed. They had moved there after her husband Will died in Aquidneck. Her death was announced in meeting just as her monstrous birth had been. It seems the governor and the ministers would not be content unless they could bury her themselves. If they could not do that, they decided to bury her with their words.

They have always thought their words most powerful.

But I think they are mistaken.

Mistress Anne knew better, and taught me better.

Every day I take my children down to the harbor. Hope toddles along beside me for most of the way, but sometimes I have to carry her. It is not so much that she tires, but that she looks up and sees her brother in my arms, and then she sits down on the path and will not walk. I do not mind. I gather her up and she quiets.

We sit on a hill overlooking the harbor. I show them the gulls gliding and swooping down looking for food. Sometimes we see the tiny specks of white circling something on the water in the distance, and we know it is a ship, and the birds are waiting for garbage to be dumped overboard.

There are many ships entering and leaving the harbor now, for Boston has become quite prosperous, with merchants of various kinds now lining the roads that run by and to the harbor. My heart used to leap each time I saw a new sail, for I would be sure that Martin would be on this ship.

But now I just point to the sail and I guess where it might have come from.

I used to look at it very hard and then close my eyes to see if I could see Martin's eyes and feel his hands on my hips again. And then I would think he is on that ship.

It is becoming harder and harder to see and feel him in my memory.

Very soon, I fear, the sight of a sail will mean only the arrival of another ship from some distant port, and so I will watch it dock, and then take my children home.

Printed in the USA
CPSIA information can be obtained
at www.ICGtesting.com
LVHW020539040624
782197LV00037B/1285